WANDERLUST

LAUREN BLAKELY

COPYRIGHT

ALSO BY LAUREN BLAKELY

Big Rock Series

Big Rock

Mister O

Well Hung

Full Package

Joy Ride

Hard Wood

One Love Series dual-POV Standalones

The Sexy One

The Only One

The Hot One

Standalones

The Knocked Up Plan

Most Valuable Playboy

Stud Finder

The V Card

Most Likely to Score

Wanderlust

Come As You Are (April 2018)

Part-Time Lover (June 2018)

The Real Deal (Summer 2018)

Unbreak My Heart (Summer 2018)

Once Upon a Real Good Time (Fall 2018)

Once Upon a Sure Thing (Fall 2018)

Far Too Tempting

21 Stolen Kisses

Playing With Her Heart

Out of Bounds

The Caught Up in Love Series

Caught Up In Us

Pretending He's Mine

Trophy Husband

Stars in Their Eyes

The No Regrets Series

The Thrill of It

The Start of Us

Every Second With You

The Seductive Nights Series

First Night (Julia and Clay, prequel novella)

Night After Night (Julia and Clay, book one)

After This Night (Julia and Clay, book two)

One More Night (Julia and Clay, book three)

A Wildly Seductive Night (Julia and Clay novella, book 3.5)

The Joy Delivered Duet

Nights With Him (A standalone novel about Michelle and Jack)

Forbidden Nights (A standalone novel about Nate and Casey)

The Sinful Nights Series

Sweet Sinful Nights

Sinful Desire

Sinful Longing

Sinful Love

The Fighting Fire Series

Burn For Me (Smith and Jamie)

Melt for Him (Megan and Becker)

Consumed By You (Travis and Cara)

The Jewel Series

A two-book sexy contemporary romance series

The Sapphire Affair

The Sapphire Heist

ABOUT WANDERLUST

The first time I met him, his sexy British accent almost talked me into giving him my number on the spot. The second time, he nearly charmed the panties off me with his wit. Then I learned he's the key to success in my new job in Paris. The man who tempts me into fling-worthy dirty daydreams has turned out to be my personal translator, and his accent is the hottest thing I've ever heard.

My mantra is simple -- **Don't mix business with pleasure.** I do my best to resist him as he teaches me how to converse with my co-workers, navigate the metro and order the perfect bottle of wine at dinner. But I also figure out how to tell the charming and clever man what I most want to say -- that I want him to take me back to his flat -- tonight.

Except there's a catch...
***

One more assignment before I take off on my big adventure...

And it involves the toughest work ever -- resisting the fetching American woman I spend all my days with. But you know what they say about best intentions. Soon, we're spending our nights tangled together, and I don't want to let her go. The trouble is, my wanderlust is calling to me, and before we know it I'll be traveling the globe to fulfill a promise I made long ago. **What could possibly go wrong with falling in love in Paris? Nothing...unless one of you is leaving.**

STAY UP TO DATE WITH LAUREN

Stay up to date on all my news, releases and sales! Sign up for my mailing list! When you sign up you'll receive a free copy of JOY RIDE, one of my hot & hilarious bestselling rom-coms!

PROLOGUE

Joy

Forget oysters. Screw candlelight and champagne. A sexy accent is the truest aphrodisiac. I'm talking a weak-in-the-knees, flutters-all-over, fast-track to euphoria.

I've tried to analyze precisely why the sound of a man's words can elicit this reaction in, frankly, millions of women. But when I break down an accent and study it like a chemical reaction, it's nearly impossible to draw a logical conclusion. The ingredients in and of themselves don't seem swoontastic enough.

And yet, accents have been known to induce major swooning.

That's why, in my professional opinion, the sounds aren't the rocket fuel for the tingles. Instead, it's the associations evoked. Italian is food, wine, and days drenched in the pleasures of the senses. Australian is the laid-back twang of a surfer. A Southern drawl says a man will take his sweet time. Oh, yes, darlin', will he ever.

But British? Dear God. A delicious British accent to my oh-so-American ears triggers wave after wave of goose bumps across my skin. My knees wobble. My stomach swoops. My skin heats. All the turned-on centers in my body are cranked to high.

A British accent is James Bond in a bottle. It's sex, it's style, it's sophistication, and it's the man who'll find his way out of any jam, save the damsel, and do it all with silver cuff links on.

Wait. Make that platinum.

Charmed, indeed.

That's why I say it's a damn good thing I'm moving to a country that won't be chock full of my personal vocal kryptonite, since I don't have the time or inclination for distractions in my life right now. Look, I don't have a single problem with the French accent whatsoever. A hot French man can *voulez-vous coucher avec* moi, if you know what I mean.

But it's a British accent that turns me to Silly Putty, so in Paris I'll be mighty fine.

Then, I meet him.

1

Joy

I'm giving myself a gold star.

I've managed the entire transatlantic flight speaking only French. Yay me! Or should I say *oui, moi*! Pretty sure that's not an official saying, but whatevercakes. Either way, I'm rocking it in the speak-French-or-die department.

I've rattled off my *s'il vous plaits* and *mercis* like a native speaker, and I'm about to break out an even fancier request as the flight attendant strolls by offering the last round of beverages.

"Would you like something?" she asks in French.

I've checked my app. The words are on my tongue for fizzy water. "*Je voudrais l'eau avec bulles.*"

With a pinch to her lips, the angular flight attendant arches a brow. "*Excusez-moi?*"

Oops. I bet bubbles was the problem. Maybe my app went a little too literally when I looked up that word. I try to talk around the confusion, to explain what I want, when I remember something I read in a travel blog once about how the French order still versus sparkling water.

I snap my fingers and smile, going for it in a whole new direction. "*L'eau avec gaz.*"

Water with gas.

I snicker to myself. The French call the sparkling variety of water gassy.

The flight attendant blinks.

I say it again, louder this time, prompting the kindly old couple in front of me to whip their heads around. Doesn't faze me. I'm naturally loud. That isn't the first time someone's blanched in surprise at my volume, nor will it be the last.

The blonde twig smiles sympathetically and says, "Of course, mademoiselle. I will bring you a Perrier."

Le sigh. She spoke to me in English. Cue the disappointment track.

But hey, I'm a mademoiselle at least. So, obviously I'm still winning at life.

When she brings the drink, it's delish. Not gassy at all, so I'm coming out ahead in the drink department, too. Optimism, thy name is moi.

Thirty minutes later, the loudspeaker crackles and an authoritative voice booms throughout the jetliner. "We are nearing Charles DeGaulle airport," the pilot intones, and a spate of nerves flutters up my chest. But I ignore them because I'm ready for this adventure no matter how daunting the drink ordering may be.

My seatmate in 2A, a lovely lady in a pink-checkered suit, smelling faintly of Obsession and tweed, shoots me a caring smile. "Is this your first time in Paris?"

She speaks in English with the most delightful French accent. Her lips are freshly glossed, like she slicked some on moments ago. Otherwise, she wears little makeup, and her hair is clipped in a loose but immaculate bun.

"I was supposed to visit a year ago for vacation . . ." I say, my voice trailing off. But I don't want to get into why that trip never transpired. She lifts an eyebrow, waiting for my answer, perhaps wondering, too. I return to my cheery side. "That didn't happen and that's A-OK. But I've always wanted to go. I wish I had studied abroad. It's one of my great regrets that I didn't."

"And now you can remedy that regret with a visit."

I nod. "I've been taking French lessons and reading all the guidebooks." Though, in fairness, I memorized nearly every one a year ago, it seems. I pored over photos on Instagram and pictures from French food bloggers, devouring everything I could unearth on Paris. "The city has always seemed magical to me, the places, the shops, the river."

"Paris can indeed be a magical city. And is this a holiday for you?"

I can't believe I'm about to utter the next words, because I can still barely believe they're true. "I'll be working in Paris. That's why I've been speaking French to the flight attendants. To practice."

Her brown eyes are warm, and they twinkle in a friendly way. "Then, next time say *De l'eau gazeuse* or *eau pétillante*. That's what we call water with bubbles. Sparkling water."

"Ohhhhhh. Information that would have been handy an hour ago," I say, smacking my forehead playfully. "I bet the flight attendant thinks I'm a typical unrefined American."

"No. Of course not. I'm sure she appreciates the effort."

"I try," I say in French.

A gentle smile is her response. It crinkles her face.

Wrinkles line her forehead, but they're soft, like the rest of her.

"It is good to attempt the language," she tells me. "And how long will you stay?"

I shrug happily. "I'm not sure. For now, it's a relocation. My company is sending me to Paris to work on a new project."

"How thrilling."

"*Je suis excitée!*" I say, trotting out more of my French.

The woman shakes her head. "No," she says as a faint blush crosses her cheeks. She drops her voice lower. "That means you are excited."

"But I am."

Her brown eyes widen, and she waves her hand over her lap. "Down there."

My mouth forms an O. "Well, shame on me," I say, and she laughs. "That's not appropriate at all. What would I say instead?"

"It depends. If you're excited to see someone, if you're excited to eat a croissant, if you're looking forward to something . . ." She makes a rolling gesture with her hand, inviting me to fill in the rest.

"Personally, I'm excited for all croissants. I think they're proof that people weren't meant to eat a gluten-free diet. Like, ever."

She laughs lightly. "Carbs are divine. So, you are definitely looking forward to croissants in Paris."

"I am." I flash a bright smile. I've been told my smile occupies all the real estate on my face. I attribute this to being from Texas. We do everything supersize. "I'm looking forward to my new life in Paris."

She smiles and translates into her language. I repeat her words.

"Very good."

"Thank you."

She hums, a soft little sound. "Paris is a good place for a new life. I believe Paris is where you go to reinvent yourself."

A few years ago, reinvention was the last thing I'd imagined wanting. I was content with a capital C.

Now, it's what I need most.

As the jet descends, I find that I am well and truly excited—not down there, but here, in my chest, in my heart—for what lies ahead.

Mostly because it's just that. Ahead.

The past belongs to yesterday.

When the wheels touch the tarmac, I bid yesterday a silent and final adieu.

2

Griffin

The way a travel book tells it, the River Seine is 485 miles long, thirty-one feet deep on average, and is spanned by thirty-seven bridges in France's capital city.

Boring.

Facts can be so terribly dull.

If I were writing a travel book, I'd surely add other details.

For instance, the river is also a home to occasional sewage overflows, it's a resting spot for love locks from the Pont Des Arts tossed in the river when angry lovers split, and it's a fairly popular watery disposal site for dead bodies, since about fifty-five of those buggers were dredged up in the Seine as recently as ten years ago.

Just picture that the next time someone suggests a dinner boat cruise down the Seine.

Yes, if I were a tour guide, I'd spend too much time

noodling on little details with my tourists, like when were the bodies tossed into the water and how long had they been earthworm meat before being given the heave-ho to their wet graves. As for the love locks, I'd ponder how many clever little bits and bobs could have been made with the damn discarded metal in the first place. Picture frames, necklaces, and the like . . . I have to imagine an entire industry could be born from the declarations of love that weigh down one of the city's bridges.

But perhaps that's why I'm not a tour guide. I find the odd facts and curiosities of a city much more interesting than monuments and guideposts.

As I ride my bike along the Left Bank, the sun rises above the horizon of the city I've lately come to call my home. I near one of the *bouquinistes* I see most mornings. His name is Julien, and he looks the part of a seller of anti-quarian books and postcards from his stand alongside the river. He sports a mustache and a beret, and he often wears a striped shirt. I asked him once if he even liked the beret. "No," he'd said, curling his lip in disdain. "It is horrible. But I sell more postcards when I wear it." Then he gave a typical French shrug.

"Bet you sell even more when you're in stripes."

A wicked grin had appeared on his face. "I do."

"*Bonjour*, Julien," I call out when I'm a few feet away.

"Why do you wear that stupid helmet?" he asks gruffly. "You look ridiculous. You're the only one who wears a helmet."

"I like what's inside it," I say with a smile as I pass him.

He huffs but waves a quick good-bye.

I slow at the light at the bridge and pedal off when it turns green. I raise my face to the blue sky and smile.

It's one of those days when I feel a little lighter, a little springier, with a mood to match the weather. Paris in the springtime is capricious, but today the sun is shining, and as I ride past groups of tourists streaming toward Notre Dame, a burst of wistfulness courses through me. It's a shame, in a way, that I'll soon be saying good-bye, since this city has been good to me. We've had a steady run— the cafés and the bookshops, the hunts up cobbled streets, and the escapades in the evenings with pretty women.

I cut across the next intersection and turn onto the sidewalk of Rue LaGrange. I veer to the right, avoiding a mother holding her toddler's hand. The mother shoots me a coarse look. She probably thinks I'm a tourist. That if I were a true Frenchman, I'd ride in the street, sans helmet, and a scarf looped around my neck no matter the weather. I simply smile in return, because nothing is going to get me down today.

When I reach the florist shop, I slow to a stop, lock up my bike, then unscrew the seat. You can't be too safe, especially in a city rife with not only pickpockets, but thieves who will do nearly anything to nick a bike. Except ride away with their crotch perched on a metal pole.

I say hello to the florist then head inside the Capstone Language Institute next door, taking the stairs to the fifth floor, whistling a happy tune as I go, bike seat in hand. Today isn't just payday. It's *cha-ching* day. It's rain-euros-on-me-for-a-job-well-done day.

This is the day I've been waiting for.

When I push open the door to our offices, I cross paths with my friend Christian, who shakes his blond head, bemused at something. Christian is a top translator at the same company I work for. He knows French and all the Scandinavian languages, even though he was raised in England from a young age.

I take a wild guess at the source of his amusement. "Jean-Paul is on a roll this morning?"

"My ears will never recover from the tale he just told."

I cringe. The fellow who runs the place and doles out the assignments is prone to TMI. Jean-Paul has never met a tawdry tale he wouldn't tell. "Just smile and nod, right?"

"I did my best, I swear," Christian says. "But I might need to find a way to erase the last five minutes from my memory. Something about a house of ill repute, three women, a bustier, and red heels. I'm not sure if the heels were worn or drunk from—"

I hold up my hands. "Stop right there, mate. That's all I need to know, thank you very much."

"You should be thanking me. I had to take that bullet today."

I clap him on the shoulder. "I'll always be grateful for your sacrifice. Did you snag a new assignment?"

He smiles impishly. "I'm booked for the week. A crew of brokers in from Copenhagen. It's a pretty penny since they're paying for my specialty."

"Nice one," I say, since Christian's a former finance whiz. "See you in the ..."

I stop myself, since if all goes as planned, I might not be here next week to see him at all.

He laughs and raises his chin. "See you on the flip side," he says, since that's his favorite American expression. He claps me on the back. "It's been good. Let's get a beer before you go?"

"Count on it."

Turning down the hall, I square my shoulders and knock on the open door to Jean-Paul's office. Even his randy stories won't derail my mood today. I can barely contain my grin. Today is bonus day, and the bonus I've been promised for my last job is big enough for me to tackle a most important item from a most important list.

"Come in."

I push on the door. "Good morning, Jean-Paul. How are you this fine Monday?"

"Fantastic." He rises, taking off his glasses and gesturing to his chair. "I had the most amazing weekend."

And he's already off and running.

"Amazing weekends are the best kind," I say, since I suppose I can endure a randy story given the bonus that's coming my way.

I take the chair as Jean-Paul drags a hand through his thick mess of gray hair. His eyes twinkle with the naughtiness of a teenager.

I brace myself as he launches into the details of a weekend that revolve around a rope, a corset, and his fourth wife, which means I'm getting a whole new tale from the one he told Christian. "But enough about me," Jean-Paul says, once he concludes by informing me that the rope burns on his wife's wrists were completely visible when she served their neighbors Sunday night dinner. "How did you feel the job with the Wentsworth Group went?"

Thank hell for the segue. "Great. The client seemed happy. The marketing executives were quite satisfied. All went well, I'd say." My recent gig was the most plum of plum assignments—one company for a few months, working with a key executive, handling all marketing material translations from French to English. *Now, let's show me the money, in the form of that absolutely delicious bonus for a job well done.*

"All did go well. Funny, that's how I felt about my first marriage, too," Jean-Paul says, a faraway look filling his eyes. "She was the prettiest." He sighs dreamily.

"Okay."

"Absolutely the best of the bunch."

"Right. Someone always comes out on top, eh?"

"Which brings me to the bonus," he says, his voice turning heavy, leaden.

It doesn't take a translator to know what that sound signifies. Hell, Google Translate could get that right.

"Yes, the bonus," I say, rubbing my palms together, my pitch rising like I can rearrange fate with a chipper demeanor. But then, this wouldn't be the first time I tried to wish away circumstances with a bloody fucking grin.

Didn't have much luck then, either.

"The good news is we have so many more jobs."

I can practically feel the bonus slipping through my fingers right this second.

"And the bad news is they'll be a week late with the bonus?" I offer, always playing the optimist. Been there, done that, have the T-shirt.

Jean-Paul rubs his hand over the back of his neck. "Griffin, it's like I say about my first wife and me. Sometimes it just doesn't work out between a couple, but they still love each other."

"I don't think that's a saying about first wives."

"What I'm saying is the client loved you, but it turns out, no fault of yours, that the marketing campaign was total crap. And the company doesn't have the money to pay the bonus since the campaign was canceled."

My shoulders sag. "They can't pay the bonus?"

Screw optimism. Just screw it, like a bike frame without a seat screws the sitter.

"It seems it is not on the map."

I fall into English. "I really wish you were taking the piss right now."

He blinks. "I'm not urinating."

"Sorry. I meant I wish you were pulling my leg," I say, using the phrase he'd be more familiar with since he learned English in American schools.

"Ah, I only wish I were pulling your leg. Yanking your chains. Taking your pisses."

I shake my head. "No, it's just taking *the* piss. Not mine. I assure you."

He flashes a smile, and it's probably the grin he used on his first, second, and third wives, because it almost tricks me into thinking everything's going to be fine. "Language is a funny thing, isn't it?" he says, chuckling as if this is the most delightful conversation in all the land. "In any case, Wentsworth said you were stellar. Most marvelous translator they've had. But you know how it goes. *C'est la vie.*"

"Win some, lose some," I add.

He snaps his fingers. "Your idioms are spot on, Griffin. That's why you'll always be in demand. As I've said, you and Annalise are some of the best when it comes to nuance."

"Yes," I agree, since my pregnant colleague is quite sharp, too. But a lot of good that grasp on idioms is now that the money is sailing away in the spring breeze.

Along with the dream it was earmarked for. I planned to use that bonus to line the pockets of an airline, pay a registration fee, and run twenty-six miles, then spend some time exploring Indonesia, the first place I ever marked on a map with a thumbtack.

It was meant to serve a certain someone's wishes.

"But don't fret," says the man who was supposed to become my former boss today but is now still my current boss. "We have new assignments coming in all the time. You're one of my top translators for all those crazy Americans who realize French is just a teeny bit harder than they thought."

I should laugh. Really, I should. Because that's the truest thing he's ever uttered.

And yet, I can't hear him over the sound of my dream trip circling the toilet.

3

Joy

In Texas, everything is big. For the last three years, I lived in a sprawling-ass house. I believe that is actually the official definition. When I spotted it on Zillow, the listing said something like that—*big-ass home for sale.*

Fine, I kid.

But it was three bedrooms and a truckload of square feet. The yard played hostess to many a barbecue—yes, my yard was female—and the two-car garage could have held a pair of fat trucks. Most of the time, it housed my Prius.

The square footage tipped close to two thousand, and the cost for all that space was way more than manageable. Such is real estate life in the outskirts of Austin.

The human resources director at L'Artisan Cosmetique, the newly acquired French division of the cosmetics giant I work for, warned me of the size disparity between Texas homes and Parisian ones.

"I must make you aware that the flats we are sending over for your consideration are not terribly large," Marisol, the human resources director, wrote tactfully in her email to me a few weeks ago. "I hope we do not disappoint you."

I promptly assured her there was no way I would ever be disappointed, even with a cupboard-size flat in Paris. She could house me in a windowless studio, in a room missing a kitchen, in a closet even. Whatever size she found, it would possess the most important feature an abode could claim—*just me.*

After living in too close quarters for far too long, I didn't need space so much as I needed *not another person.*

All that square footage hardly mattered when I shared it with someone who Svengali'd everyone around him. I learned what's truly valuable in real estate is how many people you let have a key.

I button my blouse while gazing out the window of my hotel room overlooking Notre Dame, enjoying the view.

Enjoying, too, that I'm the only person who has a key to this room.

As I slide the last button in, my phone buzzes from my back pocket. There's a note from Stephen, the apartment manager at Paris Perfect Places, confirming that tomorrow morning he'll give me the key to my furnished rental flat, 2B in a cute little building in the 5th arrondissement.

By "little" I mean less than four hundred square feet, which in French real estate is evidently considered a "luminous" thirty-eight square meters. That's precisely how the flat was advertised.

Except . . . something seems off as I reread the message. The address for the flat looks odd. I was pretty sure I rented something on the third floor, not the second.

I tap out a reply. *You mean 3B?*

Stephen's response is swift. *Yes, 2B!*

Okay, something is clearly lost in translation, but I don't think I'll be able to sort it out right now. I fire off a typical *I can't wait* response, translating it into French, but then I stop myself. What if "*I can't wait*" in French turns out to mean "*I want to rub my lady parts against you*?"

Instead, I cycle back to what my seatmate on the plane taught me, and I use one of her replies then hit send.

My stomach growls. It's nearly nine, but my jet lag woke me up at five, so my stomach is basically saying *I hate you, bitch, feed me now*. My appointment with Marisol and the translator isn't for another hour, but since I'm wide awake, I decide to take off for a stroll toward Notre Dame. Because I can, and because no one's here to stop me.

Stepping away from the window, I toss a light green scarf around my neck, wrapping it jauntily and pressing it to my nose. The smell of silk and cedar drifts into my nostrils. As I let the fabric fall, I catch the faint whiff of honeysuckle, too. That's my favorite scent in my favorite perfume that I can finally wear again. It transports me instantly to a hammock under the sun and to long summer days as a teenager when I started to daydream of boys. I spritzed some on this morning when I dressed, since I brought my budding collection of little perfumes with me on the plane in my carry-on. All less than three ounces, of course.

I grab my shades and leave the hotel room, saying *bonjour* to a maid on my floor, the concierge in the lobby, and the doorman by the exit. I'm like Belle in the opening sequence of *Beauty and the Beast*. *Bonjour, bonjour, bonjour*.

This city will be everything I imagined. It will be more than wonderful. Paris is my great escape, and it begins today.

The doorman holds open the door, and I step outside. Cue the music video. Paris, here I come. Just try to wipe the grin from my face. It's impossible because everything around me is so very French.

Like the looming sky-blue wooden door of the building next to the hotel. A knocker that looks like a cherub holds center court. What a funny little decoration for what appears to be an office building, and the very architecture suggests that the structure is a few centuries older than my home state.

I chuckle as I rub the bronze cherub's hair, then I snap a cell phone shot. I send the picture to my sister, Allison.

On the other side of the hotel is a café. My heart skips a little faster because it's everything the photos promised me. Small chairs with round wicker seats and tall, black backs spill onto the sidewalk. There's barely an inch of room between each little circular red table, but no one cares. Parisians sip their coffees from teeny cups while reading the newspaper, or brooding, or talking to a companion. Men wear scarves around their necks and trim pants with fine leather shoes. The women dress in heels and . . . black. So much black. Skirts, jeans, sweaters, pants. The melody of voices that falls on my ears aren't speaking big, bold, brash English. The foreign words are music; they're the soundtrack to my new life.

I walk to the end of the block, staring at everything with hungry eyes. I devour the sights, the delicate iron latticework on the balconies, the green and blue street signs displaying words like *rue* and *boulevard*, the curling calligraphy on shop fronts, from the boulangerie to the boutique to the patisserie. Even a pharmacy across the streets looks fancy, with a sign in emerald-green glass. The streets curve and angle, and I try to inhale Paris all at once, as if I can capture the magic of it in one big blink of the eye. Just to be safe, though, so I don't forget it, I take a few more pics, sending those to my sister as well.

I stop in the middle of the sidewalk, mouth agape, when the River Seine comes into view.

I gasp.

I'm here. I'm really and truly here. And that winding ribbon of water is proof that I'm not in Texas anymore. I'm so far away from where I used to be, and I want to drink it all in, eat it all up, savor it.

"*Oomph.*" I stumble, my feet wobbly on the pavement.

A French woman mutters something at me under her breath since, oh yeah, I just whacked her arm due to my complete lack of attention.

"Sorry," I say.

She lifts her chin and huffs.

"Well, *excusez-moi.*" Two can play at that game. But she's clear across the street by now, so I smooth my hands over my blouse and keep on keeping on.

If that's my only faux pas today, I'll take it.

I stride to the corner and wait at the light, marveling at the familiar silhouette the famous church cuts against the sky. The sight tugs my mind back to the plans I made for a trip here more than a year ago. The flights were booked, the hotel secured. I'd mapped out a fun itinerary, with time to play ultimate tourist and time to explore the city's nooks and secrets. That was what I most wanted to do. Uncover the city. Peel back its familiar layers and find the unexpected underneath.

Notre Dame was part of the trip, naturally. I like the sight of stained-glass windows and the smell of stone and old books.

But the trip was canceled.

Like so many other things.

The memory of the arguments that ensued, the

drama, the debates, and then, finally, the unraveling chores—calling airlines, unbooking hotels—smacks me like a slap in the face, and I wish I could erase them from my mind. Erase my ex.

That's one of the reasons this new job was so easy to say yes to. I wasn't running away from a love that went sour, but I won't deny that the prospect of all those miles —glorious miles, an ocean, and a continent between us— lubed up the path to "yes" quite easily. I can still recall the Friday afternoon at the lab when the email from L'Artisan landed in my inbox. I'd just finished working on some new formulations for a hair spray fragrance, and I'd tugged off my goggles and peeked at my phone.

Re: Inquiry

The subject line had intrigued me. Sure, it might very well have been an inquiry about trying a BRAND-NEW EXCITING SUPPLEMENT THAT REVERSES THE AGING PROCESS. Heck, I'm all for anything that actually does reverse aging. Whoever said one should grow old gracefully clearly never woke up one morning after her thirtieth birthday surprised to see—shudder—lines on her neck.

In any case, I clicked it open, stat, and found something better than the fountain of youth.

Would you be interested in relocating to Paris to oversee the fragrance lab at L'Artisan?

I nearly dropped the phone, and trust me, I have steady hands.

I replied so quickly I was sure I'd lose any negotiating power on account of overeagerness, but I was equally sure I didn't care.

Hell to the yes.

Though I phrased my reply more professionally.

Two months later, I'm here, heading to my first

meeting on French soil. Maybe I'm not Belle twirling with her basket in her blue aproned frock across the countryside. I'm me in jeans and boots, navigating my way through a major metropolis on the way to see Marisol. We planned to meet the translator L'Artisan hired for me—a lovely lady named Annalise who studied science at university, so she's perfect for the job, Marisol had said.

As I wander along a side street, window shopping at all the boutiques, my phone rings.

"Hello," I say cheerily when I answer, and Marisol asks me how I'm doing.

"Well," I tell her, then ask the same of her.

In French.

Yay me.

She answers, then slides into English. "I hope your first day here is good so far. I wanted to let you know we must cancel the meeting with Annalise. She's the translator we hired for you, but she's no longer available."

"Oh no."

"It's okay," she says reassuringly. "She's pregnant, and her doctor put her on bed rest due to some complications. She's going to be fine, but she cannot do on-site work, naturally."

"Of course," I say, instantly understanding.

"Capstone also assures me they should be able to find someone quickly for you. We want your transition to be as seamless as possible. We can have your translator help you with anything you need to make this easy."

"I appreciate all you do," I tell her.

"We're so thrilled to have you. I can still meet you for coffee, if you'd like? I'm nearby. Or I can send you to a fantastic bakery that's not too far from where we were going to meet."

"A bakery sounds perfect." I don't want to inconvenience her just for the sake of being social, especially since I want to start on the best foot possible.

She gives me the address, and I repeat it.

"I will update you soon. Now, go have a croissant, sit by the river, and enjoy your morning."

L'Artisan has been treating me like a rock star. I suppose an advanced degree in organic chemistry will do that for you, as well as eight years' experience as second-in-command at the fragrance chemistry lab at a major US cosmetics firm. That's why L'Artisan convinced its parent company to relocate me to Paris. To introduce our efficient style to their niche products. But I need this position just as much as the company needs me. Back home, I'd stalled out in my job. I was second, not first, and there was no room for advancement. The head of the lab was going exactly nowhere. That made it even easier to say yes to the new job.

I end the call, tuck the phone into the small purse slung over my chest, and cross the street. I repeat the address that Marisol gave me out loud, but I'm not entirely sure where I am, other than heading closer to Notre Dame. I plug the address into my GPS and realize the bakery is a block away. Easy as pie.

Or eclair, I should say.

As I cross the street, I spot an older woman tugging a small, wheeled shopping basket behind her. A baguette pokes out the top of the basket, and I want to take a photo of it. So I do, raising my cell phone and clicking. Then I notice something at the corner of the street—a man locking up his bike. He wears a helmet. From my vantage point, perhaps fifty feet away, I can tell he's handsome. Tall and trim, he wears dark, fitted slacks, and a light blue button-down shirt. The combination is somehow both casual and sharply dressed. He has that European look about him. Well, duh. I'm in freaking Europe. But what I really mean is—he looks like he belongs here. He has a certain ease about him. A comfort in his body and in his surroundings, in his style as a man who rides a bicycle in France. He owns this city, he knows it, and yet he doesn't flaunt it. That's what his easy stride and casual smile tell me, even from a distance.

When he takes off his helmet, I catch a glimpse of a chiseled jaw, and as he puts the helmet on the handlebars, I check out a rear end that would make angels weep.

I sigh happily, enjoying the Parisian view. Thank you very much, Europe, for sculpting some fine asses on your men. I'm just going to let myself savor the sight as he turns toward the door of the bakery.

Okay, savoring done. Time to savor some carbs.

I reach the bakery and open the door. The scent of fresh bread calls out to me, warm, doughy, and delicious.

I enter and inhale the lovely aromas, then take my spot in line and ogle the display case. There are apricot tarts, raspberry cakes, caramel eclairs, and bread, bread, bread. My mouth waters.

I stare at all the luscious food that's so darn enticing I barely realize the man with the cute butt and fine jaw is standing in front of me.

When it's his turn, he says hello to the woman at the register.

An involuntary shiver runs down my spine.

He said that in English.

And not just any English.

But *British*.

4

Griffin

I'd have kicked a rubbish bin in frustration if I were that type of guy. Instead, I gave myself fifteen minutes of drown-my-sorrows time. For the first seven, I leaned against the barricade at the river, sighed heavily, and stared glumly into the water. Then for three minutes, I opened my wallet, unfolded the piece of paper I keep in it, and reread the words imprinted on my memory.

3. Visit Indonesia. Run a marathon there. Travel across the country, then everywhere.

So, yeah. That's been tabled. It wasn't even my dream, but I annexed it when I had to. Adopted it, if you will, when the dream's owner died.

Then, for the final five minutes, I wandered. Contemplating.

Travel everywhere. Love the idea, but I haven't saved quite enough yet to pull it off. I need to scrape together a little more, and with the bonus gone, I need more work.

Only I don't have more work yet.

But here's the thing. Bread can solve nearly every crummy situation. *Nearly.* That's why I'm here at the bakery. Marie is behind the counter, wearing an orange apron that's covered in flour. Her thick black hair is held in a hairnet.

I say hello to her in English, and she answers me back the same. It's a running joke. The first time I came here, I was talking on the phone with a friend from home, and she greeted me in English, assuming I didn't know her language.

She was surprised when I switched to her native tongue, which I do again right now. I order a baguette, and we chat briefly. *Am I having a good day?* she asks. I don't need to unload on her, so I tell her my day is fine.

"Did you find the rugelach in Le Marais that I told you about?" she asks as she bends to the case to grab the bread.

"It was amazing. And if I keep eating that I will balloon up," I say, patting my belly and puffing my cheeks.

She laughs and waves a hand dismissively. "Don't even go there, young man. You're too skinny. You haven't an ounce of fat on you."

That might not be precisely true, but she's correct that I'm trim. Running and biking has that effect on the physique.

"And you are too good to me," I tell her, then hand her two euros for the bread.

I grab the bread and say good-bye as well.

"*Bonjour.*" The greeting comes from the woman behind me.

I turn in the direction of the voice. The American voice. The confident, strong American voice.

"*Je voudrais un croissant chocolat.*"

But she's all wrong, so I jump in. "It's *pain au chocolat*."

She furrows her brow. "What did you say?"

I repeat myself. I can't help it. In my line of work, it's a natural reaction to offer up the more appropriate translations for Americans. I ought to tune out conversations.

But *this* American? I don't want to tune her out.

She's so very . . . red.

Rich auburn hair spills down her shoulders, landing in the kind of big, soft curls that look like they take hours to achieve, with loads of potions and lotions and many fights with heated devices that do all sorts of things to hair. But she hardly seems the high-maintenance type, since she wears a red-checkered bandana like a headband. Jeans hug her legs, a pretty maroon blouse accentuates her lovely assets, and boots make her even taller. Cowboy boots.

She's statuesque.

Good thing I like tall birds.

Good thing I'm even taller.

Wait. Am I really thinking of picking up a woman in the bakery?

Of course I fucking am. I love American accents. I love the boldness. I love the confidence. I love the way American women own who they are.

Like this one. She's stunning, especially with those pouty red lips.

"That's what we call a chocolate croissant," I add.

"We?" she echoes. "That's what *we* call a croissant?" She arches a brow, but not in a haughty way. More like a "you don't say" way. She points at me playfully. "You don't really sound like you're part of that *we*. But I'll still give you a big old *merci beaucoup* for helping me."

When she smiles, it's like a sunbeam. A full-wattage grin.

"You're correct. *They* call it that. I simply partake of its deliciousness."

"You should partake of chocolate croissants. I hear the ones at this boulangerie are to die for." Then she winks at me and turns to Marie, who's watching our exchange with avid interest. The American woman orders properly this time, and Marie fetches the pastry for her.

I head out, but I dawdle. In fact, I'm pretty sure I'm on pace to set a record for sheer sluggishness. Just a few more seconds, and she should be exiting.

She strolls out the door, bringing the scent of chocolate with her, and for a fleeting moment I imagine she tastes like chocolate.

She stops in front of me. She takes a bite of the croissant wrapped in a waxy paper and chews. She hums her praise for the food. "This is a delicious chocolate croissant." Then she brings her fingers to her lips. "Oops. I meant *pain au chocolat*."

"Very good. And I apologize if it seemed out of line to correct you. I didn't want to see you commit a faux pas."

"*We* didn't mind," she teases.

"*We* are so glad to hear," I add.

She takes another bite and rolls her eyes, presumably in pleasure. When she finishes, she says, "So you're a Prince Charming rescuing damsels in distress from language faux pas?"

"Something like that."

"So gallant."

"I aspire to gallantry every day. Though sometimes it expresses itself in odd ways."

"Funnily enough, if you can ensure I'm getting access to one of the best chocolate croissants in all the city, then I'm good with those odd ways."

"Do you like . . .?" I pause, and her green eyes follow my gaze to the treat in her hands.

"I do. Very much." She points at me with the end of the croissant. Her eyes are inquisitive, studying me. "You're not French."

"You're not, either."

"But that's obvious."

"And it's obvious I'm not as well."

She smirks. "You're British."

I feign surprise. "What gave it away?"

"The accent might have been a tip-off."

"Damn." I snap my fingers, as if she's caught me. That makes her smirk a little more. "You're American," I toss back at her.

Her eyes widen, and she appears positively astonished, playing along. "However could you tell?"

She waits, tapping her toe, evidently expecting me to say her voice since that's what we've been chatting about.

"You want to know the giveaway?"

"I do."

I lean a touch closer to her. "Your smile."

That only makes her grin grow wider. She tries to contain it. She tries valiantly, it seems. But she has no luck. "They don't smile in France?"

"Not like that. Not like you do."

Yeah, I could flirt all day with her. That accent. Those eyes. Her hair. She's a welcome distraction. I almost don't mind my plans being massively derailed since it's given me this unexpected encounter, and I don't want this encounter with her to end. "What's your name?" But before she can answer, I shake my head, and hold up a hand. "Wait. Let me guess."

"Oh, by all means. Guess my name, Daniel."

I laugh. "Daniel?"

"Seems like a good English name. Was I wrong? Is it Harry? William? Clive? Oliver? Henry? Rupert? Alistair? Archibald?"

Laughing, I blurt out, "You can't possibly think I'm an Archibald?"

She waves dismissively. "Right, of course. My bad. You must be Archie."

"If I'm Archie, then how about you? Are you a Jennifer?"

She shakes her head.

"Amy?"

Another shake.

"Stacy, then?"

"Nope."

"You must be Katie?"

She rolls her eyes. "Try harder, Archibald."

"Taylor? Hannah? Madison? Chloe? Avery?" Every name yields a no. "I've got it." Her eyes widen. "Judy? You must be Judy."

She laughs loudly. "Judy? You think I'm a Judy? While it's quite a pretty name, let's be honest—when was the last time you met an American Judy who was under fifty?"

"When have you met an Archibald who wasn't bald and over seventy?"

She gives my dark hair a once-over. "True, you're not bald. But why would you think only an American would have those names? Jennifer. Amy. Stacy," she says, imitating me.

"Perhaps the same reason you picked Harry and William."

"I picked them because I like princes."

"Well, perhaps I like American-sounding names," I counter, and her green eyes sparkle as she laughs.

"They do seem quintessentially American, don't they?"

"They do."

"Does that mean you think I'm quintessentially American?" She brings her hand to her chest, and my eyes follow. Because . . . breasts.

I allow myself a second to admire the potential of hers, then I refocus. "Quintessentially American is a fine thing to be."

I'm about to throw in the towel and ask her real name, when her phone brays. It's the loudest thing I've ever heard.

"So sorry, this is my . . ." But she trails off as she answers the phone. "*Bonjour*, Marisol."

Her brow furrows, and she listens intently to her call for ten seconds, twenty seconds.

And I've crossed the line.

I can't stand here and wait any longer. That would be rude. Her phone call is my cue to go.

I give her a tip of the hat. "Good-bye, Judy," I whisper.

For a moment, her brow furrows, almost as if she's surprised I'm taking off.

Then, she smiles brightly, waves her fingers at me, and mouths *good-bye, Archie.*

She turns the other way, her croissant in one hand, her phone to her ear in the other.

I let myself enjoy a few seconds of the view of her walking away.

Then reality swoops back in. I'm no longer flirting with a sexy American woman as if I don't have a care in the world. Instead, I'm left here holding a baguette and my helmet, wondering what I'll do next to earn the money to take the trip my brother wanted to take.

5

Joy

The line stretches for a hundred feet or more. It's almost as if, well, it's as if everyone has heard of this place.

But I'm not going to let a long line deter me.

Nope. I have sunglasses and no place to be today—except for a destination I wanted to visit on the trip that never was.

I grab a spot at the back of the line queued up to enter the north tower at the cathedral of Notre Dame. Literally everyone is taking photos. And I'm not exaggerating. This is one of those times when *literally* literally applies.

Except me.

I set up an Instagram account a year ago, thinking I'd fill it with everything I longed to see in this city on that trip.

It went unused, and my shutterbug ways remained limited to the mundane, to everyday items I didn't want to forget. The filter in my furnace so I'd remember which brand to buy. A shot of my insurance card when I renewed my license. Proof of a deposit to show the bank. My camera roll is littered with daily reminders of tasks, and only tasks.

I believe Paris is where you go to reinvent yourself.

That's why I'm here.

To start over. To embrace life, opportunity, and beauty. And since change is the name of the game, I decide to capture what inspires me. I gaze at the spires of the cathedral, its massive archways, the sheer enormity of the fairy-tale-esque cathedral. I look at the real thing, but then, since I don't want to forget it, I snap a photograph.

As I stare at the intricate stone carvings in my camera app, I flash back to the Englishman from earlier today and imagine standing here with him, continuing our conversation. The possibility is so potent, I can see him. I can smell the faint scent of sweat and wood from his aftershave. I can hear the proper notes of his voice. If he were with me now, would we still be tossing increasingly ridiculous names at each other? Would we have moved on to other topics, like how many times he's seen this cathedral, or the fact that I've never set foot in it before? Would he have said, "Go on without me. I'll just wait for you here?"

My shoulders tighten as those far too familiar words echo in my mind.

Those were words Richard used, and I wince as I fall back in time to more than a year ago. I was invited to New York to speak at a conference. He wanted to tag along, he'd said. See the sights while I spoke on a panel and attended meetings. He'd visit the Empire State Building, see Central Park, stroll around the Village. But the day of my panel, he woke up and said he was in too much pain to go anywhere. He'd stay behind at the hotel. *Don't worry about me*, he said. He texted me on my way to the conference. *It's not so bad. I'll be fine.* He texted me when I arrived at the Javits. *Spoke too soon. Back is killing me.* I told him to consider calling a doctor. He texted me minutes before my presentation. *Can barely move now.*

Please call a doctor, I texted before I went on stage.

It was the worst presentation I'd ever done. I was so worried about him.

As soon as it ended and I emerged from the cavern of the convention center, I called him. He didn't answer. My heart hammered with worry, with fear that he'd truly taken some sort of turn for the worse. After a gnarly cab ride to the hotel and a mad dash through the lobby to the elevators, I found him sound asleep in the room.

When he awoke later that day, he said he'd turned the ringer off to take a nap, but he felt better and was ready for dinner.

We had sushi that night, and he asked how my talk went. I didn't bother telling him that I sucked. He felt better, and that was all that mattered.

In fact, he'd said at dinner that night that he would feel well enough to go to Paris in a few months. But when the trip drew near, he claimed flying made his back worse. He'd need more pills before he could fly. So many more, he'd told me. So many that I should go on without him.

I didn't.

I don't know what Richard is doing now. He's still in Austin, and I'm far, far away.

Right here, right now, I decide Archibald the Baguette Eater would have happily waited in line with me, cheerfully climbed the steps, and playfully confessed his name to me at the belfry. By the gargoyles, he'd have whispered it in my ear.

When I reach the main entrance, I don't go inside the church. I march up the corkscrew stone staircase, my breath coming faster as I scale the more than four hundred fan-shaped steps. But I won't let a few stairs stop me from seeing the gargoyles at the top of the towers.

I happen to like gargoyles.

They're badass sentries, fiercely standing guard over the holiest of holy places. As light shines at the top of the stairs, my breath comes hard and fast, my thighs burning from the climb. When I reach the gallery on the north tower, I'm outside at the top of the most famous church in the world, and it's spectacular. The city unfurls hundreds of feet below me, the river winding through Paris, the Eiffel Tower standing tall at the edge, the Louvre staking its famous claim by the water, the hills of Montmartre rising high.

It's breathtaking.

I stare off in the distance, delighting in the view, when something catches my attention out of the corner of my eye. I snap my gaze in its direction.

I'm looking at an elephant.

Holy smokes. There's an elephant perched next to a gargoyle.

It's a stone elephant, sitting on his big butt.

He's not grotesque. He's simply . . . an unexpected elephant.

And that's exactly what I wanted to see. Something that surprised me. Something that makes me rethink my day, my opinion. I grab my phone and snap a shot of the elephant. This photo isn't a reminder for my to-do list. This shot has meaning—it signifies the opposite of regret.

I can't regret the cancelled vacation.

If I'd have come here with Richard, he wouldn't have ventured up these steps, and I'd have felt bad going without him. That's on me. I would have wanted to climb them, but I'd have chosen to stay on the ground with him.

Now, I feel sated, because of this elephant. It feels like my reward. Maybe even a reminder to shuck off the guilt that sometimes weighs on me. Let it go, and focus on the future.

Honestly, my only regret so far in my first twenty-four hours in Paris is that I didn't snag Archibald's phone number. That man was more delicious than the croissant, and it would have been fun to have a glass of wine or a cup of coffee with him.

I give myself a virtual smack. I don't have time to let my mind wander to romantic interludes and flirty men. Extricating myself from a toxic relationship had felt like a Herculean feat at times, but I succeeded. Now I'm on the other side of manipulation, of lies, of the huge albatross of guilt that anchored me to Austin for far longer than it should have.

When I reach the ground, my phone buzzes. There's a text from my sister.

Allison: I miss you so much it hurts, but you look like you're having a blast! Keep the pictures coming and keep on enjoying life!!

I tell her I miss her with the depth of a black hole, but that I'm loving it here, too. I resolve to keep snapping photos— but to make sure they matter, that I'm both capturing life and living it well. I post the elephant as the fitting first image on my Instagram feed—#firstdayinparis #unexpectedsights #greatviews #lookaround.

When I close the app, I spot a message from the man with the rental company.

Stephen: Bonjour! The flat we arranged for you is all ready for tomorrow's meeting. The studio is perfect.

I furrow my brow. I didn't plunk down a security deposit on a studio. I opted for a one-bedroom on the third freaking floor.

Joy: I look forward to it. You mean the one-bedroom on the third floor?

His reply is instant.

Stephen: Yes, the studio on the second. It is beautiful.

I sigh. Call me crazy, but I think Stephen might be trying to yank me around. I want to call Marisol and ask her advice, but I don't want to be a burden. I sort of wish the sweet little old lady from the plane had given me her business card, since she seemed the fairy godmother type, and I bet she'd know how to magic wand her way out of this mess for me.

But alas, I'll need to handle this little situation on my own.

Back at the hotel room, I find an email from Marisol. The agency already has a new translator for me. His name is Griffin, and he studied biology in school so he knows the complicated technical lingo for the job. That's key. Though it's not necessary for him to understand how chemical reactions work, a scientific background and competence with terms that might flummox other linguists is an absolute necessity. Also, he's quite good at idioms, both in French and English, Marisol writes. If I approve, the agency can let him know.

I tap my finger to my lip, a plan brewing. I wonder if he's good at dealing with rental agents trying to screw an American over. I hope this new translator is like Archibald, ready to save a lady about to commit a faux pas.

I call Marisol and tell her Griffin sounds great. "Will you ask if he can meet me tomorrow morning?"

"Yes. He's ready to start right away."

I give her the address of the rental. "Nine thirty. I can't wait to meet him."

6

Griffin

When someone you love dies, you hear more platitudes than you'll ever want to hear in your entire life.

When one door closes, another opens.

It was his time.

Someday, this pain will make sense.

As for the last one, what the hell? How does that even make sense in a store selling pillows with stitched-on platitudes? In a shop peddling magnets with sayings? Who buys that, let alone believes it?

But someone must because it's been served up to me. I've heard my fair share of clichés in the last year since my younger brother, Ethan, died in a mostly unexpected way.

And I grin and bear it, every time.

Because ultimately, people mean well when they utter hackneyed sayings in the wake of a loss. What they mean is *I'm so sorry*.

Yeah, me, too.

Still, I'm not a fan of banalities. I could do without hearing one, say, ever again.

But back at my flat later that afternoon, a particular one pops into my head when Jean-Paul calls, though it has nothing to do with life and death.

He tells me that because Annalise has been put on bed rest, he has an assignment to fill. An American chemist needs a translator who can handle on-site work, and someone familiar with scientific lingo. The job as this woman's personal translator will last for at least three months as she transitions from the US to France. The company wants a translator for four hours a day, leaving the rest of the time free for me to work on written translations for other clients, spanning a variety of industries. Most gigs are short-term, lasting only a few days, resulting in occasional days off without pay. But this assignment is plum. Three-month jobs don't come around often, and the regularity, coupled with the chance to keep up with afternoon work, means I can sock away the rest of the money I need for my trip.

When one door closes, another opens.

Plus, the pay is higher than average since it requires special knowledge. I'm not a scientist. Not even close. But I have a ridiculously handy degree in my pocket that helps immensely when it comes to scientific terminology —marine biology.

When I finished school, I didn't have a sodding clue what I wanted to study at university, so I picked something that might transport me to interesting places. To all the spots around the globe that I'd earmarked to visit *someday*. The sapphire waters along the coast of Greece. The islands that make up Indonesia. Belize, a scuba diver's paradise. Growing up outside London, we didn't partake in scuba too often, but that sounded precisely like what a marine biologist ought to be doing all day long—exploring warm waters.

My choice of study might also have come from the weather. That winter was an unusually cold one in England when I selected my major subject, and marine biology sounded tropical.

So, yeah. My reasons were clearly thorough.

I never wound up exploring coral reefs off the coast of Australia or swimming with the sea turtles in the Cayman Islands. But after university I landed a gig at an aquarium, translating its descriptions of exhibits. The degree has helped me nab many sweet translation gigs since I've kept up my fluency in scientific names and terminology.

This new job sounds promising.

"The client knows only enough French to be dangerous," Jean-Paul says.

"I know the kind."

"Indeed. The kind who orders in French then thinks she can sustain an entire conversation about politics because she managed to correctly ask for salmon."

I laugh. "Well, you know the saying. It's a big upstream jump from salmon to politics."

Her name is Joy, and my first order of business will be to help her sort out some confusion with the apartment rental company. That should be a breeze, and a chance to impress her so she'll happily keep me around for the entirety of the contract.

The next morning, I head out early, and since I'm not due to meet the client for another twenty minutes, I grab a table at a café near the place she's going to be renting. As I drink my tea, I work through a French crossword puzzle that requires some seriously intense linguistic gymnastics. But I like this kind of mental stretching—it keeps my mind limber and ready for whatever challenges a job might throw my way. As I fill in each clue, I make note of the words in other languages I know—Spanish, Italian, some Portuguese—so I don't forget the ones I'm not actively working in.

When I finish, I close the app and drain the rest of the tea. As I do, two thoughts occur to me. The first is that tea has rapidly improved in this country and can finally hold a candle to what I grew up drinking. The second is that another door is reopening right now.

A sexy-as-hell door.

I rub my eyes.

It's a mirage.

But it's not a mirage. It's real, and it's brilliant luck.

Judy is strolling down the street, heading in my direction. She wears huge green sunglasses, with lenses the size of pizza pies. Her hair is twisted high on her head, with several loose strands escaping to curl over her shoulders. Dark jeans are lucky again to embrace those long legs of hers, and a ruby-red V-neck blouse completes the I-want-her-number-right-fucking-now look.

I set down my cup, raise a hand over my eyes to shield them from the sun, and call out, "Good morning, Judy. Are you following me now?"

She startles, stops in her tracks, and looks around.

"Over here. I'm five feet in front of you."

She spins, and her eyes land on me. She blinks, then a smile crosses her lips. "Perhaps you're following me. You did look like a stalker, Archie."

I stand and offer her the chair next to mine. I'm not letting her go this time. I have fifteen minutes before I meet the scientist lady, and I'm going to get Judy's number and land a date with her. Nothing less. "Would you like to join me?"

She peers into the white ceramic cup in front of me. "Of course you drink tea."

"As if there's anything else to drink in the morning."

"I only drink coffee."

"Funny, they have that here, too," I say, nodding at the red awning over Café Rousillon.

She checks her watch, and the furrow in her brow tells me she's adding up the minutes.

Time to press onward.

"This place is fast. And it's good coffee, I'm told," I say, determined to convince her. I shoot her a grin, finishing with the real reason I want her to pull up a chair. "Besides, if you join me for coffee, there's a good chance I can convince you to tell me your real name and give me your phone number."

She laughs. "You're a determined one."

"When I want something, I can be."

Her smile widens. "Since I'm early for my appointment, let's see how convincing you, and the coffee, can be."

She takes the seat and I sit, too, rubbing my palms. "All right, let's do this. Any particular type of coffee suit your fancy? Café crème, café au lait, café noisette?"

She lowers her shades, peering at me over the tops of those frames. "By coffee, I thought you meant a big fat Frappuccino caramel mocha, since that's quintessentially American, right?"

"Of course. And order it just like that."

She laughs and takes her sunglasses off all the way. Her green eyes are intense, some of the darkest irises I've ever seen.

"Your eyes are stunning. Hard to look away from," I tell her.

"Your baby blues aren't so bad, either, Archie."

"Thank you, and while I'm being blatantly honest, let me just say I had been hoping our conversation yesterday would have lasted longer." A small part of me still finds it odd to opt for such directness with a woman, but then, life is short. No point playing games anymore. "I quite enjoyed chatting with you."

She inches closer. "And while you're being blatantly honest, I'll do the same. I enjoyed chatting with you as well, so I'd say it's a good thing we've bumped into each other today."

The waiter weaves through the tables, and I catch his attention, quickly ordering another tea. I turn to my companion. "How do you take your coffee?"

"Black, please, with a little cream," she asks, hopefully.

I sigh heavily. "That's a tough one to order," I joke, then I tell the waiter what she wants.

When he leaves, Judy is staring at me.

"What is it?"

She shakes her head. "It's just funny. You're like my personal food translator."

I laugh. "That's my job." I fix on a stern expression. "And I take it quite seriously."

"I'll keep you with me then. Even though I could have ordered a café au lait. I'm not that terrible at French, am I?"

"I don't really know how terrible you are," I say, teasing. "We can find out if we do this again. I'd love to take you out. Would you like to have dinner with me?"

Her lips part, and I'm practically waiting to catch her *yes* in my hands. But it doesn't come. Just a rush of air over her lips, then she presses them together, and stares down the street. She flicks her gaze back to me. "You don't even know how long I'm in town."

"You don't know how long I'm in town, either," I counter.

"True."

"So, is that a no? Also, to answer you, I live here. For the moment."

Her lips quirk up. "I live here, too. For the moment, as well."

"Then we should go out again. After all, how can we be assured we'll bump into each other again? You have to admit this was pretty damn good luck this morning."

She smiles. "It does seem strangely promising."

The waiter returns with our beverages, and Judy raises her little cup to clink with mine. "To chance encounters."

"I'll drink tea to that."

After a swallow, I put down the cup and look her in the eyes again. "You haven't said yes. Do you have something against devilishly clever men who are exceptionally good at ordering both hot beverages and delicious pastries?"

She laughs loudly this time, and the older couple at the table next to us scowl in unison. Judy brings her hand to her mouth, feigning embarrassment. She collects herself, and her expression shifts. There's a twinkle in her green eyes. "I'm not opposed, but I still don't know how well you could navigate a chocolate shop, for instance."

A burst of possibility flares in me. She's closing in on a yes. "All those confusing chocolate flavors. You'd want to make sure you chose the right one."

"Absolutely. After all, who wants to take home a milk chocolate truffle when there are dark chocolate ones to be consumed?"

"No one does. Simply no one, Judy," I say as she takes a sip of her coffee.

She points to the cup. "This is quite good."

"So it's a yes then to a date where I take you to a chocolate shop and personally ensure you don't suffer with milk chocolate?"

She nibbles on the corner of her lip, then takes a deep breath. "Look, that sounds fantastic, but the truth is I just got out of a very bad relationship, and I'm not looking for anything."

Her bluntness makes me want to thread a hand in her hair and kiss her lipstick off. Then again, everything I know about her makes me want to do that.

"How fortuitous. I'm not looking for anything, either." I lower my voice, my words just for her as I lean a little closer, a feat made easier by the lovely proximity of these tiny chairs. "Except to get to know you more."

She sighs. "I really need to focus on work and my new job. I honestly don't think I can make time for anything else."

"I need to focus on work, too. Which makes me think we're on exactly the same page. Keep it casual. Keep it light."

She inhales deeply. "Stop making this so difficult."

I smirk. "Does that mean you're having a hard time saying no?"

"You're a terrible flirt."

"And terribly convincing with my flirting, yeah?"

She swallows, and a strand of her hair blows gently in the breeze. I brush that strand off her shoulder. When my fingertips touch the fabric of her shirt, her breath hitches. She raises her face, and her eyes lock with mine. "You're saying we could be not looking for anything together, Archie? Just exploring?"

I raise an eyebrow at her wordplay. "Yes. Let's explore . . . together."

She licks her lips and nods. "Give me your phone, and I'll give you my number."

I'm ready to punch the air.

In an instant, I whip out my mobile and hand it to her. She clicks open a text message, taps in her number, and then hands the device to me. "Send me a text, Archie. With your real name."

As she sips her coffee, I type and hit send.

Her phone buzzes from inside her handbag. Grabbing it quickly, she slides her finger over the new message, a mischievous glint in her eyes.

As she reads, her smile erases itself.

"Nice to meet you, Griffin." Her voice is heavy. "I'm Joy."

7

Joy

Well, that's a bit of a downer.

To say the least.

Honestly, I was getting a bit excited—and by excited, I do mean *down there*—at the possibility of both shopping for sweets and aimlessly exploring with this handsome man.

Both of those *might* be euphemisms.

But the point is this—a little diversion with no strings, no ties, might have been fun. Something to keep me busy on the occasional evening while I focused on work during the day. But now . . .

"You're really Griffin?" I ask, each word coming out stilted.

"You're really Joy?" His voice is leaden.

I point to my chest. "Your client."

He taps his breastbone. "Your translator."

I flash him a wan smile. It's reflected back at me.

Griffin blurts out, "You don't look like a chemist."

My brow knits. "What does a chemist look like?"

He scrubs a hand across his jaw, and the look in his blue eyes—concern, worry—tells me he realizes he just goofed. "I just meant . . ."

"Oh, please. Do tell me what you meant." I rest my chin on my joined hands and bat my eyes. I'm baiting him, but I want to make sure he's not a sexist pig. The last thing I want is for the guy who's about to become my mouthpiece to have some sort of issue with my job or role.

He stammers. "I just . . . didn't think . . ." He waves a hand at me. More precisely, at my chest.

"You didn't think scientists had breasts?" I ask innocently.

He shakes his head in a flurry and lifts both hands in surrender. "No, no, no, no, no." He fires off each denial like a round of ammunition. He stabs a finger against the tiny table, and it wobbles. "Also, I knew you were a woman since they gave me your name, so yes, I'm well aware that scientists can have breasts."

Okay, so he's not a chauvinist. I breathe a sigh of relief, and I think I know why he made the *you don't look like a chemist* comment now, and I kind of can't resist toying with him. It's been so long since I had someone to spar with. Someone who wanted this kind of rat-a-tat-tat game of verbal badminton.

"You just didn't think they'd be breasts you'd want to touch," I say pointedly, because there's no need to pretend we aren't attracted to each other.

He blinks. His expression is curious, as if he's trying to process the oddity of my remark. "You're quite blunt, and it's ridiculously attractive, so maybe you ought to stop that now."

I laugh and decide to go easy on him. But only a little.

"Stop being blunt? That'll be mighty hard, but I'll do my best. Maybe you can stop being ridiculously attractive, then, too? Sound fair?"

He laughs. "Absolutely." He takes a deep breath, then meets my eyes. "Does that mean I'm forgiven for thinking your breasts are fantastic, or forgiven for thinking you weren't a chemist?"

"Only if you admit you thought I'd have beakers with me, a white lab coat, and Coke-bottle glasses."

"I don't think I completely thought you'd look like a nerd, per se . . ." He sounds like he's trying to avoid saying something.

I drum my fingers on the table and take a sip of my coffee. "What did you think I'd look like?"

He drags a hand through his hair. "I didn't think you were a chemist because you're fucking gorgeous, and I don't know any gorgeous chemists so I suppose, yeah, maybe I did think you'd have a lab coat on, rather than a stun-me-with-your-stupendous-figure-and-incredible-eyes-and-pouty-mouth costume on."

And for that, right there, I can't be mad at him, not even a little. "You're too much, and I wish you were still Archie," I say, shaking my head, letting the reality sink in that the man I momentarily contemplated having a fling with is now most decidedly off-limits. I don't believe it's a written rule anywhere, but if there were, I'm pretty sure banging my translator would be in the chapter on *Very Bad Judgment Calls*.

He points a finger at me. "And if you think I'm stereo-typing chemists, then you're guilty, too, since you seem to think Brits all have stuffy names," he says, as if he's caught me on something as well. He straightens his shoulders, adopting an admonishing look.

"Because of Archie?"

"And Alistair and Rupert." He crosses his arms. He's too damn adorable.

"Fine, so we're both stereotyping. But what's the stereotype of a translator, then?"

He scratches his head. "Hmm. Good question." He screws up the corner of his lips. "I suppose just tall, dark, handsome, and completely charming."

I shrug. "Funny. I was going to say, 'Good with tongues.'"

He laughs then leans across the table and whispers in that ridiculously sexy accent, "I'm very good with my tongue."

Shivering, I let the innuendo waft over me. Then I try not to linger too long on mouths, or lips, or tongues, especially since we shouldn't be going there. "I guess I'll never know now."

He frowns.

I let my shoulders sag. But then I adopt a smile. "Since we're both stereotyping, I'm afraid I'm guilty, too."

He lifts his cup and takes a drink. "How so?"

Breezily, I answer, "Naturally, with your tall-dark-and-handsome costume on, I thought you were a hot male model, and clearly I was wrong."

As the waiter zips by, Griffin catches his attention and makes a scribbling gesture. "*L'addition, s'il vous plaît.*" He returns his attention to me. "Question. Why do we need to say *male model*? As if I could be anything but a male model? Why not just *model*?"

"Models are usually women."

"And chemists usually aren't beautiful women I want to shag, but now suddenly can't."

Shag. Dear Lord. The way he says it, the fact that he says it, the sheer sexiness of that word in his delicious accent triggers a wave of goose bumps over my skin. Here it is—the great admission that we weren't just heading toward a date. We were going to explore aimlessly together, with that exploration being conducted in a clothes-free mode.

Le sigh.

Le big, heavy, kick-my-toe-against-the-ground sigh. "Fine. You're not a model, I'm not Judy, and we're not going to explore together, since we can't shag."

He heaves a sigh, too. "Yeah, I suppose that's how it has to be."

That's for the best, surely. I didn't come to France looking for a no-strings-attached fling. In fact, I'm probably better off focusing squarely on my new job, my new home, and my new life. But, for a few seconds there, I was enjoying the possibility of a little tryst. Of getting lost in something that felt like the opposite of guilt, the opposite of too much attachment. Something that felt only good.

Perhaps I was looking for an antidote to my ex and I didn't even realize it.

A pill of bliss. A drink of pure desire.

It's been so long since I experienced that pull with someone. After more than a year together, the spark between Richard and me had faded, and before he'd been injured, I'd been ready to rip the Band-Aid off. We were drifting, two magnets stripped of their charge.

Then he had his accident.

I cringe inside, my stomach twisting at the memories —the harsh, cruel memories of how everything changed. How I stayed longer than I intended.

Now, everything has changed for me once again.

Time to zero in on *why* I'm here in France. I have a brand-new chance in my career. I've been given a great gift with this job, and the fresh opportunity to succeed in my field. I can't afford a distraction like a tall, sexy British man who'd kiss me senseless, knock the breath from my lungs, and then take me hard by the terrace window, all of Paris at my feet as he pleasured me.

Whoa.

Talk about getting ahead of myself.

I wipe the triple-X version of this man from my mind.

My brain is pure as the driven snow again.

"Let's just start fresh." I hold out a hand. "I'm Joy Danvers-Lively. It's a mouthful, and it's taken me years, but I've finally found it in me to forgive my parents for saddling me with their last names hyphenated. So cruel, don't you think? They each kept their last names, but made that double clunker my problem."

"It is a lovely name, all three words," Griffin says with a smile as the waiter brings a little slip of paper.

I point to the bill. "I can get it. Expense account and all."

Griffin shakes his head, snatches the receipt, and says, "It'll be our first and only date it seems, so at the very least, I ought to be a gentleman."

First and only. My heart drops a little at the stark truth, even though I know it has to be this way.

He grabs a few euros from his wallet, leaves them on the table, and rises. As he stands he extends his hand. "Griffin Thomas."

We shake. I'll admit, I want to yank him close and kiss the hell out of that handsome face. But I'm going to be good. This man is about to become my voice, and I can't take a chance. The job is too important, the chance to carve out a new life too valuable. I don't want to risk it by doing something foolish like boinking the person I'm supposed to spend so much time with.

"And it's not even a quintessentially British name," he says as we weave away from the tables and to the sidewalk.

"Yes, Griffin Thomas does in fact sound more like a male model's moniker."

He tuts. "Don't be silly, Joy. If I were a male model, my name would be something ripped straight from a list of macho and sexy names." He takes a beat as we reach the corner of the cobbled street. "I'd be Blaze."

I crack up. When I catch my breath, I say, "You've clearly given this some thought."

"You haven't?" He adopts the most serious look. "Don't you think that would be a fantastic name for a model? Blaze Dalton. Admit it, if that were my name, I'd have no choice but to be a model." Demonstrating, he gives a smoldering look as we turn onto the side street, passing a sundial on the side of a building. "A *male* model."

"Blaze Dalton, Male Model, PI," I say, like a TV announcer. "They'd make a TV show about you. You'd solve crimes, and you'd probably even be a nurse, too. Blaze Dalton, Male Model, PI, Moonlighting Nurse."

"For when you need a crime solved and a bandage to go along with it."

"Where are you from, Archie Blaze Dalton Thomas the Translator Male Model with a first aid kit?"

He chuckles, as we stroll past old buildings with names on the buzzers like Mercier, Bernard, and Dubois, heading toward my furnished flat. "I grew up outside London. French mother, English father, bilingual in French and English since I was little. My parents still live outside London."

"Are you close with them?"

He nods. "I text them often, and ring them once or twice a week."

"You are a good son."

"I try. And what about you? Where are you from?"

"Born and raised in Austin. Went to school in San

Francisco. Worked long and hard not to have a Texas accent."

"Why?"

I nudge him with my elbow. "I didn't want people to stereotype me. To say I had a Texas drawl or what have you."

"You don't really have a Texas drawl," he says, in a perfect imitation of a standard American accent. It's hilarious to hear him slide from his sophisticated voice to one I'm so accustomed to.

And yet, I've had enough of men from there.

"Never speak like that again," I tell him.

He laughs. "I'll stick to Archie talk."

"You do that."

We navigate a stretch of sidewalk that's perhaps two feet across, and it delights me. The streets here are so different from the wide concrete ribbons back home, and I find their oldness, their foreignness, so damn charming. The street curves and narrows as we close in on the end nearest the river. I point to the addresses above the doors. "Almost there. Now that the housekeeping is out of the way, are you ready for your first big assignment? Because it's time to kick ass and take names. I have a hunch this company is trying to pull a fast one on me, and I've no idea why."

He nods intensely. "Yes, my boss mentioned your concern. And now you have Blaze Dalton, Male Model turned Translator turned Kick-ass Fixer of Problems with Furnished-Flat-Leasing Agencies, at your service."

I quirk up my lips, giving him a challenging stare. "But can you say that in French?"

"*Mais oui.*" He rattles all that off, and I don't know if he said peas and carrots or that ridiculous title, but either way it sounded hot.

Except "hot" is precisely how I can't think of Griffin anymore.

I take a look at the handsome man who'll be spending many of my days with me. Shame that he won't be my French booty call, since I quite enjoy chatting with him. Since the moment I met him in the bakery, we'd begun an effortless repartee. That kind of banter is hard to give up. But, I don't have to let go of that side of him, since he'll be in my life in this professional role. Maybe he can become something else, too. Something I need even more than a lover. "I have an idea, Griffin."

"I happen to be quite fond of ideas," he says.

This feels even riskier than flirting. This is exposing my true heart. "Would you be interested in being friends with me?"

When his smile spreads, nice and slow, it warms me from the inside out. "I would very much like that, Joy."

8

Griffin

Friend is such a loaded word. It can mean all sorts of things. Cover all manner of relationships. It's a blanket term that can suggest something deep and abiding, or something casual and relatively meaningless.

It can apply to the most important relationships. My brother was my best friend, no question. Since I've lived in Paris, I've made plenty of new friends. Christian is a good mate. Always up for a drink, a laugh, a night out. We share a common background—both of us have English dads and mums from other countries. Mine's French, his Danish. I have plenty of other friends here, too—some French, some English, some from many other places.

Most—wait, make that all—I didn't want to shag first.

I'm not saying men and women can't be friends.

It's just harder to be friendly when you start wanting one thing, and then you need to press the brakes. Actually, slam on the brakes is more like it with this woman.

But I can no longer think of Joy as the stunningly hot American with the quick tongue and fantastic tits. Instead, I have to reroute all brain circuitry to consider her as not only a client, but also the direct route to getting the very thing I want most—money for a ticket out of town. I suppose a friend is precisely what she should be.

What she should *only* be.

It's a good thing she wants that. It's a great thing we're setting clear boundaries now. They'll help us as we work together over the next few months.

"Friends," I say, rocking back and forth on my toes. "Like a good mate."

She blinks, then smiles. "Sure, I'll be your mate."

Even though it'll be hard to think of her that way, I'll soldier on. "Before we go in, tell me more about why you think they're trying to screw you over."

She fills me in, telling me she placed a deposit for a one-bedroom flat on the third floor on a road near the river, but the rental agent now insists her place is a studio on the second floor. Her eyes narrow as she tosses out possibilities. "Did he rent mine to someone else? Is he trying to swindle me? Does the third-floor flat have a better view, and now he's thinking because I'm a foreigner that he can pull the bait and switch and give me the crappier one?" She raises her index finger. "Most of all, what would Blaze Dalton do?"

"Hmm," I say, stroking my chin, sliding into my role as the model turned PI. "Do you think it's possible something was lost in translation?"

She rolls her eyes then pokes my chest. "What's lost in translation is my money for my flat. I don't want him to take me because I don't know the language."

"Got it. Basically, you want me to go in guns blazing, full-on male-model investigation style?"

Her eyes crinkle as she laughs. "Yes. But wait, I can't just be the helpless gal."

I arch a brow. "I thought you wanted me to do the talking?"

"Of course. But I don't want to roll over like a doormat." She shudders, like that thought is abhorrent. She stops outside a small yellow boutique peddling little pencil cases and makeup bags with French sayings that draw Joy's attention. Tapping her finger across one, she translates the words out loud. "Life is a dream."

"Well done. You hardly need me."

"Ha ha." She swivels and faces me, her eyes fierce. "Here's the plan. I go in first, and you wait, say, across the street."

I narrow my eyes. "Explain the part where that's helpful."

She waves her hands animatedly as we resume our hunt for twenty-eight, the number of her building. "Because I'll get the lay of the land. Assess the situation. Determine if he's still trying to pull a fast one. If I get the apartment I want, great. Then I'll pat myself on the back for not being a damsel in distress. If I don't, then I give you a signal, and you strut in and do that thing you do."

"And what's that thing I do?" I ask curiously.

"You know. That *vous veux pépé le peu je ne sais quoi voilà oh là là*," she says, sliding into a nonsensical imitation of the French language. "And boom, done. Problem solved."

I stop her, setting a hand on her arm. "Since we're friends, I feel I must tell you this, but that plan makes absolutely no sense."

She squares her shoulders. "It makes perfect sense."

"How so?"

"Because it's fun." Her big green eyes sparkle. "Do you have something against fun?"

When her eyes glitter like that, it's almost as if fun is something she hasn't quite experienced in a while. I weave my index and middle fingers together. "Fun and I are like that. But you're aware that the whole secret code thing won't necessarily help you score the flat you want, yeah?"

She sighs, on the path to relenting. Then, she stops in her tracks like a dog digging in.

"What? Are we here? You said twenty-eight. It's the next one," I say.

She clasps her hand to her mouth and points a few feet ahead. I follow her gesture to a tall pink door. It's wood, carved ornately at the handle, and is the brightest shade of neon pink I've ever seen in this city. "Yes, Joy. It's a hot-pink door. Paris can be a colorful city."

Her eyes drift up to the blue square number atop the stone doorway.

Twenty-eight.

A sound slips from her mouth, like a high-pitched whistle.

"Okay, so that's your building. Are you offended by pink? Did you have a bad experience with a Barbie Dream House? Or does it remind you of Pepto-Bismol, perhaps?"

She shakes her head, drops her hand, and grabs my arm, tugging me into the doorway right before the apartment. Her voice turns to a whisper. "It's like seeing a pair of Christian Louboutins."

"Okay. So that's good then? You like Louboutins, I presume?"

"I don't just like them. I'm in love with them. I can't control myself around Louboutins. I don't care about whether he's tricking me. I want nothing more right now than to live in that building with the hot-pink door."

This woman is a hoot. She's a wild, over-the-top whirlwind. "You can't be serious."

In an instant, her expression turns deadly serious. "It's pink, Griffin. *Pink*."

"Yes, I know."

She points at it. "It's literally the cutest, coolest, most unnecessary door in the entire city, and therefore I must live there."

"How does one thought follow the other?"

"Have you ever bought a purse because it's irresistible? A necklace you didn't need? Perfume because it's decadent?"

"Oddly enough, no," I deadpan.

"Well, I have. And the door is the same. I want to live there because it's everything that makes Paris different and special. Because I would never find this door back home. Because it has no purpose except to beguile me with its absolute, utter cuteness. And that means you're going to have to handle this whole mess for me because if I go in there, I'll say yes to anything."

I drop a hand to her shoulder, my tone deadly serious. "I understand your predicament. The door is like a good game of rugby. You're powerless when it comes on the telly."

She arches a brow. "Rugby? Ha. More like football. The real kind. But if that helps you understand it, let's go."

As Joy emerges from the doorway and closes the distance to number twenty-eight, a thin, goateed man with glasses strides up the street, chattering away on his mobile. His voice is soft, but I pick up a few words, something about *not that place* and *you know why*, and then *sorting it all out*.

I furrow my brow, not liking the sound of those words.

When he ends the call, he spots my companion. "Hello! You are Joy!" He takes her hand and shakes. "I am Stephen. Good to meet you."

"Yes, nice to meet you. This is my friend, Griffin."

I take his hand and shake, speaking in English since that's how the conversation began. "Good to meet you."

He looks at Joy. "You want to see the flat now and take the key?"

"Yes, the flat on the third floor," I say, quickly switching to French.

"Oh, you speak French?" he says, segueing instantly as he unlocks the pink door that has, evidently, rendered Joy incapable of anything but ogling. It's a door, for fuck's sake. Sometimes I think I will never understand women.

"I'm familiar with the language," I say as we stride into the foyer.

He laughs. "Familiar. Good one. Then I need to tell you something. I feel absolutely terrible, but we can't rent her the place she wants."

"She gathered that, but what's the story, man? She's not going to pay more for some crappy place."

He brings a hand to his heart. "I would never ask her to do that. Never. Do I look like a slimy salesman?"

"Of course not. But when you tell her you have something on the third floor, and she gives you a deposit, and then you tell her it's the second floor, you have to know that sounds exactly like you're trying to pull the wool over her eyes."

"No. I would never do that. I want her to be happy. You have to let me explain what happened and show you the other one I have in mind for her." Stephen gestures to the marble floor as Joy's eyes drift down and widen. I think she might be falling in love with the floor, too. She mouths *so adorable*.

All the more reason to stay strong for her.

Stephen stops at the winding staircase, then drops his voice to a whisper, his nose crinkling in disgust. "Cigarettes."

Joy's eyes widen, and she recoils. She understood that word for sure. "The previous occupant smoked?"

Stephen nods, switching to English as he speaks to her. "Yes. It will take at least one week to clean it."

Joy cringes. "I can't wait a week."

He holds up a finger in excitement. "Okay. That's why I have another one for you."

"Why didn't you just tell her that?" I ask in French.

"Because my English isn't perfect. And I have a beautiful place for her that I want her to *see*."

"I hate smoking," Joy says in French, and I smile at her, even though that's a relatively easy phrase to translate. Still, it's good she knows a little bit. She returns to English. "I won't go anywhere near a place that smells like cigarettes."

The man laughs and smacks my shoulder. "See? Your lady cannot stand cigarettes. You know that about her, right?"

"Of course," I say, quickly, before it occurs to me what he truly means by *your lady*.

"We only found out yesterday when the previous occupant moved out. It is against our rules, but what can you do? Now we have to clean it out, and it's awful. She won't like it. She sent me a long list of likes and dislikes. I'm sure you know them all."

"Yes, of course," I say quickly, even though I pretty much only know that chocolate croissants, coffee, and adorable entryways are on the top of her list of pros.

"But the studio we have is quite large, and we will give her a discount. I wanted to explain this to her, but I thought it best to do it in person." He turns to Joy. "I'm so sorry for the trouble."

"It's okay," she says, beaming.

"And I will show you the studio now. I think you will like it," he says with a smile, gesturing to the stairs. "Be very careful. This is an old building, and it has a narrow wooden staircase."

Joy's eyes twinkle as she takes the first step. She makes a sound like a squeak. "Oh my God, I love it. It's uneven."

I roll my eyes as I laugh. "First the door, now the uneven steps. Remember, you do have to walk up these every day."

She marches up, head held high. "I don't care. They are the complete opposite of my big fat driveway back home. Therefore, I love these uneven steps."

When we reach the second floor, Stephen heads to a door at the end of a narrow hallway and unlocks it, opening into a relatively well-lit and admittedly spacious studio.

Joy wanders in, running her hand over the slim kitchen counter, along the back of a black leather couch, and then over the frame of a window that lets in a decent amount of light, considering it's on the second floor.

She turns around. "It's not bad. I had just hoped for more light." She looks at me. "Know what I mean?"

I nod. "Yes. You do love your light," I say, since I'm quickly learning Joy doesn't just like things. She falls hard for them. She's a woman who goes all-in. And, like that, my dirty mind slips to thoughts of things I'd like to put all in her.

Crap.

Must clean filth from brain now.

I glance at Stephen. That does the trick. He taps his finger against his lip. "Hmm."

"You have a way for her to have more light?" I ask.

He takes a deep breath, claps his hands together, speaking to us both. "Okay, I like you two. I want you to have a good deal. You are young lovers and have so much energy. I have an idea."

My instinct to correct mistakes kicks in. "We're not—"

Joy steps on my toe. Hard. If there's one language I understand thoroughly it's *shut the fuck up when I smack you*. I zip my lips.

"This might not be to your taste," Stephen says to me, switching to rapid-fire French again. "The flat I have in mind is one we don't rent often. It's usually just on Airbnb for those who want a true Parisian experience, and can brave the stairs." He tips his forehead to Joy. "I have a feeling she might like it. She has a certain exuberance about her," he says with a wink, and I nod in acknowledgement then turn to Joy.

"He says you're exuberant, and he has something else that you might like."

She wiggles her eyebrows. "Exuberant is my middle name."

Stephen smiles. "But it's on the sixth floor. You'll need to climb up the uneven eighty-four steps every time to reach this place. We don't have a lift."

I nod and give Joy the overview.

To my complete non-surprise, she says, "I want to see it."

We climb. Up and around. The steps groan and shriek their displeasure with every footfall. This is precisely the type of climb no one wants.

When we reach the top floor, Stephen unlocks a door and tugs it open.

Once inside, Joy gasps. She blinks, taking in the sun-drenched flat. The living room is dripping with natural light. It's bathed in it, and Joy marches to the windows, places her hands on the edge of the floor-to-ceiling shutters that open onto a tiny terrace, and gazes outside. Honestly, she's in a perfect position for all the things we can't do anymore. I do my best to imagine she's thinking deep thoughts about turtles or hamburgers, and that helps me navigate my way out of the dirty zone.

She spins around. "And it has parquet floors, too. Gah!"

I laugh. "Maybe wait till he gives you more details and a price."

But she can't even wait, because she pushes open the door to the bedroom. "More windows," she calls out, and when she strides out of it, she points to an open set of stairs at the end of the living room. "Where do those go?"

"Ah, yes," Stephen says with a quirk in his lips. "We have a rooftop terrace here. Like a garden."

Her eyes widen, and she heads up the stairs and momentarily out of sight. I follow, quickly joining her on the roof. Potted plants and flowers line the edges, and an iron railing rises four feet high. She wraps her hands around it and stares at the endless view of Paris. "Everything," she whispers, wonder in her tone. "I can see everything."

Stephen cuts in. "This one is a little bit more. Because of the terrace."

She turns around. "I'll take it."

Stephens smiles and shrugs. "It is perfect for lovers, no?"

Joy wraps a hand around my arm, squeezing my bicep. For a moment, I'm speechless, all from her hand on my arm. It makes no sense why it should feel so damn good.

But it does, and her touch sends a wave of heat through me.

Now I'm thinking how very perfect this flat is for lovers.

And cursing that we can't test out the window, the garden, the terrace ... not to mention the bed.

Then I remember Stephen's question, and Joy's foot digging into my toe, and perhaps she needs me to play along.

"It is perfect for lovers." I drape an arm around her shoulder, and she lifts her face to mine. In the span of a second, it's as if Stephen is gone, and there's just this woman and me, and all I can think is how much I'd like to press a kiss to those perfect red lips.

Perhaps she can read my mind, because she dusts her lips against my jaw, and that barest touch triggers a rush of heat in my body. I'm not even sure why we're playing this game, but I also don't really care.

When she lets go of me, she says, "I can move in today. Is that okay?"

Stephen nods. "Excellent. I will switch the paperwork. Let me go call the office to get that started."

He heads down the stairs, leaving us on the rooftop garden.

I scrub my hand over my jaw. "Why did you want to go along with the whole young lovers thing?"

"Because that man is a romantic. I could see it in him. In the way he looked at us and seemed to catalogue how we interacted. Some part of him liked the idea that we were a thing. Doesn't hurt anything for him to think that." She nudges me. "Besides, we almost were, right?"

"We almost were."

"It didn't bother you to play along, did it?"

"Not in the least."

"I suppose we can go back to being translator and translatee, Blaze." She winks and heads down the stairs.

I'm alone on her roof, staring at the city. This woman might be the toughest client I've ever had, since I'm going to spend every second resisting her.

9

Joy

I'm ready.

All I need is one last accessory—the finishing touch for nearly every outfit. Perusing the antique silver mirrored tray perched on the bureau, I consider which perfume is most appropriate for a first day. Nothing too intense. Something incredibly subtle. Most of all, something classy.

I choose one that smells faintly of a soft, dewy path in the spring woods, with a lilac bush at the end. A collector sent me some from her stash—a sampler tube—and I've cherished it. I daub some behind my ears then set the tube next to the scalloped edge of the mirror. The mirrored tray is new, purchased from the Marché aux Puces this weekend, from a grizzled old vendor with yellowed teeth, a cigarette dangling between them as he played cards with another fellow, barking out a price. I wanted it so badly, I didn't even attempt to bargain. I simply paid what he asked.

Now, it's Monday morning and time to go. I grab my shoes and slip them on, shoulder my Kate Spade bag, then lock the door behind me.

Down the six flights I go, with my head held high.

Hmm.

That's a little dicey.

Fine, the stairs are hard to navigate in heels. I have determination in spades, but I also wasn't whacked with the stupid stick. I return to my place, take off my Jimmy Choo sling-backs, drop them in my bag, and slide into a pair of flip-flops. I hoof it down the eighty-four uneven steps.

With each footfall, I say silently *I love my rooftop*. It makes it that much easier to manage the insanity of six flights.

When I reach the bottom, I'm not breathing hard. You are.

Anyway, I've pretty much acclimated to the time change, and I've mostly acclimated to these steps. One thing I've absolutely adjusted to is my rooftop. Last night, I drank a glass of white wine while sitting in a wooden chair, watching the lights from the Eiffel Tower.

Not too shabby.

Butterflies flap in my belly as I cross the foyer in my building, my flip-flops slapping on the marble floor. Setting a hand on my stomach, I try to quell them. But I'm not sure I can. It feels like the first day of school, and I'm jam-packed with jitters.

You're going to do great.

It's what my parents told me this weekend over Skype.

It's what Allison said in a text. *You'll be fabulous!*

It's what my co-worker Jeanie from Texas said in an email. *You will be a rock star!*

It's what I desperately want to believe, and so I give myself thirty extra minutes for the commute, and I head for the metro.

When I walk down the steps, it's not just crowded. It's like a vacuum-packed bag of coffee grounds. The platform is stuffed with people, shoulder to shoulder, jostling, squeezing, working their way to the front of the crowd as a train slides into the station. As I make my way through the sardines, I have to make a decision—push forward into the train that's clearly eaten too much at Thanksgiving, or turn the hell around and catch an Uber.

Duh.

I hightail it away from the rumbling train, because as much as I want to be a Parisian, I don't want to show up at work sweaty, stinky, and covered in the scent of half a million others because I'm damn sure that's how many people are on that train.

I'll just slink away and slide out of here.

"*Excusez-moi*," I mutter. "Pardon." I wedge myself between two suited guys, sliding through, and then bump past a sturdy woman carrying a large box. I blink—mostly in admiration. She's a tough dame, navigating this mess.

I'm pushing against the crowd, gripping my purse tight to my body like it's a baby in a Björn, and beyond the rows of heads I can see the steps. Almost there.

Then, a sharp, stinging pain radiates from my left foot.

"Oh crud," I mutter.

I try to lean to my right foot, but there's no room, and all I can feel is this stabbing sensation in my instep. That's when I realize my great mistake.

I am a magnificent idiot.

I'm wearing flip-flops in the city, and someone just stepped on my foot with the hard sole of a shoe.

A few minutes later, I make it out of the crowd, hopping around. My foot is bleeding.

I really need a male nurse with a Band-Aid right about now.

* * *

With an oh-so-very-attractive Little Prince Band-Aid plastered on my foot—incidentally, the Little Prince is a licensing whore; he's on everything—I open the door to my Uber ride, and the driver whisks me away to my new offices in the 7th arrondissement. I peer at my foot, studying it. All things considered, I don't think the little licensor has ever looked so dapper as he does next to a pair of Jimmy Choos.

I'll be at work shortly, with only a Band-Aid as proof of a little morning struggle. I sink into the leather seat as the car weaves through the streets.

But then something crazy happens when a car drives in morning rush hour.

It's called . . . wait for it . . . traffic.

I curse. I mutter. I tap my foot. I peer out the window as if I can make all the honking Peugeots and Saabs and Audis disperse by sheer force of will.

Doesn't work.

I look at the time. It's eight-fifty-five, which means I'm going to be late on my first day. I fish around in my purse for my cell phone, and fire off a quick text to Marisol.

I'm so very sorry. Stuck in traffic. Be there soon.

I tuck the phone away then stare out the window like a dog, watching the beautiful buildings pass by at the pace of escargot.

At last, the car pulls up to the curb of a busy block, and I thank the driver and get out. Briefly, I lift my gaze and stare at the office building in the business-y section of the 7th arrondissement, swing my gaze to the street sign, then heave the heaviest sigh in the history of Europe.

I'm on Boulevard Bosquet.

And my office is on Rue Bosquet.

I punched in the wrong street name in Uber.

I groan. I frown. My shoulders sag.

A skinny man walking past me tosses a rueful smile in my direction. "It's Monday," he says, knowingly.

At least, I think that's what he said.

Ten minutes later, I make it to the offices of L'Artisan Cosmetique, making me fifteen minutes late, and fifteen tons irritated with myself.

Griffin waits in the lobby. He wears dark slacks that fit well, leather shoes, and a crisp, white button-down shirt. His jaw is smooth, with a freshly shaven look. Briefly, I imagine him in front of his bathroom mirror, running a blade over his jaw. There's something so sexy about a man with only a towel wrapped around his waist staring into the mirror as he shaves.

When he sees me, he smiles, then his smile disappears. "You okay? You look flustered."

I hold up a hand, like a stop sign. "I can't even today."

He laughs. "'I can't even' doesn't translate."

"They haven't figured out how to express the ultimate frustration yet? Well, the French need to get on that, stat."

"I'll send a note to the International Consortium of Idioms and Internet Sayings," he says, walking me to the elevator.

"Have you been waiting for me this whole time?"

He nods. "But I kept myself busy with some Spanish crossword puzzles."

I shake my head, frustrated. "I tried to be a half hour early. Instead, I have a Little Prince Band-Aid and an inability to distinguish between rue and boulevard."

"Ah, yes. It's a trick we use to ferret out you Yanks. Is it working?"

"Quite well, it seems," I say, then step into the elevator with the handsome man.

Nerves crawl up my throat. "I'm so pissed at myself for being late."

"Don't be so hard on yourself. You're adjusting to a new country."

I sigh. "All the more reason to be on time," I say as I stab the button for the sixth floor.

As the doors close, Griffin lifts his chin and looks me over. "You smell pretty."

A grin takes over my face. He's speaking my language now. "Thank you."

"It smells like . . ." His voice trails off, and he shakes his head. "Can't place it."

"Lilacs," I supply.

He snaps his fingers. "That's it. I have a terrible nose. Ever since the hospital, I think."

I furrow my brow. "What? Were you really a nurse?"

He curses under his breath. "No. Sorry. Didn't mean to be a downer."

"You're not a downer at all. I'm curious now, though."

"Someone in my family was in the hospital for a while. Passed away. But we're all fine," he says, fixing on a cheery grin. "Now, did you bring a lunchbox and a sandwich for your first day?"

I shake my head, unable to segue into this playful zone so suddenly. Not with this lump in my throat from that news. "Griffin, you don't have to just wipe it away," I say as the elevator slows. I wrap a hand around his forearm, trying to comfort him. "You don't have to be tough for me."

"Ah, but I do. Because this is your day, and I'm fine. I want you to have a great day at work."

I peer at him. "I know, but it sounds like you went through something."

He raises his chin. "Let's focus on you, Joy. That's why I'm here."

I sigh, but I understand fully. We don't always want to talk about hard things. In fact, we don't often want to at all. Sometimes work is much easier to zoom in on.

Just in case though, I try one last time. "Are you sure?"

"Positive."

I try to put his comment out of my mind.

When I make it to the offices, Marisol is waiting for me. I'm nearly blinded by her beauty. She's tall and white-blonde, with cheekbones carved by goddesses. She's even more stunning in person than she was over Skype—that's how we did the interviews.

"So good to meet you officially," she says, a warm smile on her face.

"I'm so sorry I'm late."

"Don't think twice about it," she says. "Let me introduce you to your team."

She escorts me to the lab where I'll be overseeing the fragrance chemists, and that's when my translator truly comes in handy.

"I'm so thrilled to meet all of you, and I'm very much looking forward to working with each and every one of you, and helping L'Artisan grow and improve and expand its reach," I say.

Griffin instantly converts everything I say into French, though I suspect most of the team understood my brief intro. That's because most French businesspeople speak solid English, so when Marisol first told me she was looking for a translator, I asked why we'd need one. As a French company, L'Artisan Cosmetique has only done business in French previously, she explained, and so all its chemists are accustomed to solely speaking in their native tongue. Sure, plenty of them know enough English for me to sit down and gab about the weather and popular movies over a Nicoise salad. Saying "hello" and "nice to meet you" is easy-peasy, too.

But being able to discuss the finer details of chemical formulations that make household products smell like a spring breeze is entirely another matter.

I'm not equipped to say those technical terms in French, obviously.

And it's too risky to assume they'll understand the precise specifics of the new production processes that I'll share with them in English.

Ergo, Griffin is here to ensure that we don't accidentally blow up our lab while testing a lavender-scented body lotion. Though, to be fair, the most likely candidate for combustion would be hair spray.

Incidentally, I invented a new scent for one back home, and it smells like a song. Every time I spritz some on my locks, I want to break out my microphone and belt upbeat pop tunes.

"*Bonjour*, Charles," I say to a young man who looks like he graduated from college last week.

"Hello, Joy," he says, his voice a little wobbly, perhaps from nerves. "Welcome to France."

"Thank you. I hear you're working on a cutting-edge new formulation for a lip balm concentrate," I say, then explain more of the details of his formulation. "I look forward to checking it out."

His brow furrows for a moment, and I can see the cogs

turning, but once Griffin does his thing, Charles is smiling and nodding.

"I look forward to that, too," he says.

I shake hands with a woman about my age, with fine porcelain skin and a nervous smile. "Nice to meet you, Adaline."

"And you."

Then, I dive into the nitty-gritty, sharing my overall approach to best practices that I fine-tuned back in Austin.

And seriously, Griffin sounds delicious speaking French on my behalf—even better when he says words like prototype, and formulation, and molecule measurements. That just gets all the combustion inside me going.

"And if I say anything inappropriate, it's all his fault," I joke, and I garner a few laughs before he translates. More laughter comes once he does.

"And if she says anything funny, it's all my fault, too," he adds in English, then he glances at me, and when no one's looking, he winks.

Like we have a secret.

And we kind of do.

* * *

Griffin is so fast that the language barrier hardly slows us down the next day in the fragrance lab. It's a little funny, too, to hear everything I say about calculations and mixes in his accented voice.

But when I explain how I want to approach a revamp of a body spritz for women, Charles asks a question before Griffin translates.

Charles has the name of the molecule wrong, though.

I share the correct one, and Mr. Sexy Chemistry makes it sound better in French.

Charles nods. "*Je comprends maintenant.*"

I understand now.

Me, too! I award myself a point for understanding Charles the first time around, even though that was a very simple sentence. But hey, I have to start somewhere.

We've set up the schedule so Griffin's here in the mornings, which is when I work with the others in the lab, and he also attends meetings with the other department heads and me. That turns out to be super helpful because when one of the marketing gals says to her colleague before the meeting starts on Wednesday that the mini chocolate tarts on the table are the worst she's ever had, Griffin whispers in my ear and warns me from taking one.

Now that's the kind of help I truly appreciate.

But I also like when he's not here with me. When I'm alone with my work in the afternoons. I like it when I don't have to talk, too. Somehow, that's easier.

Silence is a language I comprehend with crystal clarity. When I inhale a formulation of jasmine for a new face cream, the scent transcends words. It evokes memories of peaceful days and private gardens. I don't need to reword or paraphrase the smell of relaxation because it's a state of mind, a place I want to visit.

Here in the quiet of my own thoughts, I take that trip.

* * *

The first week cruises by, and I'm busier than I ever was at home. My brain is tired, but the kind that feels like a good workout, as if I've been using every muscle in it for cerebral exercise. I've been trying vainly to understand what everyone's saying, but all I manage are words here and there. I'll key in on a verb—ooh, that means *to buy*—or a noun—someone mentioned the waste bin—but by and large, I'm floating in a sea of incomprehension. When I return to the office after lunch, the receptionist greets me in French then English, but as I walk down the hall, everyone is talking in their language.

I wish I understood them. I wish Griffin were here to translate the chocolate tart gossip.

Not because I'm a nosy nelly. Though, a little bit of me is.

I want to understand them because I feel blind. Deaf. Mute.

I'm operating at half power, with switches in me turned on and off. A fuzziness lingers in my head when I walk into a bakery, the grocery store, the cinema.

I get by. But words and phrases float over me. They're darkness—they're clouds. No matter how pretty they are, they don't light up my day.

As I leave on Friday, my mind drifts to a book I read years ago where a blue-haired girl is gifted languages by her adoptive father every year on her birthday. It's a fantasy tale, but nevertheless by the time she's eighteen she speaks many languages.

And she doesn't have to learn them.

The gifts he gives her simply turn a switch in her brain. She shifts from not understanding a word to comprehending each one.

Lucky bitch.

I want that magic pill.

When I near my flat, a bus rumbles past me, and I stare in its direction, trying to read the billboard on the side of it. A giraffe wears a red trench coat, and the only word I can make out is *art*.

Because it's the same freaking word in both languages.

I try and I try and I try, but the letters swirl and dance, and it's as if I'm at the eye doctor, squinting at the *EFGD* in the eye test but seeing only squiggles.

When the green bus rolls away from the stop, a cloud of fumes sprays from its exhaust. Coughing, I rub a hand over my eyes.

I resume my pace, turning the corner of my block. I blink. Something feels funny in my eye. Like a bug or a piece of dirt. I rub again as I pass the café where I met Griffin for coffee. When I look at my curled fingers, there's a filmy circular lens on them.

I stop in my tracks, spin around, and look for a window. Something to peer into as I pop my contact lens back in. But it's already drying in my hand.

I consider jumping in frustration Rumpelstiltskin-style, but instead I woman up in the middle of the sidewalk, holding my eyelid open, and pop that bad boy back in my eye.

Ouch.

It hurts going in dry like that.

But I'm near my flat, and I have contact lens solution.

Eighty-four steps later, I correct myself.

Since I don't take my contacts out every night, it slipped my ever-loving mind to bring contact lens solution to France, and this eye hurts like the dickens.

I trudge back down the steps, around the corner, and to the pharmacy.

As I scan the shelves, it's as if I've hit a brick wall. I don't know the words for contact lens solution. I don't know how to find the solution because EVERYTHING LOOKS DIFFERENT HERE.

That means I'm going to have to go to the counter and do that thing I detest. *Fail.*

I'm going to fail at speaking the language. I'm going to fail at accomplishing this most basic errand.

My confidence frayed to a thread, I make my way to the counter and ask for contact lens solution in a hideous amalgamation of broken French and English.

The quizzical look on the pharmacist's wrinkled face tells me I'm botching it. I take a deep breath and try again. Pointing to my eyes, leaning my head back, acting out what I need. Soon enough, he understands me.

When I'm back at my flat, I rinse the lens and put it back in. I pour a glass of wine and head to my roof. Sighing deeply, I flop down in the chair as the pink sunset tugs the sun beneath the horizon. As I take a sip, twilight starts to settle in, casting the city in a soft, pale light from the Seine all the way to Sacré Coeur.

There's so much I love about Paris, and yet it feels even more foreign than when I first landed here more than a week ago. I'm like a fish trying to swim upstream, but I don't know which way the currents will pull.

From my vantage point, with buildings bathed in a warm, gentle glow, everything feels possible. But I know that once I venture down the stairs and beyond the pink door, it's like a battlefield on the streets. Of beauty and frustration.

I'm going to need more than charades to survive in this city.

I reach for my phone.

Joy: I'm drinking wine on my rooftop. It sounds perfect, but I still miss you.

Allison: I'm on my lunch break eating at In-N-Out Burger.

If you're jealous of me you're crazy, even though it is
In-N-Out.

Joy: The one American food I miss.

I switch gears and track down the email of a perfume
blogger I connected with in Austin through an online
forum of other scent-obsessed gals. An American living in
Paris, Elise has become an Internet friend, and when she
learned I was moving here, she told me we must get
together. She's been traveling for work but said she'd
return this week, so I send her a quick note and then gaze
at the skyline, wondering what everyone else is doing on a
Friday night here in Paris while I'm all alone.

Wondering what Griffin's doing.

My phone dings. That's quick for a reply.

But when I open the text, I see Griffin's name.

10

Griffin

I probably shouldn't be thinking of Joy as I run eight miles in the late afternoon, cruising through the Luxembourg Gardens for the last bit, as a hip, new band blasts in my ears.

I definitely shouldn't be thinking of her as I shower, after crushing my previous personal best for those eight miles.

I absolutely shouldn't be picturing how she'd look in this shower with me right now. But it's such a fantastic image that I cut myself some slack as I take care of business.

I suppose that also means I shouldn't be thinking of texting Joy as I jog down the metro steps and squeeze onto a crowded train heading to the heart of Le Marais tonight. But given where my filthy thoughts have taken me on my travels so far today, checking in with her hardly seems inappropriate in the spectrum of inappropriateness.

Besides, I'm only being helpful, I tell myself.
I nearly believe it, too.

Griffin: Scale of 1–10. How was your first official week as a Parisian? Obviously, your mornings were excellent since they were spent with me.

Once I'm on the train on the way to meet Christian, I open her quick reply.

Joy: My mornings were indeed a highlight, though I'm still hunting for the best chocolate tart in the city. Also, I'm hardly a Parisian. More like a transplant-Parisian.

Griffin: Ah, yes. I've heard of that species of foreigner in my marine biology studies. Very dangerous if you don't know how to handle them.

Joy: And I bet you do! Anyway, it was great and awful at the same time. A bus was obnoxious enough to spew its fumes on me this evening, which caused me to knock out a contact lens, which meant I had to go to the pharmacy to buy contact lens solution.

Griffin: That sounds not ideal, but not exactly awful.

Joy: Oh, trust me, it was six ways of awful when I tried to tell the pharmacist what I needed. I butchered the language like it's never been sliced before.

Griffin: I highly doubt you slaughtered words. You could have called me. I would have been happy to help.

Joy: That's kind of you, but I need to be able to function as my own errand girl.

Griffin: Sure. I get that. Don't forget we're friends, and friends help friends buy *solution pour lentilles de contact*.

Joy: Show-off.

I laugh as the train rumbles underground, nearing my stop.

Griffin: Anyway, it takes years to learn the language. Don't beat yourself up over contact lens solution. Are your eyes better?

Joy: Perfect. I'm using them now to enjoy the fabulous view from my rooftop. Thank you again for helping me snag this place. It's truly beautiful.

Griffin: You scored it with your swift decision-making, hatred of smoke, and love of pink doors.

Joy: You helped immensely. Just as you've been immensely helpful at work, too.

Griffin: Well, you're one of my favorite clients. But shhhh. Don't tell the others.

Joy: It'll be our secret.

Briefly, I wish we had other secrets. Or really, I wish that we could. And I kind of wish we were having this conversation in person. Before I can think better of it, I send another text.

Griffin: What are you up to tonight? A group of us are going out for drinks and general carousing in Le Marais. Have you been there yet? You should join us. We don't bite.

Joy: Thanks for the invite! But this wine has gone to my head. I think I might call it a night. I have a busy weekend buying nail scissors and laundry-drying racks. Also, biting isn't always a bad thing.

On the spectrum of inappropriateness, Joy appears to

have joined my team. I grin as I write back.

Griffin: Biting can be a very good thing. Anyway, the night is young. If you change your mind, call me. Otherwise, good luck with the scissors and laundry.

Joy: Good night, friend.

Griffin: Good night, friend.

When the metro slides into the station, I step off the train and ring my parents. My mum answers on the third ring. "Griffin, good to hear from you. Are you okay?"

"Mum, I'm fine. I promise," I say, wishing there was a way I could ease her worries. I don't think she'll ever answer a call from me without expecting the worst.

"Oh, good," she says, relief in her voice. "How's work?"

"It's fantastic. I have a new client," I say, then I tell her briefly about L'Artisan and Joy, and she enquires about my marathon training. I tell her I'm improving my times then ask how Dad is doing with his effort to learn how to cook, since he decided to take cooking classes a few months ago—I suspect to keep occupied.

"He made me bangers and mash. It was dreadful."

"Naturally. Tell him to make you something good, like coq au vin," I say, since she likes her French food much better than the English fare.

"No. I can't let him ruin my favorite dishes."

We chat for a few more minutes, then I say good-bye, finding a welcome measure of peace because I've managed, on a regular basis, to fulfill another one of my brother's wishes.

It's probably the easiest one of all.

P.S. Be nice to Mum and Dad. It's hard for them.

* * *

My brother was a runner, a cross-country standout in primary school. With his blond hair, blue eyes, happy-go-lucky spirit, and success on the field, he was a magnet. At lunch, guys and girls alike flocked to him. After school, he always hung out in the center of a crowd.

Since he was younger than I was, I had free rein to put him in his place. Make sure his success didn't go to his head.

"I bet you can't catch me," I'd told Ethan one morning while he was lacing up his trainers. He was fifteen. I was sixteen.

He laughed. "Seriously? You're seriously thinking I can't catch you? You twat. You'd never be able to keep up with me."

I scoffed. "You'd be huffing and puffing and have no clue what just happened when I passed you," I'd said as I parked my hands behind my head on the couch at our home. "Just last night I dreamed I ran a marathon. Came in first place. And it was my first time running it. No doubt that'd happen."

"Then get on your shoes and let's go see how that dream becomes your nightmare."

I rolled my eyes. "Fine."

He was right.

He did kick my arse.

But I was right, too.

I was faster than I'd expected. I enjoyed it more than I'd thought I would. Or maybe I simply enjoyed the competition. We were only thirteen months apart, so we found ways to compete in nearly everything—sports, girls, school, video games, even ridiculous things like who could clean our room fastest when Dad told us to get on our chores, stat. Later, he beat me in the race to run a marathon—he finished one prior to the accident.

We also ran a 10K together a few months before he was paralyzed. That was the ultimate competition. We were neck and neck the whole time, but I pulled ahead at the end and bested him.

"You wanker," he'd said, panting and out of breath at the finish line. But he had a wicked grin on his face, and for a fleeting second, I wondered if he'd let me win for some reason. I'd pushed the thought out of my head, though, preferring to believe I'd won on my own.

Later, when he was in his wheelchair, his legs unable to work, his arms nearly useless, too, he'd said, "You know I let you win the London 10,000."

"You did not," I told him.

"I so did. It was easy. Right there at the end? You remember?"

"You can't accept that I beat you fair and square," I'd told him as I heated some soup for his lunch at his flat in London.

"You can't accept that you were beaten by a cripple."

I spun around. My jaw was set. My shoulders were tight. "Don't say that word. Ever."

He rolled his eyes. He was quite good at that. "I've accepted it. You should, too," he said. It had been one year since he was struck by a drunk driver while heading home from a night out with friends.

"Even if you've accepted it, I don't want you using that word. Also," I said as I turned back to the stove, "you ought to accept that you had the full use of your legs for the London 10,000, and I still beat you." I smirked, and he promptly tried to ram his wheelchair into me.

He was unsuccessful. "We'll race again. I'll beat you this time just to prove it. Even in a chair."

"You're on."

As I navigate an uneven patch of sidewalk on my way to meet Christian, I can't help but think Ethan would have found a way to race again. I also can't help but think how lucky I am to be able to easily manage the streets of Paris, even when the sidewalks turn cobbled, even when the street corners are so narrow they'd never be able to accommodate a motorized chair like his.

Some days, I'm acutely aware that everything I can do with ease, including the most basic physical accomplishment of walking, are things my brother was unable to do for the last three years.

I can't take a second of my life for granted.

Even if that means going out with friends on a Friday night. *Life is for the living*, Ethan said one evening when he was too sick from an infection to make it out of his house. *Don't stay home. Get out. Enjoy it. Enjoy it extra for both of us.*

"I will," I whisper as I walk, talking to a ghost. "I will."

Then, I do my best to shove off the thoughts, focusing on the here and now.

When I reach the bar, I find Christian already draining a glass of beer. He's shouting at the TV—a ref just called a penalty against the Danish team, a quick glance at the screen tells me.

"Did you see that? That's so bloody ridiculous," he says, gesturing wildly to the TV.

"Yeah, your team deserved it."

"No way. The refs all have it against us."

I laugh as I grab a stool. "That's it. No one likes the Danes except, you know, everyone."

He flashes a smile, his teeth gleaming white. "It's because we're so good-looking. Tall, broad, strapping."

"And humble, too. Don't forget that."

When the bartender comes by, I order a pint and drum my fingers along the bar as I wait.

The game goes to a commercial, and Christian pulls his gaze from the set. "So, you're stuck here in this shitty city with us riffraff for another few months."

"Yeah, Paris is awful."

He flashes a smile. He loves Paris. He once told me his dream job was to become a kept man of some gorgeous French woman. Preferably, she'd be a few years older. Younger women don't hold his attention. A woman a few years older? That sparks his interest. And ideally, he'd service her needs every night and stroll along the river every day, he's said. He hasn't found her yet, but I do admire his dedication to the dream.

"How are you handling it?" he asks, his tone a touch more serious.

"It's not too bad. It's only three months. Especially since the client is a fun one."

Christian arches a brow. "Fun? As in female?" He lets the last word linger, like it has more than two syllables.

I laugh. "Did I say the client was female?"

"No, but I highly doubt you'd say a male client was fun. You want to bang her, don't you?"

It's like he can read my mind. "No," I say, with denial operating at full blast in me.

"Liar."

Thankfully, the bartender arrives with my beer, giving me a temporary reprieve. "Thanks, man," I say, then slap a few euros on the bar. The bartender nods and drops them in the till.

After a swallow, Christian stares at me. "Waiting."

"What are you waiting for?"

He smacks my shoulder. "Just admit it. You said she's fun. Therefore, you fancy her," he says, adopting a singsong teenage girl tone.

"Fancy is so snooty. You can just say 'I have the hots for her.'"

He points his finger at me. "You admitted it. I knew it."

"Bastard," I mutter.

"So you fancy her. What's she like?"

An image of Joy pops into my brain. Curvy, clever, witty Joy. Long legs, fantastic hair, lush lips. A sense of humor that goes on for days. A smile like sunshine. Not to mention a certain zest for life I haven't quite experienced before. From the pink door, to the terrace, to her boldness in asking for contact lens solution and croissants, she's something else.

"She's fun and smart and brainy and a little crazy," I say, though that hardly seems to sum her up.

He shudders. "I try to stay away from the mad-as-a-hatter ones."

"Crazy in a good way. Crazy, like, she has this wild sort of energy."

"Ah," he says with a nod. "I like wild. Wild is one of my favorite traits."

"I'll drink to wild."

"And you have the hots for the wild woman you translate for. How's that working out for you?"

"It's fine. I'm keeping it totally professional." I take another drink.

He nods. "That's the only way to do it."

"Getting involved with a client is a terrible idea," I say, since it's something I need to keep telling myself.

"Don't I know it." Christian dated one of his clients a few months ago, a fresh out of business school gal. It didn't end well, since the client basically decided she wanted to have hot Viking babies with him. Fortunately, her attempts to sink her claws into him coincided with the end of the assignment, which also coincided with her returning to Denmark. She tried hard to convince him to return with her to Scandinavia. She even claimed she might be pregnant. She wasn't.

He'd never been so happy to see a client leave this country.

"And don't you make the same mistake," he says, his tone deadly serious as he raises his glass and takes a drink.

"I won't," I say quickly.

"You can't mix business and pleasure. We're lucky to have the jobs we have. We have uncommon skills. We can't fuck them up by screwing around."

"Absolutely."

He sets down the glass and sweeps his arm out wide. "Besides, we live in a city of beautiful women. And you know what advantage we have over the rest of the blokes?"

"What's that?"

"Dickhead. You know."

"Gee, could it be that we speak their language, but we have the cool cachet of being from someplace else?"

Christian offers a wolfish grin. "Women love men who aren't from where they're from. They love the other. The outsider. The foreigner. The mystery. And so, we are morally obligated to enjoy the bounty of beautiful ladies here in Paris and to bring them the ultimate pleasure."

I raise an eyebrow. "*Morally?* It's a moral obligation?"

He bangs a fist on the bar. "Complete and total moral obligation. We can't shirk it. It'd be like a soldier abandoning his regiment."

"It's a duty, then?"

"One I'm fully committed to honoring. And you should be, too. Hell, isn't it an item on that bucket list of yours?"

Item number two, in fact. *Sleep with all the French women.*

I haven't followed it to the letter. Or the spirit, either. But I feel Ethan would be pleased that I've done my part to carry through on some of his wishes—I've enjoyed the hell out of my nights here in Paris over the last year. "My brother clearly thought of everything."

Christian is one of the few people I've shared the details of my brother's list with. He's an easygoing guy, and he has a brother, so he gets it. You don't question their last wishes. You just honor them. "You know I'm happy to pick up the slack on that one. Should you need it," he says with a casual shrug.

"How noble of you to take on such a terribly burdensome bucket list item."

"I'm thoughtful like that. Let's see if we can honor it tonight."

I flash back on the list I keep close to my body, and my heart. There's something else on it that Ethan wanted me to do. I tap my chin, as if deep in thought. "Besides, it'll help me knock out another item for Ethan."

"What's that one?"

"*Help someone you care about achieve their dream.*"

"And who is this person you care about?"

"You, tosser."

"I love when you both compliment me and insult me in the same sentence."

"Piss off."

He raises his chin. "What's this dream you think you're helping me with?"

"Isn't it only your greatest wish? To be a kept man?"

He bats his crystal-blue eyes. "I can't wait. You're going to help me accomplish my goal to retire at thirty with a hot, rich woman who wants me to service her all day and night? I fucking love you." He reaches across to clap me on the shoulder. "You're a true mate, Griff."

I laugh, and toss back the rest of the beer. "You already retired once," I say, since Christian made gobs of money in the markets, which gave him the luxury to do what he wants now. "But you never know. Maybe she'll walk through the door in a few minutes, and I can say I accomplished that one."

Honestly, I've no idea why helping someone achieve a dream was one of Ethan's wishes. He never elaborated on it. But he wrote it down, and therefore I must do it.

"Maybe we'll find one for you, too," Christian suggests.

Except when a group of pretty women wearing clingy dresses and sky-high heels saunters to the bar to chat up Christian and me, I find myself with zero interest in them.

And an immense interest in texting the woman on the rooftop on the other side of the river.

11

Joy

I should stop. I really should stop. I can't even blame it on the accent this time. After all, you can't hear an accent over text messages.

Besides, his texts aren't even terribly naughty.

They're funny.

Even when he teases me.

He texted me on Friday night, sending me photos of everyday objects with their French and English translations. A streetlamp. A bicycle. A billboard with the word *Saperlipopette.*

Griffin: Obviously, this means gadzooks.

Joy: Clearly. What else could it mean?

Griffin: Here's another. *Loufoquerie.* It means clowning around.

Joy: Are you trying to teach me French words I'm least likely to ever need? Because the contacts and the croissant translations were helpful, but how do you expect me to use *loufoquerie*?

Griffin: Oh, ye of little faith. Let me give you an example. "It's a Friday night full of all sorts of *loufoquerie* and you should be *loufouquering* with my friends and me."

Yes, that one sounded dirty. Very dirty. I might have spent some time in bed that night thinking about loufoquering Griffin, and I don't mean clowning around.

Now, it's Sunday morning, and I'm off to meet Elise. Her blog and its descriptions of perfumes have expanded my mind—she never says *this smells like an iris*, but instead she'd write *one whiff and you'll be tending to a window box full of freshly blooming irises, their petals carrying a hint of a warm spring breeze*. I take a small sampler tube of Linger, a rare brand, since it was discontinued a decade ago, and I tie a silver bow around it. I can't arrive empty-handed. That would be rude.

I drop the gift into my purse, and a new text winks up at me on my phone. I slide it open, and it does funny things to my chest and to my belly. Butterflies flutter all around.

Griffin: Bonjour.

It's not even the word. It's that he texted me good morning.

It's going to be a hard three months.

Correction. Two months and three weeks.

Joy: Bonjour to you, too! How did I do with that? Admit it, you're impressed.

Griffin: So very impressed. Next, you'll be telling me you bought scissors and a laundry-drying rack with ease.

As I head to the metro station, I feel a little sheepish. I didn't accomplish any errands yesterday. I spent the day exploring my arrondissement and eating ice cream.

Once I'm safely inside the metro—yay for sparse Sunday morning traffic and Converse sneakers—I tell Griffin.

Joy: I spent the day exploring. I avoided errands. I ate ice cream. It wasn't as good as I'd hoped. The ice cream, that is.

Griffin: I'm an expert at avoiding errands. I can't believe you didn't call me for errand-avoiding company. Also, the best ice cream is on Île de la Cité. Have you been yet?

Joy: No. But now I'm fantasizing about a cone.

Griffin: Today. Four p.m. Berthillon. Your fantasy comes true.

The smile that spreads across my face is wide and radiant. It's not a date. It's nothing at all like a date. It's a friendly outing.

And I can't wait.

Joy: In that case, I'll be there. Assuming I don't botch the subway again. I tried to go to the Louvre yesterday and wound up at Moulin Rouge.

Griffin: Seems someone was looking out for you. :) The Louvre is overrated.

Indeed. I drop my phone in my purse and sit back on the subway seat, rattling underground all the way to Place D'Abbesses, where I exit at the famous Montmartre stop. I'm six stories underground, and since that's a piece of cake to me these days thanks to my Uneven 84, I take the spiral steps all the way up to street level, where the famous umbrella-like green awning of the metro stop awaits.

I stare at it and snap a photo. I post it with a #favoritesinParis, then head to Place du Tertre, where the caricaturists gather. I glance at my watch. I'm meeting Elise in thirty minutes. This spot is so ridiculously touristy, and I can't resist. One of the caricaturists makes eye contact, and I remember my French words.

"How much?" I ask in his language.

"Ten euros."

I'm ready to pump a fist. I can do this. *Oh là là.*

My sister will get a kick out of this caricature. I take a seat and he begins chatting. In French. I don't understand a word he's saying. I pretend he's telling me I have a very expressive face and a fantastic smile, and he admires my adventuresome spirit so much. *Not everyone would venture up to Montmartre by herself, but here you are braving a new city, experiencing all it has to offer. Don't worry about the ex. You did what you could. You helped where you could. Not everyone wants to be helped, you know?*

He raises an eyebrow, waiting for an answer as he sketches.

"*Oui. C'est vrai,*" I reply. *Yes, that's true.*

After all, I'm having a pretend conversation with him. I might as well answer what I imagine him asking.

I know it was hard to finally say good-bye, but you'd tried so many times before, and besides, you were stuck, he was stuck, and he refused to get help for his addiction. Once he was injured at work and hurt his back, you did everything you could to help him recover. You took him to doctors. You took him to endless doctors' appointments. You sought out every possible treatment for him. But the only option he wanted was more and more OxyContin. And then another pill, another, and then another. You tried to get him help, but he didn't want it. Besides, you weren't in love with him anymore. You hadn't been for a whole year, since before he fell off a ladder. You can only try for so long until there is no more trying to do.

"*Oui?*" The man smiles at me, asking me his question.

"*Oui.*" I return his grin, though I've no idea what he asked.

"*Voilà!*" He presents me with my caricature, and I laugh at the elongated chin and huge lips, and my hair that looks like windswept curtains. My eyes are huge—saucers in my face.

"Beautiful," he says, and I understand him.

"Thank you."

I pay him, roll up the drawing, and tuck it into my cavernous purse as I leave the square with the café, turning onto a curvy street that climbs the hills in Montmartre. Breathing deeply, I let the scent of the ivy that curls over the walls of a brick home on my path flood my nose. The street bends, and I imagine Picasso himself walking these roads. I'm hardly an artist, but sometimes I craft scents and seductive compositions, and I suppose that's the closest I come to making art.

As the street bends once more, a heavy green door etched with curling ironwork panels comes into view.

That must be Elise's home. A dual citizen, Elise has lived in Paris for several years now. She was born in Manhattan to French parents and raised in New York City. But she returned to the City of Light several years ago and can move seamlessly among the French and Americans, from what I've gathered.

I reach the door and ring, and soon a voice floats over the buzzer.

"Come in."

The emerald-green wooden door spills into a courtyard teeming with yellow tulips. I've gained entry to a secret lair simply because I have the passcode—a love of perfume. The door swings open, and a pretty, petite brunette with black glasses and high cheekbones steps out and tosses her arms around me.

"My new American friend in Paris," she declares, the sleeves of her maroon top fluttering.

"Hello, my new French–American friend in Paris. Your courtyard is gorgeous," I say, once I untangle myself.

She waves a hand dismissively. "I do a little gardening."

I hold up my thumb and forefinger. "Just a little."

She ushers me inside, and bless her, she has a bottle of champagne on the living room table.

I think I love her.

* * *

Two hours later, I'm buzzed, happy, and laughing.

"Try this one," she says as she reaches for a bottle on the marble table in her living room. A delicate tray hosts several vials and tubes of her favorites. "It's Euphoria."

"Will it make me feel amazing?"

"It will make anyone want to seduce you. No man is powerful enough to resist this scent."

"Why? Does it smell like pizza and beer?" I ask, thinking Richard was weirdly powerful enough to resist all pretty scents. He curled his nose up at them, covering his nostrils, asking me to please, please, please never wear perfume in the house. It gave him a headache.

She slaps her hand on her thigh. "You're very funny." She hands me the bottle. "Here you go."

I've already washed off the ones I've tried on so far, so my wrists are bare when she spritzes some on. I bring my hand to my nose and inhale. "Mmm. It's a tropical garden, and I've just strolled past a mango tree, where the fruit hangs low and ripe."

She whistles her appreciation. "You need to write my blog for me."

"Well, you don't want me to say something simple, like

it smells like mangoes," I say drily. "Your blog taught me better."

"The best perfumes take you on a trip. They whisk you away to a place, to a time, to a memory."

I sigh happily, picturing a tropical island while I'm in her very French, very rich home. Elise owns an advertising agency. The perfume blog she writes in her spare time.

"I was worried," I admit with a contented sigh.

"About what?"

"Would we get along? Would you be snooty? Would I be a terrible guest, since my French is abysmal?"

"You'll get there, and of course we get along. We share a love. And you are wonderful and not a douche. Did you like my American word? See, I haven't been gone too long from the United States."

"Just say douchecanoe and you'll be good to go at proving your dual citizenship."

"Douchecanoe," she says with the most impeccable French accent, and we both crack up.

"Brilliant."

"*Merci*. And how are you liking Paris? You must be fighting off all the French men all the time."

I scoff. "No, not at all. I haven't even had so much as a French kiss."

"You've come to the most romantic city in the world, and you haven't even kissed in the City of Light?" Incredulity is her new middle name.

"There's no one." But an image of the handsome man I spend half my days with flashes before me. I can feel my lips curve in a grin as I imagine Griffin's handsome face.

Elise must catch my expression because she arches a brow curiously. "Are you sure?"

I inch closer, even though we're alone. "Well, my work translator is a total fox."

She laughs. "Fox. Do tell."

I spill all about Griffin. How we met. Our rapport. Even the texts he sent.

"British and French. He sounds delicious. You should take a lover," she says, then raises her glass.

I nearly spit out the bubbly. "Take a lover?"

She nods, her expression fiercely certain. "Yes. You are attracted to him. He's attracted to you. It makes perfect sense to me."

I shake my head, bemused. "You're so French."

"Why not do it?"

"We work together. It would be complicated when it ends, and it always ends."

"Then don't complicate it. That's what we do well here. We've learned to take our pleasures—our wine, our perfume, our chocolates. Eat them, savor them—enjoy them. You never know what tomorrow brings. We should enjoy every day, and eat it like a fruit."

"If that's the case, I want my days to taste like peaches."

She wiggles an eyebrow. "You should eat a banana."

I laugh. "You're going to be a very bad influence on me."

"I might be. But you won't regret great sex. Seriously? Have you ever regretted great sex?"

I set my glass down. "It's been so long since I've had it, I'm not sure I remember enough to regret."

"That saddens me so much I need another glass," she says, grabbing the bottle and offering me some.

I wave her off. "I shouldn't have any more." I glance at the time. "I need to take off. I have to meet Griffin for ice cream."

"Where? Berthillon?"

I smile. "How did you know?"

"It's only the best in Paris. He probably wants to feed you ice cream and get you in bed."

"Is that a thing here? Ice cream and sex?"

She nods sagely. "Like I said, we love our pleasures in France."

I point at her. "You're trouble, Elise. Total trouble."

She smiles. "Of course I am. Maybe you need trouble. Maybe you've spent the last few years doing what you thought you should, and now it's time to do what you want."

I blink and square my shoulders, surprised she can read me so easily. "How can you tell?"

"I can see it in your eyes."

I take a beat before I answer. "You might be right."

When I leave, I can't help but wonder how right she is. If I should pursue more. I know, rationally, it would be a mistake, but with all this champagne and perfume in my head, everything feels possible.

12

Griffin

We're friends.

Friends go out for ice cream.

Friends stroll along the narrow streets in the little island in the middle of the river. One friend could stare at another friend as she licks her ice cream like it's a fucking blow job.

Whoa.

Rewind.

That's not what friends do.

Friends don't picture talents with tongues.

But for a moment, I don't bother trying to trick my mind into being merely mates with Joy. Her tongue strokes across the raspberry ice cream with such lavish attention that I can't think anything but filthy thoughts. When her lips kiss the scoop, I nearly groan with lust.

She exudes sensuality, and she smells divine. I swear every time I'm with her, a different scent trails in her wake.

I have no clue what it is, but today she reminds me of a lush waterfall, and I picture tugging her under it and kissing the hell out of those raspberry lips as the sun warms our skin.

So yeah, it isn't easy trying to be friends with a girl you want to shag. I swear I can hear Ethan laughing at me. "Good luck with that one," he'd say with a wink.

Oddly enough, I crack a smile at the imagined retort, laughing softly as we meander past a café where waiters prep for the oncoming dinner rush.

Joy tilts her head to the side, curious. "What's so funny? Do I have ice cream on my nose?"

My finger makes the most of the opportunity, as I brush it along the tip of her nose. "All gone now."

"Seriously?"

I shake my head and take another lick of my coconut ice cream. "I was just teasing about the ice cream. Truth be told, I was thinking of something funny."

"Are you going to share? Or will you keep all your comedy a secret?"

"Just something I imagined my brother saying."

She arches a brow. "Is he a funny guy?"

My heart squeezes as if I'm being strangled. It's not that I don't want to tell Joy; it's just that I don't want to ruin this day. A part of me feels guilty for thinking that, but I also know once we open the Pandora's box of heartbreak —the *my brother lost the use of his legs, most of his arms, and he lived like that for three years before dying in the hospital while trying to fight off an infection; I miss him like crazy and now I try to live out all the dreams he was never able to realize* conversation—we'll be venturing into deeper, darker waters.

I want to stay in the shallow end and eat ice cream.

I say *he was* in my head, before I finish the sentence

aloud with, "Very funny." I change gears. "Now that you're enjoying the best ice cream in Paris, do you want to hear all about this island's role in French history?" I sweep my hand out grandly to encompass all of Île de la Cité.

"Ooh, are you going to regale me with tales of Heloise and Abelard? Of the former royal residence turned into a prison during the French Revolution? Or will you show me the statue of Henri IV because for some reason that's greatly important?"

My eyes widen as I glance at her. "Such sarcasm. I'm ridiculously impressed. I had no idea you had such a store in you."

She wiggles her eyebrows. "I think it might be the champagne I had at Elise's."

"I can't believe you didn't save any champagne for me," I tease.

"Do you like champagne?"

I whisper conspiratorially, "Love it. Maybe even more than a pint. Don't tell a soul."

She places one finger on her lips, sealing our little secret. Then she gestures to the buildings and the streets. "Truth be told, I don't mind those historical details. I've studied guidebooks about Paris, and I read about Heloise and Abelard, and I think if some romance writer wants to pen a completely taboo story, she ought to do a modern retelling of a nun falling for a man. Now, that would be risqué."

I hold my free hand up high, as if I'm lighting up a marquee. "*The Vixen Nun.* I can see it now."

"Starring Blaze Dalton as the modern-day monk."

"I've been meaning to tell you that Blaze also moonlights as an actor."

"Naturally." She brings the ice cream to her mouth

once again and hums her approval after a long, lingering lick.

With the strength of an army, I tear my gaze away. "So, you don't like traditional tour-guide info?"

"Oh, I do like it, actually. But I like the odd little tidbits even more. In fact, I already went to Notre Dame, but my favorite was the elephant."

I bring my hand to my heart. "The elephant. Seriously, you need to stop talking right now."

"Why?"

"If you say anything more, I'll think you're perfect."

She scoffs. "Because I liked an elephant?"

"No. Because you *noticed* the elephant."

Joy shrugs as we amble down a cobbled street so picturesque it could be in a movie. Planters hang from window shutters, and an old-fashioned ironwork sign perches above an antique shop. Ivy has had the courtesy to crawl across nearly every building wall. "I like learning about what's right in front of me, but also what's undiscovered. However, I suspect you prefer the latter. Why don't you show me something on the Île de la Cité that I won't find on every single walking tour? Like that one." Lowering her voice, she tips her forehead across the street. A man wearing trousers and a short-sleeved white shirt walks backward, talking animatedly to a group of a dozen or so tourists, all snapping pics on mobile phones or cameras as he tells them a story of how Marie Antoinette served time as a prisoner in the Conciergerie.

Nothing wrong with history. I love it. But I also love what's not in the books.

Evidently, Joy does, too, and this little discovery is like a burst of electricity in my chest. I'm buzzing with awareness and possibility because it feels like she knows me.

Like she's speaking the language of my heart. "I'll show you something that people rarely see."

We finish our cones as we stroll past a café with a chalkboard menu and mint-green chairs placed on the sidewalk. Joy stops to take a photo, then she studies it on her phone. She lifts her eyes and tugs the fabric of my shirt.

"Look!" She points to the awning.

I study it briefly, finding nothing noteworthy. "It's a red awning. Is this another pink door for you?"

"No, silly. Look higher. There's an angel carved into the stone above the awning."

I squint, finding it. A small little fellow with wings and a bugle, occupying no more than six or seven inches.

Once more, Joy takes a photo. "I saw an angel my first day here, but that was on a door knocker. It's so random. I love how completely random this is."

"I've never noticed it before. Nor have I seen any angel door knockers," I say, scratching my jaw.

"Maybe there are angels watching over the city," she muses.

I arch a skeptical brow. "You don't seem like one of those angels-are-watching-over-us people," I say as we resume our pace.

"I'm not really. As a scientist, I'd be more apt to think the planets were watching us. But some people do believe in angels, and I like knowing what people believe because it helps me understand the world better. And now I shall post that chubby little dude on Instagram," she says with a flourish, raising her arm then stabbing her finger against the phone with panache. "Hashtag: their eyes are everywhere." She adopts a spooky laugh.

"Beware of angels," I intone, my voice going dark, too.

We make our way to the edge of the island, to the royal

palace that became a court and a one-time prison. There, I show Joy one of my favorite gems, situated on an obscure side of the Conciergerie.

But I don't even need to direct her to see it. She's the rare person who looks up long enough and high enough to see what's in front of her.

An ornate gilt medieval clock, lavishly decorated in gold and set against a royal-blue background, the twin statues of Law and Justice framing the timepiece.

I gesture to it. "This is the city's first public clock and its oldest public clock, given by Charles V to the city of Paris in 1371. But it's hardly included on tours, even though it mattered so much more to French people than a statue of a king."

"Why did it matter so much?"

"Because before 1371, Parisians were pretty much wandering around wondering what the hell time it was," I say with a chuckle.

She laughs, too. "See? I like those details. Tell me more. Why didn't anyone know the time?"

"No one could afford their own clocks, and watches hadn't been invented. A big public clock like this helped the citizens know when the baker, the butcher, or the tailor opened and closed."

Joy shakes her head in amazement. "We take so much for granted."

"And before then, there were only sundials."

"But then you don't know what time it is when it's cloudy," she adds.

"That's the rub."

Her brow knits, and then she snaps her fingers. "I swore I saw one the day we found my apartment. I'm not even sure it was working."

"The city is full of sundials, too. Some are useless and

don't work. Some still tell time in the most ancient of ways. It is a little-known fact that Paris is the French city with the greatest number of sundials. There are about one hundred and twenty around the city."

"Why so many?"

"I'm sure there's a logical reason. Like scientific societies met here or were studying the stars, but I have my own theory."

"Yes? Do tell."

"We're obsessed with time," I say seriously, then I train my gaze on the golden arrow ticking its way around the seconds. "Not just Parisians. It's part of being human. We waste time, and we want more of it simultaneously."

"And yet, we rarely spend it wisely. We often simply squander it."

Her thoughtful tone hooks into me. All these ideas I marinate on she already knows the answers to. "I think we're searching for lost time. We don't ever find it, but that doesn't stop us from hunting for all our lost hours."

"Maybe that's why there are so many sundials," I speculate. "Maybe the French knew sooner than anyone else that we would always be seeking more time. There is literally never enough." For a quiet moment, we stand in front of the clock as its hands tick forever forward. "What I love most about these little curiosities is picturing everyday life in this city—like when the baker is open."

"Which reminds me how glad I am to be alive today. I love knowing the time, and I love knowing thoroughly modern details that Google tells me, like *what's the nearest boulangerie that's still open?*"

I smile at her, and translate her question into French. Then I point at her purse. "Now ask Google."

She nibbles on the corner of her lip but does as told, taking out her phone and speaking the question into the search engine, as I repeat the words in a low voice for her. She's stilted as she speaks, and her pronunciation is nothing to write home about, but it gets the job done, because the pleasantly robotic voice answers from her phone in French.

"The nearest boulangerie is on the corner of Rue de Lutèce and is open until six."

Joy thrusts the phone in the air, victory-style.

"*Très bien*," I tell her.

When she tucks her phone away, she says, "Whenever I hear the time, though, it reminds me that I still feel sort of lost in time. Like when I first came here."

"How so?"

"From jet lag at first, but also there was this constantly hazy feeling of being neither here nor there. I'd left America, but I didn't feel truly here, either, but caught someplace in-between. Was I seven hours ahead, or seven hours behind? Even though I'm acclimated now, I hardly feel like I'm grounded here in Paris."

"You're still converting the hours back to US time?"

She nods, and a sad look passes over her eyes. "Maybe I always will."

"That's not a bad thing. Your family is there. Your point zero is the United States, and all your references are across an ocean."

"But I'm here," she says, her pitch rising as she digs her heels in, "and I want to feel like I belong."

My eyes roam her body, her silhouette framed by the river behind her. Her red hair blows in the breeze. She is an oddity, a bold, bright, brash American woman in this European place that's both ancient and thoroughly modern. Paris is full of curiosities, and I'm pretty sure she's one of them. "I think you belong here," I tell her with a warm smile.

Her eyes light up, glittering. As I look into them, it occurs to me they're a color I've never seen before. The green is vibrant, but not overwhelming. Those are not emerald eyes. That would feel unreal, like a template for fake contacts. Hers are a sage green, and I can't look away.

I swallow as if I can drink down this flare of desire I feel for her that's physical but also something more. There's some fine thread connecting us, though I don't know what it is. I'm not sure how to name it.

Or if I want to.

All I know is I like it—too much for my own good.

"I can show you all the sundials I know of," I say, and the words come out like gravel. I clear my throat. Fuck, it sounds like I invited her to bed. Maybe that's what I meant to do.

"I would love that," she says, tapping my arm. She squeezes my bicep. "But I'm going to need to teach you something. It's not fair that you're doing all the work."

"It's not work. It's all pleasure." Especially with her hand on my arm.

"Be that as it may, I will have to take my turn showing you something you might not know about this city. Like exploring the flower markets?"

I'd pretty much say yes to any place she wanted to take me right now. "You smell like a flower. Like some tropical plant," I blurt out.

Taking her hand from my arm, she runs it down her neck. I want that hand to be my tongue. "It's a new perfume. Do you want to smell me?"

I nearly wobble in my shoes. I want to smell her, taste her, touch her. I want to lick her from her ankles to her thighs. I want to press my lips to the hollow of her throat.

"I do," I rasp out.

She lifts her chin and gently taps the side of her neck.

I dip my head toward the crook of her neck, bending until my nose is inches away from her bare flesh. The scent of lush gardens floats into my nose as I close my eyes and draw a deep breath. My skin heats, and my bones hum. My nerve endings snap to attention.

Along with other parts.

My nose brushes against her skin, and a quiet noise seems to escape her throat. A hitch in her breath. As I draw one more delicious inhale, that sound shifts to a murmur, and I can picture her wrapping her hands around the back of my head, yanking me close, and urging me to lavish attention all over her neck, up to her ear, then to those lips I don't want to resist.

But I do resist.

I step away. "It's getting late. I believe you still have scissors and a laundry-drying rack to procure."

"And I thought you were an expert errand avoider."

"It is a top skill of mine, but I can't wait to hear you ask for scissors in French."

She blinks. "I have to perform in French for you?"

I laugh. "Yes. Hop to it."

She's not half bad at the store when I teach her how to ask for the items she needs. Once we leave, she fixes me with a serious stare. "I really owe you after all you've done for me today."

I shake my head. "You showed me something I've never seen before. That's pretty impressive."

She scoffs. "Spotting one little angel statue hardly compares to you treating me to ice cream, a clock, and your astonishing switcheroo skills when it comes to words."

"I don't agree. I think we're even."

"Hardly," she says, doubtful.

"Look at it this way—you kept me company on a

Sunday afternoon when I might otherwise have been tempted to do something dreadfully boring, like dishes."

"If you say so."

"By the way, what is that tropical flower you smell like? My nose is terrible. I can't distinguish scents at all."

"Was it a flower?" A flirty little smile crosses her lips. "Or was it the scent of the Sunday afternoon when you devoured ice cream and wandered through the city until the clock ticked close to twilight, and your companion wondered how she could ever thank you?"

My throat goes dry. My skin heats.

This woman.

We stop at a street corner along the Seine. I step closer to her, savoring the view of her pretty face for one last moment. A streetlamp glows softly behind her, a halo of light framing her copper hair. "If you insist, I'm sure you'll find a way to repay me somehow," I say, then I do what the French do. I kiss her right cheek then her left, catching one final inhale of today, then I say good-bye.

The truth is she doesn't owe me a thing. As I walk home, I let my mind replay the afternoon with her. Someday, when I'm searching for lost hours, these are the ones I'll want to find.

13

Joy

"What time does the nearest cheese shop close?"

I pose the question to Google in French as I near my office building on Thursday of that same week.

Like a responsive robot, she answers me. "The nearest cheese shop is on Rue Cler, and it closes at five."

Tra la la.

I'm learning French by osmosis. I've been picking it up and not even realizing it, and now, look at me. Owning the cheese deets. *Paris, I've got you figured out.*

With my phone close to my mouth like it's a mic, I chat more with Google until I reach the entryway to L'Artisan Cosmetique, where I tuck my handy-dandy new friend into the side pocket of my Kate Spade bag. Before I know it, I'll be conversing with my colleagues in the elevators, in the halls, in the break room, all thanks to this magical, fantastic device known as a smartphone.

Smart indeed.

Heck, I probably won't need Griffin soon, and that'll honestly be for the best. That man is temptation made flesh. It's not just that he's handsome. It's not only that his accent makes me want to hump his leg. It's that he's so damn attentive. He listens to me. He *cares*. And he does it in a way that goes beyond his responsibility as a translator. He does it as a friend.

But even though I wanted to haul his fine body against mine when he drew his nose along my neck the other day, I resisted. Relationships are messy stews. They boil over, and then you're left cleaning up a big old spill of something you don't even want anymore. Besides, getting close to someone makes you lose sight of what you want in life.

I'm so damn lucky that I have this chance to focus on my career, and I don't want to torpedo it by letting a little thing like lust overwhelm me. Whoever said you can have your cake and eat it, too, clearly was never involved with a man like Richard.

I shudder at the mere thought of his name then steer my brain toward happier ground.

Like chocolate tarts and that fantastic new pair of royal-blue wedge heels I picked up yesterday on sale at the shop on the corner. They look fabulous with the red skirt I'm wearing today, if I do say so myself.

I head inside my building and press the button for the elevator, letting thoughts of flirty British men, and inconvenient American men, and my own mistakes in staying too long fall out of my head, like leaves fluttering to the ground.

When I reach my floor, I find Griffin chatting with Marisol, and a flare of jealousy ignites in my chest.

I stop in my tracks, trying to process why on earth I'd

feel envy. He's effectively a contractor with our company. She's signing off on the checks to pay him. It's only natural they'd chat. I'm sure it's a simple conversation about work forms or payday.

When I reach them, I say hello, and they both shift to English, which pisses me off for some odd reason.

"Good morning, Joy," Marisol says. "We were chatting about how awful running can be."

I furrow my brow. They're *supposed* to be discussing paperwork.

"I'm training for a marathon," Griffin says, a frustrated look in his pretty blue eyes. "Had a brutal run this morning. The kind where I ask myself why the hell I'm doing it."

I didn't know he was running a marathon.

Marisol sighs heavily, chiming in, "It was the same for me. I'm a runner, too, and it was just one of those days."

The flare inside me burns brighter, turns hotter. It scalds my skin. I hate running so much, and I hate that Griffin is bonding with my HR manager even more, and the thing I detest the most is that I'm having this kind of incendiary reaction to them having a conversation. "Well, you should take up people watching. That's my favorite form of exercise, right after shopping," I say with a practiced smile, and it's only when I stroll toward my office that I realize the words came out more haughtily than I intended.

Or perhaps just as haughtily as I intended.

Ugh. I suck. I drop my forehead onto my desk.

"You okay?"

I raise my head at the sound of Griffin's voice. He stands in the office doorway, studying me. I offer another smile, hoping it's more authentic than the last one. "Fabulous. Ready to tackle the day. Since, you know, I didn't run this morning."

Oops. I went there again.

He lifts an eyebrow. "Is something about running bothering you?"

"What? No. Why would that bother me?" I glance at the clock. "Meeting time."

When in doubt about your bizarre emotional reaction to something, practice avoidance.

Fortunately, the meeting provides the perfect opportunity to do precisely that.

In the conference room, we discuss time-to-market for the new body spray, and then we brainstorm product plans for our lavender lotion. Next on the agenda is our wish list of items. That excites me, as developing new products is a true passion, especially when Griffin translates and tells me they want to explore making perfume.

My ears prick with excitement, and my heart pounds faster with possibility. I sit straighter as I ask questions about what they might want, scribbling down ideas in my notebook as quickly as I can.

By the time the meeting ends, my brain hurts again—from trying to comprehend what they said before Griffin translated for me.

And failing.

I need him so badly, and today it's ticking me off because I don't want to feel jealousy. I don't want to feel longing. I don't want to want to kiss him so damn badly it's like a persistent ache in my chest.

I want to be friends, just friends.

I need to put myself in a time-out and try to sort through the barrage of emotions I didn't expect this morning.

Naturally, I retreat to the ladies' room. Once inside, I

take out my phone and check my messages. My sister replied to my email that had my Montmartre caricature attached to it.

Allison: Oh my! Never has a likeness of you and your big mouth been so accurate! Also, love you madly, and miss you much.

That brings me a smile and makes my heart hurt the slightest bit. Understanding my sister is so easy, but understanding everyone here is so hard. I'm more home-sick for English than I want to be.

But I'm not going to be visiting that familiar place anytime soon.

* * *

That afternoon, I sequester myself in the lab with blotters and vials and tubes. Griffin is gone, as he usually is at this time. Off running, or doing written translations, or meeting beautiful French women who run, or having sex with trim French women who whisper dirty French things in his ear.

Gritting my teeth, I reach for a tube of synthetic orange blossom molecules.

Nearby, Charles is working quietly, too.

I swing my gaze back to my own work, wishing I felt comfortable casually asking him what he's working on, bantering about the day, gabbing as we test formulations. *Hey there, Chuck. What's shaking? How's the body lotion formulation going? Does it smell amazeballs?*

Oh yes, it's fantastic. Want a sniff?

Why, thank you! Oh my, that is wonderful. You're so talented.

I followed the process you outlined in the meeting last week. And yes, I think the process is amazeballs, too.

Yeah, that conversation doesn't happen, even though I make a mental note to look up the correct translation of "amazeballs" later. Clearly, such a critical word in English must have a French equivalent.

But I can't say any of that, so I offer a professional smile and return to my work. Today, I'm fine-tuning a formulation for a body lotion. It's close, but not quite there. It needs that final top note. Something that makes customers want it. Something that makes them think of their happiest moments.

Orange blossom isn't cutting it. It's too close to a cleaner in this blend.

Closing my eyes, I try to picture all my favorite days, but my memory isn't cooperating. Unpleasantness intrudes, images of Richard calling me the day he fell from the ladder, telling me he injured his back and was being taken to the hospital. My shoulders curl inward, tensing. I'd been ready to break up with him before that fateful call. I'd known I wasn't in love with him anymore. But how do you break a man's heart the same day he breaks his back?

You don't.

You woman up.

You stay. You help. You do everything you can.

Until you can't do any more.

When I open my eyes, I try to will away the unpleasant images. I can't brew the scent of guilt. I can't bottle our antiseptic relationship.

As I stare at the white-tiled walls of the lab, I cycle through some of the most pleasing scents. Vanilla and jasmine. Honey and rose. Peach and apple. You can't go wrong with peach. It's like bread; it's like puppies. It's impossible to dislike the scent of peach.

But I can't find the vial I need when I search for it on the shelves. Sighing, I grab my phone, double-checking the words on Google Translate.

"Do you have the peach?" I ask Charles in French, adding the dilution amount.

His eyes light up. "Yes."

He rises, reaches for the tube, and hands it to me.

"Thank you."

But when I mix it up, the scent is too strong, too intense. And I know why. I asked for the wrong variation. Because my pronunciation is as good as a garbage can.

"Do you like it?" he asks me in his native language.

"A little," I tell him.

It's a lie.

I can't stand it.

Mostly, I can't stand myself.

When I leave work that night, I take out my phone and curse it. "You're only good for bakery information."

The phone beeps. "I can give you bakery information," the robotic woman answers.

I curse at her.

"I'm sorry. Can you repeat the question?"

"Ugh."

"I did not understand you. Can you try again?"

I bark into the phone. "Where is the nearest bakery that's still open? I desperately need a peach tart."

"I'm sorry. There is no bakery open."

I imagine she adds, with a snicker, *you pathetic idiot.*

I go home, wishing for a tart but needing so much more. I head to my rooftop and text my sister.

Joy: What's shaking, sugar?

Her reply is swift.

Allison: Can't talk. At work. Skype later?

But later I'll be asleep, and once again, I'm lost in time. Stuck between two worlds. I don't exist in my old world any longer, and I don't fit into the new one.

Once upon a time I thought it would be easy to escape into a new life. But there's nothing simple about starting over. I write back to Allison saying we'll talk another time. As I close her message, I find a text from Richard that came through earlier in the day.

You were wrong. I'm not addicted. My new doctor says my previous doc didn't know how to manage the pain. Hope you're having fun in France.

Seething, I narrow my eyes and stare daggers at my phone then shout at it, "I'm not having fun. Not today. Not at all. And you're wrong, you ass. You're fucking wrong."

Gripping the phone harder, I consider chucking it. Tossing it far across the rooftops of Paris for the crime of delivering Richard's message to me, as well as tricking me into thinking a search engine could solve my language woes. But that would be cruelty to my smartphone, and my phone has, bakery misunderstanding aside, been pretty good to me. I set it on the chair.

Then I tromp downstairs to my bedroom, marching to my silver tray with my favorite scents. I snatch up a little tester tube of Obsession, and spritz it on my wrist. Next, I grab Angel, with its chocolate and caramel notes, and spray some on my other hand. Like a dog sniffing for food, I hold my nose up high and let the mixture of scents feed my olfactory senses. If Richard were here, he'd cough majestically, dramatically even, and tell me my perfume gave him a headache. He'd fling his hand on his forehead as if to prove his point. That wasn't why I wanted to end our relationship, but it was one more Jenga block in a teetering tower.

A tower that came crashing down.

Tonight, I celebrate my freedom from him by dousing myself in all the scents he abhorred. By the time I'm done, I smell like a ten-cent whorehouse. I cackle as I twirl in my bedroom. Yup. I'm a regular mess right now. But I don't care, I don't care, I don't stinking care.

I do a little jig. I can finally do whatever I want in my own sweet time in my own dang home.

But admittedly, the scent of me right now is a wee bit overwhelming so I hop into the shower, wash myself clean, and pull on yoga pants and a sweater.

I return to my new favorite place, sinking back into the chaise lounge on my rooftop garden. With a cooler head, I grab my phone, delete Richard's message, then go to his contact information. My thumb hovers over his name. I could delete him, too. I could even block him. Instead, I resolve to ignore him if I hear from him. After all, there's nothing I can do for him anymore. I put down the phone and stare at the twinkling lights glittering on the Eiffel Tower.

I gaze at them until they turn hazy and blurry. I might have moved on from my past. I might be letting go of a relationship I stayed in far beyond its expiration point. But I haven't fully stepped into my new life.

And I know why.

The answer doesn't reside in Google.

It can be found in those lights.

In where they flicker.

In what they represent.

I text Griffin and tell him I have a proposition for him.

14

Griffin

There's one word a woman can utter that gets a man's blood flowing south instantly.

Okay. That's not true.

There are about twenty thousand that produce that effect, because when you fancy a woman, nearly anything remotely sexy can drive you crazy with desire for her.

Imagine if she says, *I'm going to take off a sock.*

Boom. Implied nudity. Hard as a rock.

Perhaps she asks, *Do you like strawberries?*

Obviously that means she wants me to eat them off her breasts. Flagpole raised.

But then there are some that are so direct, so spot on, she might as well be saying, *I'd like you to fuck me hard all night long.*

Which, for the record, might possibly be my favorite thing a woman could ever say to me. In fact, I might need to make that my own personal addendum to the bucket list.

At the moment, though, the word is *proposition*.

As I walk to the restaurant Joy has chosen on Rue de Bac, I keep replaying that deliciously inviting message.

I have a proposition for you.

What could it possibly be but some fantastic arrangement where we shag all night and still get along for work? No strings, no pain, no heartbreak. Sign me up right-the-hell now. That would be fantastic. A promise of orgasm-drenched nights, capped off by an uncomplicated good-bye when I take off for Indonesia in a few more months, finally visiting the places around the world Ethan and I marked on a map when we were younger.

As I round the corner, Christian's words have the temerity to appear in the forefront of my brain.

Don't you make the same mistake. You can't mix business and pleasure. We're lucky to have the jobs we have.

We *are* lucky to have our jobs. I don't disagree with his basic premise, but I doubt Joy's proposition will jeopardize mine. Besides, I really only need to keep my job for the next two and a half months. That's all she needs me for at her company, and then I'm gone. Who knows where I'll end up after I take off on my great adventure? We made so many marks on that map. If I found it, it'd be full of pinholes, I'm sure.

Travel everywhere, Ethan wrote.

He can't. So I must.

There's simply no way that Joy's *have hot sex with me every single night starting now* will interfere with my bigger plans. I can juggle business and pleasure. I can enjoy the woman, the gig, and the checking off of each item on the bucket list.

When I reach the door of Gabriel's, a restaurant

started by a French-Brazilian cook who's now become a rock star chef in New York City, I'm more certain than ever that I can have my cake and eat it, too. Preferably off Joy's soft, supple belly.

With that enticing image front and center, I smooth a hand down my black shirt, push open the door, and head inside.

* * *

She lifts her glass of wine in an elegant hand, and all I can think is the proposition is coming now. She's going to hit me with her *take me to bed and do very bad things to me* offer this second. She's been cagey and she's been coy, insisting we order drinks first and then appetizers. What an alluring vixen. In return, I'm going to have so much fun torturing her exquisitely in bed. Driving her wild, touching her everywhere, putting my mouth all over that enticing body.

I raise my glass and tip it to hers, clinking. My eyes drift to her hands, picturing how inviting they'll look above her head as she writhes on the bed.

She takes a sip, and I can't stop looking at those lips now. Those red, pouty, full lips I've wanted to get to know since the day I met her.

Oh yes. I'm going to get my wish.

She murmurs, "Mmm. This wine is so good."

I take a drink, too. "It's fantastic."

She runs her finger along the rim of the glass. "I do love a good wine. My friend Elise says I should take more advantage of the pleasures Paris has to offer."

"You really should," I say, shifting an inch or two closer in my chair.

The restaurant is small, and the tables are lit with low

candles, shimmering faintly. Exposed brick walls give the eatery a cozy feel. The weather outside has turned chillier, as it often does in April. Maybe Joy is thinking I can warm her up.

She arches an eyebrow playfully. "You also think I should partake of all the pleasures? Wine, food, dessert?"

"I think your friend Elise is brilliant, and I think you could even expand that list of pleasures."

"And what else should I put on my list? Maybe languages?"

I blink. That's not what she's supposed to say. "Languages?"

She smiles, big and wide. She sets down her glass and spreads her hands on the table. "As I said, I have a proposition for you. Here it is."

"Yes, hit me up." Obviously, it's the language of sex she wants me to teach her. The words and phrases that will take her straight to O-town every night. Funnily enough, I'm pretty damn fluent in that language as well as the many others I speak. "I'm conversant in many tongues."

She laughs, tossing her head back, her throat long and inviting, her red hair curling in lush waves over her shoulders and down her chest, curtaining those fantastic breasts. I nearly growl with the realization that I will finally get properly acquainted with those beauties.

"You and your talent with tongues." She shakes her head, amused, then clears her throat. "That's actually what I want to talk to you about."

I was right. Fist pump.

I've never answered an implied question faster in my life. "Yes. The answer is yes. We can start tonight if you want."

She furrows her brow. "We can?"

"Absolutely. After dinner?"

"Really? You don't want to start, say, now?" she asks, stammering a bit as if she didn't expect my response.

I'm surprised, too, since I didn't peg Joy as the get-it-on-at-a-restaurant kind of woman. But I pride myself on being flexible. I glance around the room, scanning for an opportunity. French bathrooms are notoriously tiny. But where there's a will, there's a way. I can make it work. Or maybe she has something else in mind. The tablecloths do afford some nice coverage. A little under-the-table manual fun? Count me in.

"Now works for me." Just so she knows I'm game for anything, I reach a hand under the table and gently stroke her knee.

She flinches for a brief second, then her eyes go hazy and she inhales sharply. "Now for wha . . .?"

"Whatever you want," I say, running my hand up her thigh.

Her breath catches, and a faint pink flush runs up her neck. Jesus. She's so incredibly sexy. She's so responsive, and I'm going to get to play her beautiful body like an instrument.

"What I want . . ." She says it as if she's mesmerized, like she can't form words because she's already so turned on.

"Anything you want." My fingers travel higher up her thigh, and her eyes flutter closed. Her breath seems to come in a rush.

She swallows then says in a bare whisper, "I want . . ."

She doesn't finish. She lowers her hand under the table, and her fingertips graze against mine. Electricity surges in me, sparking through my veins. Lust vibrates everywhere as my dirty mind spins so many possibilities. Places, positions, times. How she'll look as a flush crawls up her chest and she arches beneath me, losing control, letting go.

I lace my fingers through hers with agonizing slowness, making it clear I'll savor her, make her feel so good. I clasp them around hers possessively, so she's keenly aware of how we'd come together. When our hands lock, she opens her eyes, and her hot gaze meets mine. Those green eyes of hers are flooded with lust, and a desire that matches mine.

"Have you decided what you want?"

The voice of the waiter snaps her focus from me.

I look up at him, silently cursing him with my eyes.

Joy snatches her hand away and sits tall. She fumbles with the menu then orders the Nicoise salad with salmon, and I choose a roast chicken dish.

"Very good. More wine for you?"

I nod. "Another glass, please."

Joy nods.

He fills our glasses and leaves.

I practically rub my palms together because we can return to the main attraction.

But when I meet her gaze, her jaw is set, her focus dead-on professional. "Griffin, I need to learn to speak French. Will you teach me?"

I freeze. What the hell did she just say? My hand tightens around the stem of the wineglass. "Excuse me?"

Her eyes widen, an apologetic look crossing them. "That's what I wanted to talk to you about. That's why I asked you to dinner," she says quickly. And holy balls, she did proposition me. But it's not for sex. It's for words. I'd like to say my heart sinks, but it's another part that deflates. Along with my ego, which has been massively punctured, too.

"That's why?" I ask cautiously, making sure I don't completely cock this up, too.

"My proposition is that I'd like to pay you myself for you to spend more time with me, actually teaching me the language."

So yeah. I basically felt her up under the table, and she wants me to teach her how to say table, fingers, and hands, instead.

"Foolishly, I thought I would learn the language simply by being here," she explains. "I figured I'd pick it up the way young people do, through TV or whatnot. Except, I hate television. I suppose I could find some French language school, but I thought maybe if you wanted to pick up any extra work or hours . . . I can pay you well."

Her voice rises at the end of her explanation, almost as if she's embarrassed to be asking. Or maybe she's embarrassed that I came on so strong.

But, in my defense, she sure as hell did seem responsive under the table.

I blow out a long stream of air, trying to reroute my errant, filthy thoughts. I reach for the glass of wine and take a hearty drink. I give myself another moment to adjust to the shift in plans, and in my pants for that matter, as well as the fact that I hit on her like a total wanker sidling up to a woman at a bar.

She keeps going, hastily adding, "It's been a dream of mine to know another language. I took some French in school, but I didn't learn enough to do much more than order food. I can't get by in this country simply knowing how to say *how much does that cost* and *I'd like a salad, hold the ham*." She stage whispers, "I hate ham."

"That's understandable," I say absently before it hits me like a whack upside the head. I've embarrassed her by coming on to her. Now she's chattering on and on because I've made her feel stupid. Time to fix this problem. "Ham is awful. Simply dreadful. You need to be able to converse about ham." I bang a fist on the table to emphasize this critical point and try to defuse the discomfort.

She smiles and laughs lightly. "Yes, exactly. I need to have conversations every day—about ham or synthetic vanilla or when the next train is coming or what I'm doing this weekend or whatever else comes up," she says, sounding natural again, and I breathe a sigh of relief. Perhaps I haven't totally scared her off with my hand-under-the-table routine. *The routine she loved*, the devil in me says.

"Absolutely. Couldn't agree more."

"Right? You get it. I know it'll take time, but I thought if you could help me, and I can truly immerse myself in the language, then I can start to feel like I belong here. I can make the progress I want to make in my career, and I can potentially achieve one of my dreams. To speak another language."

My spine straightens. All the noise in my head disappears as I key in on that word. *Dream.*

An image of the sheet of paper I keep in my wallet snaps into crisp focus.

6. Help someone you care about achieve their dream.

That item from Ethan's list has always been a tough one for me. I haven't been quite sure how to tackle it, so I've put it off. Now I know. Now I get it. This is how I fulfill that wish. This isn't Christian's satirical commitment to find a rich vixen. This is real. This matters to Joy. And this mattered to my brother.

"Yes," I say, clear and confident.

She beams, her eyes sparkling, her smile stretching wide. "You will?"

"Under one condition," I add.

"Okay," she says, curiously.

"You can't pay me."

"What?"

I swallow thickly and look her in the eyes. "It's an item on my bucket list."

"Are you sick?" Her tone is laced with concern.

I shake my head and steel myself to tell her. "No. It's my brother's list."

"Is he ill?"

"He was. When you asked me about him the other day, and I said he's very funny, that wasn't entirely true." I take a breath, remembering Ethan toasting me when I landed the job at the aquarium several years ago, saying the job sounded great but a little fishy. I'd rolled my eyes, telling him to try again with a better pun. He never stopped the fish jokes, and I'd do nearly anything to hear another one. "He *was* funny. He died more than a year ago."

"I'm so sorry," she says, her hand stretching across the table. She threads her fingers through mine, and I can tell I'm forgiven for my wayward action before. This isn't a prelude to seduction. It's the gesture of a friend. Perhaps I need that more at the moment. Maybe we both do.

"Yeah, me, too. Sorry I didn't say anything the other day. I guess I should have but . . ."

She shakes her head, dismissing the notion. "We only say things when we're ready. You weren't ready then."

Her response warms some cold, brittle part of me. The part that's been on ice for the last year. "I think I just wanted to enjoy that day with you. I didn't want to bring anything sad into our Île de la Cité adventure." I take a breath then dive into the deep end. "He was in a car accident four years ago. Hit by a drunk driver, and wound up in a wheelchair. Couldn't walk. Could barely use his hands. I helped take care of him. Which is a really weird thing to say—that I *took care* of my adult brother."

"Why is that weird?" Her voice is soft, and her hand squeezes mine.

"You just don't expect to be in that position. Maybe I was Blaze Dalton, in a way."

A faint smile tugs at her pretty lips. "Were you?"

I shake my head. "Not really. He had carers, or aides as you call them. But, you know, they're not family. And we don't live in a castle or on an estate. We all helped. Mum. Dad." I shrug. "What else can you do?"

"You can't do anything else." She swallows roughly. "I'd do the same for my sister, Allison. You just have to help."

"I was getting ready to move to Paris shortly before the accident. We'd even talked about going together maybe, Ethan and I. He was keen on the idea . . ." My voice trails off momentarily, as the memory of our plans sharpens, images of those days, jogging in London, plotting our next steps, snap before my eyes. "But that didn't happen. I stayed in London, writing marketing materials for the exhibits at the aquarium and doing translations of them for French visitors. That old marine biology degree came in handy after all, since it enabled me to have a job near home, which meant I could help out, along with my parents. Ethan was so tough, though. Sturdy in his own way. Not saying he was happy about it, but he didn't let it get him down. At least, not like you'd think it could get you down."

"That's incredible. It takes a lot of internal strength, I imagine."

"He had that." I sigh. "And the rub is, he was actually managing well enough with his lot in life before he came down with an infection. That's what did him in." I shake my head. "The damn irony of it. He died because he couldn't fight off a basic infection. But before that, he'd even managed to still work."

"He did?"

"He was an online DJ, so he was fortunate to be able to keep doing a job. Set up a home studio and all that. He drew some contentment, I suspect, from having a modicum of independence. His voice still worked, after all. But he was always very physical. An athlete. And he wanted to do so many things—travel, explore, run more marathons."

"That's why you're training for a marathon," Joy says, like something has clicked into place for her.

I nod. "Exactly. It's on the list. Third item. He desperately wanted to do another, so there's a race in Indonesia I'm planning to do in a couple months. I've always wanted to go there, spend some time wandering around when I'm done."

"I hear Indonesia is beautiful."

"And warm."

"Always a plus."

"He wanted to do other things, too. He wanted to zipline. Skydive." I shudder at the last one. "I told him that I loved him to the depths of the ocean and back, but there was no sodding way I was skydiving for him, so he'd better keep that off his list."

"Did he?" she asks with avid interest.

"Thank the Lord, he did. You couldn't get me to skydive if you paid me. But 'live in Paris' is on the list, so

I'm doing that. And so is 'help someone achieve their dream.' And that"—my voice softens—"that I can do, too."

"You really don't have to do this for free," she says, her voice thin, like it pains her to accept that there's no fee.

I lean closer, locking my eyes on hers. "But I want to, Joy. Don't you see?"

"You'd be doing something massive for me. This isn't just a *let's be friends and eat ice cream and sniff flowers and perfume* request."

That reminds me how very much I like sniffing her neck. "But I'll gladly do that for free, too." I wink.

She laughs but then erases the humor a second later. "I really want to be fair and compensate you for your time."

"This is fair to me. This is immensely helpful. You'd be doing something vital," I say, my tone intensely serious, brooking no argument. "I *need* to do this."

"Griffin," she says, but I can tell she knows she's not winning this debate.

I shake my head and squeeze her hand tighter. "Let me."

She shrugs, her lips curving in a soft grin. "Okay."

"Let's start now," I say, switching to the language she wants to learn. I do what I've been doing for her all along. Translating. But this time, I make her say the words back to me. Then I do something that'll drive her crazy. I don't speak English first anymore. During our meal, I talk to her in French about simple things, making her answer in her best stitched-together attempts, correcting her every time she needs it.

By the end of the dinner, she looks exhausted.

She lays her head on the side of the tablecloth. "May I take a nap now?"

I pat her hair. "Poor Joy. Dreams aren't always easy."

When the bill comes, she reaches for it.

I do the same.

But she has the check in her fast little fingers already. "No," she says, quickly standing. "If you're teaching me French for free, I'm paying for dinner."

"You can't pay for dinner."

She scoffs. "Try and stop me."

She bolts from the table, bag in hand, and strides to the waiter, who's clearing another table now. "*Voilà. Merci.*" She hands him her credit card.

She returns to me, a smug smile on her face. "Oh, by the way, one of the things we American women are quite good at is getting what we want. And sometimes that means blowing through a restaurant like a bull in a china shop." She shimmies her hips in some kind of victory dance that's no doubt supposed to be in-your-face, but it makes me want to kick back and watch her move that lush body.

I laugh and hold up my hands in surrender. I should be more devastated that I'm not taking her home to screw her tonight, and an hour ago, I was. But oddly enough, I'm not feeling that way any longer. Maybe because I'm one step closer to something even more important—finishing the list. Getting out of town. Wandering across the world, as I've always wanted. I've stayed still in London and Paris for the last few years. My innate wanderlust is calling to me. Ethan knew it was a strong force in both of us and perhaps fulfilling the travel wish would be the easiest one for me.

Since we were lads, we wanted to see the world. We'd stay up late, poring over maps and atlases, looking up photos of the craziest, wildest places, then we'd plot how we'd eventually make our way around the globe. We wrote endless lists of our eventual conquests. We pushed pins into maps of the world, intrepid explorers plotting our trips. The Northern Lights in Iceland, the crystal-blue waters lapping beaches in Thailand, the neon streets of Tokyo. We'd sleep under the stars when we had to and when we chose to, as we traversed South America, checking out the tip of Argentina after we traveled through Buenos Aires. We'd hit every continent. We'd avoid the Amazon on account of anacondas, and we vetoed Mount Everest, too, after reading *Into Thin Air*, one of the many adventure stories we tossed back and forth, its pages dog-eared many times over.

"I'm not going to die on a snow-capped mountain with icy air blasting me," he'd said when we were in school. "When I go, it better be on some tropical island, surrounded by women in bikinis, serving me drinks."

"When I go, they won't be serving me drinks," I'd said, always upping the ante. "They'll be serving *me*."

"In your dreams."

In the end, that's all they were to him.

But not forever, since I'm still here to live them. Some have already come true, and more will. Including another one now, thanks to the woman smiling at me by the door, waiting.

We leave the restaurant, strolling down the avenue as the soft golden lamplight bathes the streets.

"The lights in Paris are different than anyplace else," Joy says, pointing to the lanterns. "There's almost a magical sort of glow to them."

"That's true," I answer in French.

She shoots me a smirk. "You're a very strict teacher."

I laugh, shifting to English so nothing is lost in translation. "Be a good student or I'll bend you over the desk and spank you."

Her eyes light up. "Maybe I want to be bad now."

I nearly groan, wanting that, too. Wanting all of that. Maybe I do still wish she'd made the other proposition, but for now I'll have to be content with being her friend, her translator, and her teacher.

"When should our lessons begin?" she asks.

"What are you doing tomorrow after work?"

She points at me. "Learning French with you?"

I nod and smile. "You're correct. And that does sound like an excellent recipe for a perfect Friday evening activity. The only thing that might make it better is where it takes place."

I slow my pace, and whisper my idea. Joy's green eyes turn bright and glittery.

"Elise did say I should partake in all the pleasures in life. She says I need more fun."

As I wander home later, I find myself wondering why she needs it.

15

Joy

If someone were to cross-examine me under oath, before God and country, I could say without fear of perjury that I've indeed found heaven on earth.

My always-working-overtime nose has never been happier.

I lean over the display case in the cool, air-conditioned, chocolate-scented bliss known as Jean-Paul Hévin near the Eiffel Tower, and my mouth waters. I will literally drool on the counter if I don't keep my jaw shut. And I don't care. Because . . . chocolate.

We're talking chocolate the likes of which my taste buds have never encountered before.

Forget fancy candy bars from upscale grocery stores back home. This is the Gucci of chocolate shops. This is my Louboutin-loving heart coming home to roost among my favorite things.

Treats.

Luxuries.

Exquisite tastes.

I point at a chocolate square beneath the glass. "What is that?" I ask the perky blonde clerk, like an eager seven-year-old pawing at a delectable goodie.

Griffin admonishes me. "*En français.*"

I narrow my eyes at him, then direct my question again to the woman in the black linen dress behind the counter. She answers and her words are gibberish to me.

But I find a response. With a satisfied grin, I declare, "*Saperlipopette!*"

Gadzooks.

Griffin's hand flies to his belly, and he nearly doubles over in laughter. "Now you're really *loufoquering.*"

Honestly, last night I thought we were going to slide right into *loufoquering.* When he held my hand under the table, I was entranced, utterly swept off my feet by the unexpected physical contact and the intensity of it, too. More so by what that little bit of contact did to me. It sent me soaring. For a few moments at the restaurant, I truly thought he was going to seduce me, take me back to his flat and pin me to the door, cage me in with those lean, ropy arms, and kiss the breath out of me.

I'd have let him.

Despite what a horrid idea it would have been, I'd have given in, I'm sure of that. I'd been on the cusp of falling into him, and then everything shifted when I uttered my proposal. But that's how humans are. We are designed to be malleable, to change gears quickly when need be. Now, my gear is in *feed me chocolate* mode.

The woman behind the counter grasps a pair of chocolate tweezers and reaches into the case.

"She has chocolate tweezers," I say in a stage whisper.

Griffin repeats that in French.

I straighten my shoulders and aim to impress him when I change the sentence the teeniest bit and say to the clerk, "You have chocolate tweezers."

She smiles. "Very good. Your French is very good."

She's lying. She's telling a bald-faced lie. But she's so sweet, and she has her paws on the chocolate I want in my belly, so I simply say, "I have a good teacher."

When the blonde places the dark chocolate ganache in my hand, I step away from the counter, ready to pop it into my waiting mouth and let the chocolate melt on my tongue.

Griffin has other ideas. He closes my fingers over the sweet. I whimper. He says something, and I furrow my brow, trying to understand. He slows down. "I need something from you."

I nod. "Yes?"

He glances at my hand. "Tell me what it smells like."

"What?" I ask as if he's gone nutso. "Why?"

He speaks in English. "You have this amazing nose, don't you?"

I laugh. "It's not amazing. It's just well-exercised."

He arches a naughty eyebrow. "Like my mouth."

Tingles spread across my chest. *This man.* Everything he says can sound dirty and delicious. I'm pretty sure he knows it, too. He does it on purpose. It's almost as if he loves to remind me that we were once going to have a brief and potent Parisian affair.

"I wouldn't really know how well-exercised your mouth is," I say coyly. Then, because he started it, and why shouldn't I continue it, I tap his top lip with my finger.

A little growl is my reward.

I open my hand, and bring the chocolate in it to my nose, letting the decadent aromas spread to my brain—

berries and lime juice. Then, I hold it under his nose. "Do you smell berries?"

He closes his eyes and sniffs. He looks so vulnerable here with his eyes shut in the middle of the store, trying to reconnect with one of his senses. I steal this moment to study his face. Those cheekbones I noticed the first day I saw him, prominent but not too sharp. That square jaw, so masculine. His lips, soft and full. The shape of his handsome face. Sometimes, there's a faint trace of stubble on his jawline, but mostly he's clean-shaven, and I like the smooth look. I like watching him, too, wondering what's going on behind those closed eyes.

"A little," he answers at last and in French. Holy smokes. I understood him! He arches a brow. "Raspberries?"

I know that word, too, courtesy of all the raspberry tarts I've snapped up at the upscale patisseries I've been frequenting. Good thing I've been walking all over this city. I need the footwork to burn off my tart work.

"I think this one is blackberries, but you're close," I say excitedly, switching back to English now.

He doesn't correct me as I continue, "And then when you bite into it, try to smell the zippy notes of the lime juice in it."

Even with his eyes closed, his expression is quizzical. His eyes scrunch more. "Smell it when I taste it?"

I squeeze his shoulder. "Smell and taste are connected. Things taste even better when they smell amazing. Scent enhances taste. It's the whole kit and caboodle."

His lips quirk. "If you say so."

He parts his lips the slightest bit. I linger briefly on the alluring vision in front of me, and the way a hot spark spreads down my chest as I stare at his mouth. Like a voyeur. But a voyeur he's invited in.

I put the chocolate square on his tongue. He chews and murmurs. His eyes open, and the blue in them is brighter than before. "It's good."

"See what I mean?"

"Now I'm supposed to see a smell? You nose people are so very complicated."

I laugh. "Did you smell the lime and the berry?"

He shrugs. "Maybe?"

My shoulders sag. "And that would be a no."

"Sorry," he whispers. "But it was tasty."

I screw up the corner of my lips, considering. "Okay, I have an idea."

"Say that in French, Joy. I've been slacking off with you."

I groan, but then, this is a sentence I can manage. I do as I'm told, then I return to the counter and ask for several more squares. I order two hot chocolates as well, and soon we head to a small table in the back corner of the shop, with a tray of chocolates and two cups of frothy *chocolat chaud*.

Yes, this is heaven.

I give him the Earl Grey ganache, telling him to search for the smoky flavor of the infused tea. "Surely, being English you know what Earl Grey tastes like," I say.

"Clearly. Since there's nothing better than a cuppa."

"Oh, I bet this hot chocolate will be better than tea. But go on." I wave at the treat.

He takes a bite, and with intense focus, he seems to hunt for the smoky scent. "I can sort of taste it. Sort of smell it." He hands me the rest of the square, and I pop it into my mouth. "How do you have such a good nose?"

I shrug happily. "Anyone can learn to distinguish smells with precision. But for me, it's my job. You just train your nose. The more you use it, the better your olfactory sense becomes." Since we're talking about talents, my curiosity turns to his impressive skills. "By the same token, how are you so good with languages? You know Spanish, too, right?"

He grins. "And Italian. And I'm learning Portuguese."

"You're learning a fifth language?"

He nods. "I take classes."

"Is that on your bucket list?"

He shakes his head. "Nope. I mean, it's not on Ethan's list. But yeah, I suppose it's on mine, in a way, even though I don't have a bucket list. It's just something I've wanted to do, so I'm doing it. I love languages. Always have."

"Why?"

"I love the way you can play with words, and how different combinations of words mean entirely different things. It's like a crazy puzzle. If you put the pieces together correctly, you can do the most incredible thing." He spreads his arms out wide. "*Communicate.*"

I flash him a smile. "Communication is incredible. I realize that more every day when I fail at the most basic forms of it."

He shakes his head. "Don't think of it as failing. Think of it as relearning. Reworking the basics."

"I like that attitude." My mind catches on something he said in the elevator my first day of work. "You said something about a hospital. That your nose had been terrible since then, and that's why you couldn't make out the lilacs very well my first day of work."

"Yes." He stares up at the ceiling. "I suppose it's right around then, if I were to try to pinpoint."

"That's probably because the smells in it were so antiseptic."

He nods. "Yes, cold. All the smells were so cold."

I nod, puzzling together why he says he can't pick up

the scents well. "I think you shut it down. Your sense of smell. There were so many unpleasant ones, and they brought painful memories along with them. Our sense of smell is closely tied to the portion of our brain that controls memories. Yours was linked with something that hurt you. So you kind of subconsciously turned off your nose."

He tilts his head. "You think so?"

"I do. It's not unusual. We sometimes shut down things that bring us pain." I raise my hand, miming turning off a knob. "But I can turn it back on for you."

He inches closer. "I've no doubt you can turn it on."

I roll my eyes. "Has anyone ever told you that you're an irrepressible flirt?"

"Did you mean an irresistible flirt?"

"Yes. That, too."

"As a matter of fact, yes. A gorgeous redhead did about ten seconds ago."

Those sparks? They flare harder, brighter, faster. Tingles spread over my shoulders, and a charge rushes down my body.

But we don't linger too long on dangerous ground, because he flips the switch once more, repeating himself in French.

I return to my mission of the moment, too—retraining his nose. Helping him relearn, so to speak. I reach for another chocolate, then another, guiding him through the scents and tastes. This one has a hint of pepper, this tastes cool because there's the faintest bit of mint, this one oozing with caramel should taste warm and sweet on the tongue.

His eyebrows wiggle. "Warm and sweet on my tongue." He repeats himself in French.

"You have a dirty mind," I say, pointedly, and now we're back here again.

"I do. And you do nothing to make it clean." He winks at me. Then he clears his throat. "But thank you for giving me such a fantastic sensory experience on a Friday night." He runs his finger down the end of my nose, and I shudder.

That's not supposed to feel erotic.

That's not supposed to be sexy.

But he doesn't tap my nose. He doesn't squeeze it. He slowly brushes the tip with his finger, and somehow that faintly sexy gesture sends shivers across my skin.

Then, we talk.

As we drink our hot beverages, we chat about the chocolate, the weather, the day, and it's as if a key in a lock turns just the slightest bit, giving me hope that the door might eventually open for me.

Not today. Not tomorrow. But perhaps soon I might be able to converse in this country's language without him.

When we finish, Griffin clears the cups and the tray then offers me a hand. We exit, but once we hit the street, I hold up a finger and tell him I'll be right back. "Wait for me."

"I will."

I turn to go get the one last thing I want for him, but as I glance back over my shoulder, I see him waiting. He tucks his hands into the pockets of his jeans, and here on the sidewalk outside the chocolatier, with the lights of the tower behind him, he's what I want to photograph. I want to snap this shot, post it on Instagram, and hashtag it "boyfriendaspirations."

As soon as that thought lands, I mentally smack myself.

I'm not sixteen. I'm thirty.

But in my defense, he's completely photo-worthy, and I have no doubt the ladies of Instagram would love this image. Instead, I take a mental picture because I want to remember Griffin waiting for me on the street, patiently, with a smile that reaches all the way to those bright blue eyes. He's not checking his phone, grumbling, or grimacing. He's waiting. Happily. For me.

Hustling back into the shop, I order one last item from the clerk. She gives it to me and wishes me a good night.

I yank open the door, hand him the wrapped treat, and say, "*Voilà.*"

He arches a brow curiously as he opens the paper. A smile plays on his lips. "I've been waiting for a chocolate tart from you." He takes a beat. "Thank you." His voice is soft, and our eyes hold. He looks at me like he did in the restaurant. With desire. With longing. He leans closer, dusting his lips to my cheek. "*Merci.*"

I. Die.

My knees go weak. My stomach executes cartwheels.

It's the barest touch, but I want to cup my hand on my cheek and hold that kiss close all night long. I'm not supposed to want this from him. But I want it. Oh, how I want it.

Then, it hits me. He's not kissing me. He's saying goodbye, European-style. The other cheek will come into play any second. My heart drops, knowing the evening is ending.

"Are you leaving? Are we done?" My voice rises, and I can't hide that the thought makes me feel bereft. I want more of his words. More of this conversation. More of his finger on my nose, his willingness to taste new things, his confidence in teaching me.

I want the night with him to unfurl into whatever comes our way.

He doesn't kiss my other cheek. Instead, he shoots me a sexy, lopsided grin that ignites the butterflies in my chest once more.

He scoffs. "Done? We're not done in the least. In fact, I'm still waiting to learn something about you, Ms. Danvers-Lively." He gestures to the sidewalk.

I could skip with happiness. The night isn't over at all. We're going to have a twilight walk in Paris, and I do believe I'll be going to bed on a cloud tonight. This is a dream. "What do you want to learn?"

"You said something last night that piqued my interest. Your friend Elise told you that you needed more fun. Why? What was un-fun about life in Texas?"

My chest tightens. Here we go.

"Why would you think it was un-fun?" I toss back, since a part of me doesn't want to ruin the flirty vibe with the archaeological excavation of my pre-Paris life.

He taps his chin, adopting a studious look. "Hmm. Could it be that when we first met, you said you just got out of a bad relationship and you weren't looking for anything serious?"

Busted.

But I'm busted, too, with the stark reminder of why I can't back him up against the glass wall of the boulangerie we're strolling past, and kiss him hard with the cobbled streets of the Rue de Grenelle as our witness. Because my last relationship weighed me down. It entangled me. In my experience, relationships are chains around my ankles. When you're finally free, you don't check yourself back into the asylum. I'm finally finding myself again in Paris. I'm stepping into the person I've wanted to be. I can't fall into the mistakes I've made in the past.

"I was involved with someone for a few years," I admit.

"At first, it was good, like most relationships are at the starting line."

"True. If they weren't, we likely wouldn't begin any," he says as we wander down the street.

I offer a half-hearted smile at the sentiment. It's both true and a little sad that so many relationships start, and yet so many end. "As for my ex, he wasn't a bad person, and we clicked at first. But after a year, I grew apart from him. It just happened. I didn't feel the same for him anymore. I wanted more out of life, out of work, and he didn't. There was no big fight. No big reason. It was just one of those things."

He shoots me a quizzical look. "No reason at all?"

I hold up my right hand as if I'm taking an oath. "None, I swear. No cheating. No lying. Just no longer feeling like we had anything to talk about. I tried to get the spark back, but when he didn't put in the same effort, I felt more alone. I was ready to end it, and that's when he fell from a ladder at work."

Griffin recoils. "What?"

"He's a contractor. He was working on a house. It was a workplace accident. He injured his back."

"That's awful."

"Exactly. I couldn't end it then."

"You couldn't?" Griffin sounds thoroughly flummoxed.

"Of course not." My response is crisp and clear. "That would be cruel. The man was in the hospital for a few days. He was in pain. He could walk, yes. But he was in constant pain from the injury."

"Right. Sure. But why fake your feelings?" he presses.

"I didn't fake my feelings entirely. He was still a friend. He wasn't a jerk," I say, bristling at the direction this conversation has taken.

We stop at the boulevard, and the light ticks as I wait

for it to change from red to green. We're nearing Champ du Mars, the park that rings the most famous icon of France.

"Well, that's good. But why stay together if you didn't love him anymore?"

He makes it sound like it was such a simple answer. But there was nothing easy about those times. "I cared about him as a person, Griffin. I couldn't just leave him when he needed someone. His family wasn't in town, and he was trying to get back on his feet."

"His family should have helped him," Griffin says resolutely. "They should have come to town."

"Well, they didn't." I wrap my arms around my chest, irritation brewing rapidly in me. I don't like being judged for my choice. "Look. I stayed because it was the right thing to do. He needed help, and I was the only one there. When I originally planned to break up with him, I was no longer in love, but he was still a good friend, a stable guy. Then, he was injured, and over time, he grew addicted to painkillers, and he turned into a completely different person. He questioned everything I did. He wore me down. He became manipulative. He wasn't like that before. The man he was when I finally left wasn't the man he was when I wanted to leave. A year later, he was someone I no longer even recognized. He wasn't someone I loved and he was no longer a friend, either." We stop at a tree inside the park, darkness shrouding us. I stare at Griffin, my eyes hard. "You're judging me, and I don't like it."

The harsh reality is he'd probably judge me even more if he knew I let myself become consumed by the madness. The drama of an injured, addicted Richard was a powerful storm, and I was caught in it. I let myself be dragged down. I let his health and my own deep, potent desire to try to fix him become more important than my goals and dreams.

Maybe that's what I really don't like.

I felt like I was losing myself then, and Griffin calling me out on it makes it all the more real.

He reaches for me, but I back up. "I didn't mean to judge. I was just trying to understand what happened, and I'm sure it wasn't easy."

"It wasn't easy, but it's like you're saying I made the wrong choice, when I hardly feel I had a choice to make at all," I say, my pitch rising.

"I'm sorry, Joy. I didn't mean to be harsh. I can tell this is a sensitive topic, and I don't want you to think I was judging you."

I purse my lips. "I feel like a fool now."

"Please don't." He tucks a finger under my chin. "I think it just bothered me that you were with this guy when you didn't want to be."

I swallow, wishing he'd take that hand off me, and wishing equally that he'd spread his fingers over my jaw and tug me close, pull my body next to his and let me sink into his arms. "I wanted to do the right thing," I say, softer this time. "Does that make sense?"

His smile is gentle. "It does, and I do understand. I was just feeling . . . retroactively protective of you."

I smile back. That's kind of strangely sweet. "Thank you."

"So few people want to do the right thing, but you did."

"I did what made sense at the time."

"Different things make sense at different times." His voice goes low, smoky almost. The sound threads into me, as if I'm drawing it into my body. My chest zings.

His hand is still on me, holding my chin. He's looking

at me like I'm the thing that makes the most sense to him right now. Like *we* make sense.

My entire body pulses with energy. With longing.

Kiss me.

Don't kiss me.

Take me.

Let me go.

I call upon some store of resistance that I've evidently packed inside me for moments just like this. "I should go."

He drops his hand from my chin.

Touch me again.

"Okay. I'll walk you home."

We head past the tower. The park in front of it is teeming with lovers. So many lips are locked together right now.

"We need a picture in front of the Eiffel Tower," he says, in French.

"We do."

When I stand next to him, he wraps his arm around my shoulder, and everything about the way he holds me possessively makes so much more sense than it should. His fingers curl over my shoulder, clasping me tight to his side. Our hips touch. I could turn my head and bury my nose in the crook of his neck. Inhale his aftershave and learn if it lingers on his skin this late into the evening. Taste him.

My body is a drum, beating loud and hot.

I grip my phone harder, trying to channel all my physical energy into the simple act of lifting it. On the screen, I catch a quick glimpse of a man and woman who look like all the other lovers here tonight. Grinning, touching, needing. But we're not like these real couples. I snap a selfie and show it to him quickly.

"Good one. I like it."

"Me, too."

That's the problem. I like it too much. I drop the phone into my purse, relief flooding me since, somehow, I managed to take that picture without tossing the phone to the ground, yanking him against me, and saying screw everything.

Including me.

"Hashtag it: anightinparis."

"Maybe I will."

"Send it to me later, yeah?"

"Of course."

He tucks my hair behind my ear and turns me to face him. "Joy?" My name comes out importantly. I meet his eyes. They're vulnerable again. "Maybe it's good, in some terribly selfish way, that you stayed with him as long as you did, since that means you're here now."

Tingles spread all over me, and my heart is full of starlight. I'm dangerously close to melting, but somehow I manage to whisper a *merci* before we leave the park.

Later, when I'm home, I run my finger over the shot of us looking like Friday-night lovers. Looking like we want to kiss, to touch, to spend the rest of the evening together. I don't post it to Instagram. It feels private, this #anightinparis. I send it only to him, then I turn off my phone before he can reply.

16

Griffin

Eight miles.

I round the edge of Parc de Bagatelle, one of the biggest green spaces in the city. The pale pink light of dawn burns off as the sun rises in the morning sky.

My heart pounds against my chest as my feet hit the hard-packed earth, and my playlist blasts a random mix of new indie bands in my ears. When I first buckled down for the marathon prep, I tried to listen to my Duo Lingo app during my training runs, but I found, at the end, I remembered close to nothing of Portuguese. When I run, I get so lost in the movement I can't focus on words, only rhythm, so I let this eclectic mix power me through.

As I leave the park, racing past a museum dedicated to the works of Monet, I have the fleeting thought that Joy would probably like that museum. I bet she likes Monet. I bet she'd gaze at the prettiest paintings in the same way she stares longingly at a piece of chocolate, a pink door, or a window box bursting with flowers. The woman loves beauty in all its forms. She devours it with her senses and feasts on it.

I try to shake away the thoughts. If I keep thinking about Joy this much, I'll want to spend every second with her.

Oh wait. I already do.

For now, I refocus my brain on the simple act of putting one foot in front of the other, in moving one step closer to completing an all-important item on Ethan's list —running the marathon in Indonesia. I picture checking it off the list, another accomplishment. Originally, I planned to explore the islands and train at the same time. But I've flipped that order around, training here now.

As I switch over to a quieter street to cut across the city, I flash back to the dream I had when I was younger. Running a marathon. It was so crystal clear, and it came out of the blue, inserting itself into my brain unexpectedly.

At the time, a marathon seemed so easy.

Something I could pull off in a cinch.

It's not easy.

And yet, I don't mind that it's hard. I don't mind that it hurts. I rather like the burn in my legs and in my lungs. I keep up the punishing pace as I near the nine-mile mark, cruising past apartment buildings, then a Monoprix and a nearly deserted Starbucks. Even at eight a.m. on a Saturday, the coffee shop is nearly empty.

We are not a country of early risers, I think with a smirk.

Then I blink. What a strange notion. *They're* not early risers, I mean. I'm not from here, so I don't know why I included myself in that sweeping statement about the

French. I'm just a visitor, really, making a prolonged pit stop on my itinerant journey around the globe.

By the time I hit nine and a half miles, a fresh burst of energy surges inside me, and I feel as if I'm flying, even as my muscles are wrung out. A new song starts, a fast, soaring number that's like a burst of adrenaline.

Another minute, another block, another stretch of the city.

Soon, soon, I cross the ten-mile mark.

Holy shit.

That's a lot of miles.

I don't stop. I should. But I don't want to. I keep running the rest of the way to my flat, finishing finally at eleven miles, when I slow my pace, panting, exhausted, spent.

But utterly high on endorphins, too.

No wonder Ethan liked this so much.

It feels spectacular, like it does every damn time I run.

I wipe my brow, unlock the front door, and head into the entryway of my building then up to the third floor. Beads of sweat drip down my body. After I enter my flat, I fill a glass of water, down it, and then drink one more. As my breathing calms down, I strip out of my running shorts, step under the showerhead, and turn the faucet to hot.

The shower is the most welcome sight in the world.

And then, unbidden, Joy joins me in it.

This is getting to be hard.

Pun intended.

This isn't the first time she's come into the shower with me. I'd like to say I ignore the visit, but that'd be a lie. As soon as the image of her pops into my mind, I'm ready to go.

We're talking a proposition-style hard-on.

I picture last night, wandering by the Eiffel Tower, tugging her close as she snapped a photo of us. God, I'm so fucking transparent. The way I touched her, gathered her near, kissed her good night like I wanted it to last until the morning—I'm doing a terrible job at playing just friends. But every little crumb, every morsel makes me want more of her. Every brush of my fingers against hers makes me want to know what more of her would taste like, feel like, look like.

I lean my head back under the stream, letting the water streak down my body, and then I take matters into my own hand. She's here with me. Naked, wet, aroused. Wrapped around me.

I groan, grip myself harder. I see her lips, red and inviting. Lips I've longed for since the day I met her. I want to kiss, taste, and right now, I want to fuck those lips. I want to slide my aching cock in that lush mouth and watch her take me deep, suck me hard.

Lust jolts through my body as I let the fantasy play out. As I watch my cock thrust deeper into that perfect mouth, as I wind my hand into her wet hair, her lips are so tight around me.

I jerk harder, tug faster, picturing what it would feel like to finally have her on her knees.

But, then I blink.

Shove the image away.

That's not how I want Joy right now. I know what my own orgasm feels like. *Fantastic.* I've been there, done that, don't need to picture it.

Instead, I want to do filthy things to her. Want to find her naked on my bed, wearing nothing but a white shirt I'd discarded earlier, unbuttoned and spread open, revealing those beautiful tits, rosy nipples, and a soft belly.

Rough, raw noises rumble up my throat as I shuttle my fist harder, faster. Rocking into my hand, I imagine crawling down her body, licking a path between her tits, kissing to the paradise between her thighs. I picture flicking the tip of my tongue over her for the first time.

Primal desire flares inside me, and I grunt as I imagine tasting her where she's wet and hot and needy. She arches her hips. Begging. Pleading. Curling her hands around my head.

I heed her call. Oh dear God, do I ever fucking heed it.

I bury my face between those thighs, and then pleasure yanks me under, rockets through me as I come hard. A shudder racks my entire body, and I press my forehead to the glass door. "Fuck," I mutter as water pelts my back.

I groan loudly, a rough and hungry sound.

An empty one, too. That felt absolutely great and utterly annoying. Because it's not real. It's not happening. And I'm going to have to fight like hell to pretend I don't want to do unholy things to her body when I see her again.

And damn, do I want to see her again.

I adjust the temperature in the shower, going luke-warm then cooler, forcing myself to stand under the stream as it chills.

Ten minutes later, I'm showered, dressed, and still wanting her. Oh yeah, turns out a shower wank doesn't evict Joy from my brain. Nor does an ice cube–temperature shower, either.

From the kitchen counter, I grab the chocolate tart she gave me last night and devour it.

I'm still hungry.

But before I root around for something else to gnaw my way through in mere seconds, I snap a photo of the paper the tart was wrapped in. There's one crumb left. She'll like this. I send her the shot.

Griffin: There's nothing quite like a ten-mile training run, followed by a chocolate tart. By the way, thanks for dessert for breakfast. It was delicious, and I thought of you.

I look at the sent message. Well, it's not totally obvious I have it bad for her. *It was delicious, and I thought of you*, I mouth to myself. Could I be any more blatant? I shake my head and sigh heavily. I set down the phone.

Maybe I ought to try not thinking about her for a full minute. I grab my phone and click open a word game. This one helps keep my Spanish in shape as I have to steer letters, Tetris style, into words. But as I form *sobra*, my phone buzzes. I exit the game so quickly that I leave the *a* free-falling. So much for playing it cool, as the letter crashes to a cruel death.

Joy: My, my. Aren't you quite the warrior? I'm still lounging in my jammies, drinking coffee and eating bonbons.

Griffin: What kind of jammies?

Look, I can't help myself. When a gorgeous woman says she's in PJs, I'm required, on account of being male, to ask what she has on. Especially since she was naked in my shower mere minutes ago.

Joy: A corset, Griffin. I sleep in a corset. It's black lace. I wear stocking and garters, too. As well as stilettos.

I crack up. She's onto me.

Griffin: Ah, that sounds quite comfy. I find it quite pleasant, myself, to sleep in a tailored suit.

Two can play at this game after all.

Joy: You don't say? I might need a picture of that.

My stomach rumbles, reminding me of the other important matter at hand. Sustenance. I open the fridge. A jar of pickles stares forlornly at me. I scratch my jaw, wondering why I even have pickles. I don't remember buying them. I take a photo of the pickles and send it to Joy. But before I can add a note to explain why I'm sending the picture, a text from her lands on my screen.

Joy: Why, I thought you'd never ask me to go pickle shopping with you. I accept. :)

Griffin: I'm starving. I'm off to get some breakfast. *Petit déjeuner* to you. I'd invite you to join me, and teach you scintillating phrases about eggs and coffee and bread, but you'd need to get out of your jammies rather quickly, since ten-plus miles of running has made me rather ravenous.

So have thoughts of you coming on my lips.

Joy: You have no idea how quickly I can get out of bed when breakfast is involved.

Griffin: By the way, have you been to the Musée Marmottan Monet? If not, it's quite lovely, and it's open today.

Joy: This will come as a complete and utter shock, but, like nearly everyone else in the world, I love Monet. Oh, and yes, you can take me out to breakfast and to see some million-dollar art, Griffin.

So, yeah, that means I'm completely transparent to her. Brilliant. As I leave, I remind myself to not make it so patently unmistakable that I like her during breakfast.

But when she arrives at the café wearing tight jeans, a light blue shirt, and a red bandana around her hair like a headband, it's a lost cause.

"You had that on the first time I met you," I say, pointing to the cloth in her hair, the ends tied in a little knot, its tails poking out under her ear.

Her lips quirk up. "*En français.*"

"You caught me," I say with a laugh.

"You remember?" She runs her fingers over the red fabric.

I nod, keeping my words simple so she understands. "I remember. I thought it was bold. You looked like Rosie the Riveter."

Her eyebrows rise. "You know Rosie? That's so American."

"I happen to like American things," I say, and when her green eyes lock with mine, I watch as understanding registers in them. As the words turn in her head till she knows what I mean.

The moment she does, her eyes sparkle then hold mine. She doesn't look away. "I like English things."

Evidently, we're both rubbish at friendship. I lean back in the chair and sigh. "Being friends, it's so easy, yeah?"

Might as well call a spade a spade.

"So simple," she says drily, her hand rising to fiddle with the bandana as if she's going to take it out.

"No, seriously. It's so incredibly you," I tell her, reaching across the table, brushing my finger against the fabric then down a soft strand of her hair. The red locks slide over my hand.

I raise my gaze. Her lips part the slightest bit as I let go of her hair. She watches as the strands fall against her chest.

She clears her throat and taps the menus. "We better order, or the specter of pickles will haunt you all day."

"Best to avoid pickle hauntings."

I tell her what I want, and when the waiter arrives, I let her order. She gets it right, and I'm more pleased than I should be.

Because it's her.

* * *

Soles of shoes echo across the hardwood floors in the quiet mansion that houses more than three hundred Monets. A handful of other museumgoers flit by, but we aren't packed like sardines.

I gesture to all the space. "The best part is it isn't crowded like the Musée d'Orsay or the Louvre."

"It's a little secret in Paris," she says as we wander through gallery after gallery of impressionist art. I switch back and forth between languages, teaching her new words and phrases as we go. She's a fast learner, with a nimble mind. She stops in front of one of the many images of the Japanese bridge the famous artist painted.

"I want to see the bridge," she says, and a burst of pride flares in me since she said that correctly on her first try.

"We should go to Giverny."

Then I stop, processing what I just said to her. The weight of it. The intention of it. I invited her to Monet's gardens. That doesn't sound like something a teacher would say to a student, but rather a man to a woman. A woman he wants to romance.

Those wide green eyes give me her yes. Then her words do, too. "I want to go."

My heart springs around in my chest, and it's the strangest sensation. A nearly foreign feeling—one I haven't experienced in a long time. The last few years have been dictated by the fallout from one unexpected event, so I haven't had the time or the inclination to *feel* anything more than the occasional bout of desire. "I've never been."

She shoots me a curious look. "You haven't? How is it possible there's a place near Paris you've never traveled to?"

"Miracles do happen."

"I'm shocked," she teases, then drops her hand and returns her focus to the painting of the bridge. "I read a novel once where paintings came alive."

"How so?"

"In the story, the Degas dancers at the d'Orsay twirled out of their frames after hours. They performed ballets in the museum. The cat in Manet's *Olympia* jumped from his painting and padded across the tiled floor once the sun fell. It was like *Night at the Museum* meets *Midnight in Paris*. And in the story, the hero could travel through Monet's bridges to other museums around the world that had one of his paintings of the bridge, since he painted so many."

I chuckle. "Sounds quite fantastical."

She laughs. "It was. It was magical. But I think that's the power of great art. It not only transports you but makes you want to crawl inside and live in it."

"Do I need to hold you back from trying to jump inside a Monet, Joy? Are you warning me of your intention to launch headfirst into a famous work of art?"

She brings her hands together in front of her, as if prepping to dive. Her eyes are quizzical as she poses the next question. "If you were going to jump inside any painting, what would it be?"

I marinate on that for a minute, considering. "I suppose if these bridges really do transport you, I'd go into one of those Monets. Easy way to travel, right? Sort of like apparating in Harry Potter. I could be at the Hermitage in St. Petersburg like that." I snap my fingers.

"Do you want to go to Russia?"

"I want to go everywhere," I say as I stare at the red and gold sunset version of the bridge in front of me.

"You're a globe-trotter, aren't you?"

"I'm an *aspiring* globe-trotter," I say. "It's what I've

wanted to do since I can remember. Pack my bags, see the world, sleep under the stars."

"We need to get you in these paintings, then."

I point at the one in front of me. "I could take that bridge to New York. Another to Boston. I bet one of Monet's bridges is in Tokyo. I've always wanted to go there, too, to see how vibrant and bright the city is."

"Then you'll go." She bumps shoulders with me. "If you want something badly enough, you make it happen."

I have to wonder if that includes some*one*, too, or if her work, and mine, will stand in the way before I chase my desire to cross all the bridges to everywhere.

17

Joy

I'm hot for teacher.

Or really, I should say *hotter*.

Every day I'm hotter for him.

But it's more than lust that I feel.

Griffin's not only my closest friend in France, he's my daily companion. It almost feels like we're two travelers exploring the world of Paris together. After hours, it's like we've taken a sabbatical from life, and we're intrepid wanderers, getting lost and found together in the streets, passages, and alleys of the City of Light. Him and me, me and him.

I've shared a house with another person, but I never felt like I wanted more *time*. But that's what it's like now. When I say good-bye to Griffin at the end of each night, my heart is a little bit lonelier, and when I wake up, that organ is eager once more, knowing I'll see him soon at the office.

When I see him in the conference room, I want to grin, to flirt, to give him a thousand private looks that only he'll understand. Even in the lab, when he translates the names of chemicals, I can hear him in my mind saying other things, like *you look beautiful* and *let me take you out for a glass of wine*.

When I leave the office, sometimes we shop, since that's where I experience the real brunt of knowing or not knowing words.

On a Saturday afternoon, we go to the open-air market on Rue de Grenelle under the Metro bridge, and he urges me to barter for a lamp I want. It's emerald green with a hanging chain as a switch. It's so deliciously antique that I can't resist it.

A stout woman with curly hair runs the stall. I ask her what year it's from. I ask if she'll take less. I tell her I will return.

Je reviendrai. Griffin wants me to say that because the French have a specific word for come back. They don't say return, he tells me.

So many words.

So many new ones.

My brain swims with new combinations of the alphabet.

As we wander to the other end of the market, buying walnuts and bread, I say the names of everything I see. And I don't just say the names. I use them in a sentence.

Then we *revenir*, and I buy the lamp.

"You're learning," he says with a proud smile.

I might have doubted the blonde chocolatier, but I believe him.

I believe him because he makes me buy contact lens solution that evening, and then he kisses me good night, lingering on each cheek. He tells me he's glad he could be there to help me at the pharmacy this time, but he's even more glad he could see me do it on my own.

The next week he shows me the coolest Metro entrances, and then we decide to find more sundials, hunting for one engraved by Salvador Dali before we track down a sundial in the courtyard of a hotel frequented by the philosopher Jean-Jacques Rousseau. "Legend has it he was in love with the woman who ran the hotel and professed as much in a letter to her one day," Griffin muses as we regard Rousseau's sundial.

"And did she smother him in kisses and say she was madly in love, too?" I ask, hungry for this romantic tale.

He shakes his head, a rueful smile on his face. "No. It was, sadly, unrequited."

My heart aches the littlest bit when I watch him walk away first. Has there ever been a crueler word than *unrequited*?

I try my best not to linger on it, telling Griffin I have something to show him. His eyes twinkle with excitement as I play tour guide this time, escorting him across the city to track down an angel three-stories tall serving as a column in the corner of an apartment building from 1860.

He cranes his neck heavenward, checking out the carving. "How did you know of this?"

"After I came across the first two angels, I did some research. There are angel statues and carvings and little hidden angels all over the city. You could add angels to your list of Parisian quirks."

He turns his eyes to me. "You think I have a list of Parisian quirks?"

I nod. "Yes. Oddities and curiosities. Sundials, clocks, Metro entrances. I think you know the most unusual details about Paris. You're a student of this city, every nook and cranny."

He shakes his head, disagreeing. "There's so much I don't know."

I stab my finger against his chest. "That's my point exactly. Every day you uncover more. You remind me of what Elise said. We should enjoy each day like a fruit and eat it."

He quirks an eyebrow as we stroll down a quiet street. "You think I eat Paris every day?"

"And you wake up the next day with another appetite and another."

He wiggles an eyebrow. "That's not the only thing I want to eat."

"You say everything like it's naughty."

"Everything should be naughty. But especially when you talk of fruit and eating. You give me no choice." We stop at the corner of the street, and he repeats what he just said in French, reminding me that he does have a choice, at least when it comes to his time and his talents. He chooses to be generous with his time. He gives of himself freely. I know he's getting something out of these language lessons. I know he's inching closer and closer to his brother's goal. But still. It hardly feels equal.

That's why I do my best to make sure the explorer in him is happy. I research places to go that are off the beaten path.

Like the next week when I take him to see antique signs scattered around the city. I snap photos of him under them and make up silly stories, and I show him more angels that I uncover, including an unusually sensual one, clearly female, that almost looks like a precursor to the Victoria's Secret angels.

"My turn to play photographer. Your turn to pose," he says, shooing me under the angel.

I give him my best pout, and he shakes his head. "Just be yourself."

"Fine," I say and flash a smile.

"Yes. That. Now post it to your feed and use the hashtag sexyasanangel."

"Please," I scoff.

He shrugs. "Just send it to me, then."

"Why?"

"Because you're sexy as fuck, and I want to look at it tonight."

A shooting star ignites in my chest. "You do?" My throat is dry.

His eyes seem to blaze with heat as he looks at me. "Yeah, but tug down the neckline just a bit, right? We'll shoot another."

I roll my eyes. "Stop it."

"I'm not joking."

I guess I'm not, either. I do as he asks, and I send it to him later. I'm not sure what he's going to do with it. I learn when he texts me at midnight.

Griffin: THANK YOU for the picture. It made my night.

That's all I need.

Inside my flat, with the light from the moon filtering through my windows, the sounds of the city flitting into my home, my hand finds its way inside my panties, where I ache for him.

Already, with one touch, I'm soft and wet and needy. My knees fall open, and my mind paints the most delicious images.

Griffin over me, licking me, kissing me, sucking me.

His hands traveling everywhere. His tongue painting a trail down my skin. His words whispering across my body.

My mind races. Speeds up. Slips back in time, too, to five, ten minutes ago in a flat across the city. There, a gorgeous Englishman stands in a tiny kitchen, opens his texts, and finds my photo from earlier that day. He hardens and groans looking at me tugging at my neckline. No time to waste, he unzips his jeans, wraps his hand around his cock, and strokes.

I moan out loud. It sounds obscene to my ears. It feels that way as I imagine him.

He doesn't even go to the couch, or the bed. He's too turned on. Too aroused. He shoves his jeans to his hips, tightens his grip, his fist tunneling up and down his hard length. He's never been this aroused. Never wanted someone so much. He fucks his hand harder, and faster, wishing it were my mouth, my hand, me.

He craves the wetness in me, wants to thrust into the aching center of my body, to take me, fuck me, have me, own me.

His thighs tighten, and he groans, a loud, feral sound. A wish for me. My name on his lips. Husky, dirty, filthy. He growls it. It's not the first time he's come thinking of me. It won't be the last.

And as I picture him climaxing in the dark, in his hand, my image blazing before his eyes, I do the same, pleasure blurring my brain.

His name is on my lips.

It's not the first time I come saying his name.

I don't think it'll be the last.

* * *

I bend my face to a huge bouquet of pink hyacinths, closing my eyes as I inhale.

"Your turn," I say when I open them.

He does as I instruct, here at the flower market in front of Palais de Tokyo. "Smells like flowers."

I swat him. I've been doing a lot of that. I can't seem to resist touching him.

We wander to the next stall, where I snap photos of purple irises, peach tulips, lavender hydrangea, and sunflowers six feet tall. He stands next to one. "Still taller," he says with a wink.

"Just a little."

He sniffs the sunflower, crinkling his nose. "This stinks."

"Sunflowers are not known for their smell."

"Which is your favorite? To smell?"

"Honeysuckle. But they don't have that here."

"Which is your favorite that's here?" He gestures to the vast display of petals and stems.

I nibble on the corner of my lips and spin, checking out stall after stall, all teeming with flowers, bursting with bouquets that light up my senses.

I point to several buckets with soft purple flowers. "Lilacs," I say, and we head to the nearest lilac stall, where Griffin guides me through what he wants me to say to the florist.

He makes me ask question after question, likely driving the florist bananas. This isn't Berlitz with Griffin. This isn't someone teaching me travel phrases, like *Can you recommend a good restaurant?*

It's trial by fire. It's immersion.

But the language isn't the only thing I'm becoming immersed in. I'm becoming immersed in him. I want to ask him more about his bucket list. I want to know what else is on it, to know what matters to him. But that feels too personal, too tender, like touching a wound that's still bruised and hurting.

After he's exhausted me, he gives me one more thing to ask for. "One bouquet of lilacs to take home. And you'll want that one," he says, pointing to the most perfect one.

When the florist gives me the price, I root around in my purse for bills and coins. But once I look up, Griffin is handing the bearded man the euros, and then my teacher gives me the bouquet. "For you."

"Really?" My heart squeezes.

"Yes, really."

I hold them to his nose. "What do they smell like?"

He inhales, then steps closer, bringing his mouth to my ear. "Like this woman I've been spending all my time with and am dying to kiss."

I melt from head to toe, my bones dissolving. I'm burning for him, aching to touch him, longing to be kissed.

As I watch him walk the other way, looking back at me once with such heat in his eyes that I'm sure he's waging the same internal battle I am, I know that this is the scent I want to bottle. I want to remember this day. I want to open the top of the perfume, close my eyes, let the scent drift into my mind, and remember what it feels like to fall in love.

But more than that, I want to remember what it feels like to fall in love and no longer have the will to stop it, to throw all the reasons out the window and let it happen, come what may.

18

Griffin

The days unfold like this. At dawn I run, then I help Joy at work in the morning. In the afternoon, I focus on written translations. In the early evening, I meet her, and we walk and we talk. I make her tell me about her day, and I ask her questions. As we wander through St. Germain des Pres, over the Pont Neuf, and along the Seine, stopping for a chocolate éclair, a café noisette, or a glass of wine, she makes strides, each day sounding better, gaining confidence. We stroll through the markets, we dart into shops, and we meander past the bouquinistes, where one day Joy chats with Julien, finding the words to buy a dozen sepia-tinted postcards of Paris.

"You've never brought a woman by before," Julien remarks to me, his voice low, his words so quick I'm sure she won't understand.

"Ah, that must mean I really like you," I tease.

He grunts. "It means you like her."

I wave a hand dismissively. "It means you have good postcards, mate."

He grumbles a thank you then hands the cards to Joy.

As we pass other stalls peddling old books, vintage posters, and *Life* magazines from decades ago, Joy asks what we talked about. "I heard the word *like*," she says, an inquisitive note to her voice.

"Good ears. He said you really liked his postcards," I say with a smirk.

"I think you're lying."

"What do you think he asked me, then?"

"Something else," she says.

"Something like what?"

"Something you don't want to tell me."

But I do want to tell her. "He thinks I like you."

"Oh yeah?"

I nod. "Crazy old man."

"Insane, clearly."

"Absolutely batty." I point to the pack of cards in her hand. "What are you going to do with those?"

"I'll send them to my sister."

"In the post?"

She laughs. "No. I'll do it the modern way. By snapping cell phone photos and sending them immediately. Instant gratification."

"*Gratification instantanée.*"

She raises an eyebrow. "Maybe you should teach me how to say delayed gratification, too."

That's what I'm living every day. But then, delayed means the gratification with her will eventually come. I have no idea if it'll always be out of reach.

* * *

We take lunch together on a Wednesday, and after we finish, we turn a corner onto a narrow cobblestoned street as the sky rumbles.

She gasps. "I've been waiting for it to rain."

"It's rained a few times in the two months we've worked together."

She shakes her head. "Not enough. I want the rain that makes me scurry under an awning. I want the rain that filmmakers can only wish for."

I arch a brow. "What's that?"

"Rain that drenches the streets. That makes them look like jewels."

Images of wet, sparkling roads unfurl before my eyes. "That's what filmmakers want?"

"They often hire crews to spray water on streets. Because the best shot in all of film is a street after a rain. It sparkles. I want that kind of rain."

"Do you really want that kind of rain, or do you just want the aftereffects?"

"I'll take the rain to get the diamonds," she says, then reaches into her bag and fishes around for something. She extracts an umbrella, a tiny little thing. But when she opens it, it wilts. The spokes don't work.

"*Merde*," she says, and I laugh.

"Such a good student."

"My umbrella is broken," she says in French.

"Even better."

"No. What's even better is shopping." She points to a store down the street where the window displays an umbrella with black and white polka dots. It's like a homing beacon for Joy, and she marches to the shop through the drizzle. She pushes on the door, and I follow her inside.

But she stops in her tracks and brings her hand to her mouth.

"The polka-dot one? The price is bonkers, right?"

She shakes her head and speaks in a reverent whisper. "No. Look." A ruby-red umbrella is perched in a metal stand, its carved wooden handle poking out the top. Running a hand lovingly along the fabric, Joy looks as if she's stroking a cat. "I'll take it."

She grabs the umbrella, heads to the counter, and buys the new one, disposing of the old.

When we step outside, big thick drops fall from the sky, and Joy opens the jewel-colored umbrella. She twirls it above her head, smiling under the cherry-red canopy she's given herself. "Join me under my umbrella?"

I don't know how she does it, but she makes everything sound like an invitation to travel to the place I most want to be right now. I take the umbrella in one hand, hold it above us, and wrap the other one around her shoulder.

She loops her arm around my waist, and we walk in the rain. She's not due back at the office for twenty minutes, and she makes no move in that direction.

She looks at me, her expression serious. "What else is on the bucket list?"

I tense as the second item blasts like a neon sign in the night. *Sleep with all the French girls.* I don't want to get into that one. "A number of things."

I squeeze her shoulder, hoping a bit of contact will deflect her interest. But she's no cat, distracted by a laser pointer. She's a brilliant woman, hungry to know the truth.

"Evasive much?" she says.

"I'm not evasive."

"Is it private? Is it a secret? It's okay if it is. I'm just curious, since it's literally the most important thing to you."

The rain slaps against the streets like a persistent, wet drumbeat. Like it's the soundtrack to this decision, urging me to open up more to her. She's helping me with the list. I suppose the least I can do is tell her what else is on it.

"I don't think you'll like all of them."

"You might as well tell me now, then."

"The first is live in Paris."

"You mentioned that. You said Ethan had wanted to. So you're doing that."

"And you know the 'run a marathon' one, so I'm working on that. Then there's 'help someone with a dream.'"

"And you're doing that."

"There are a few others I've done already, too."

"And those are the ones I'd dislike?"

I shake my head. "No, but you might like this one. *Number five. Have six-pack abs.*"

Her eyebrows wiggle. "*Oh là là.*" She eyes my stomach. "You've accomplished that?"

I pat my belly. "You're welcome to check for yourself."

She darts her hand sideways, patting my abs over the fabric of my shirt. She slow claps. "Well done, Griffin. Well done."

I stop to take a quick bow then keep walking.

She nudges me. "And yet, I don't think that's the one I'd dislike."

I steel myself then say it. "The second is 'sleep with all the French girls.'"

She jams an elbow into my side. "What a little piggy."

I laugh as the rain hammers the ground, and we take refuge under an awning. "I told you that you wouldn't like it."

"Did you do that? Sleep with all the girls?" The question seems to taste bitter to her.

"Do you really want to know?" I toss back.

"That's a yes, then."

"Why are you asking if you don't want to know?"

She huffs. "Just say you didn't."

I narrow my eyes, trying to figure her out. "Are you jealous?"

She scoffs. "Not at all."

I hold up a thumb and forefinger. "A little?"

"Not in the least."

I smile. "Good. Because I didn't." Then I add, "Not all of them, at least."

"Oh, you're awful."

"I swear, I didn't go overboard on that. Obviously, it's an item you follow to the spirit not the letter of the law. But cut me some slack. I'm a thirty-year-old single guy living in Paris."

She stares at me with narrowed eyes. I wrap an arm tighter around her. "Would it make you feel better knowing you're the only one I want to sleep with now?"

She blinks. "Really?"

"This surprises you?"

"Yes, it does."

"You think I want to sleep with other women?"

"I don't know."

"Do you want me to want to sleep with other women?"

She breathes out heavily then whispers a *no*.

A jolt rushes through me. God, how I want to touch her. "Do you have any idea how much I've wanted to get you naked since I met you?"

"No. How much?"

"So much you really ought to stop asking about other

women. I don't think about other women. I think about you. All the time. So much it drives me crazy. So much I want to say screw the friendship rules and kiss you senseless."

"Would you? Kiss me senseless?"

Life is short. Events can change everything in the blink of an eye. Plans can crater. You have to take your chances. This is the chance I most want to take. "I would absolutely kiss you senseless."

She leans against the wall under the awning, the red umbrella still over our heads as the rain pounds down. With my free hand, I reach for her face. She shudders when I touch her—a beautiful, sensual shiver that seems to move through her whole body.

From this. From my hand on her face, cupping her cheek.

I'm keenly aware that I want this first kiss to be spectacular for her. I want it to be everything for her. A kiss she remembers for all time. When I'm gone in some far-off land, and she's still here, I want her to linger on this kiss.

I take my time, memorizing every second. The way her lips part. How her eyes stay locked with mine. They darken, shining with desire, with longing. A flush crawls up her neck—that delicious, seductive neck I've been dying to kiss for so long.

Once you have a first kiss with someone, you don't get a do-over. You have to make it count. Make it worth every second of anticipation. "I don't just want to sleep with you. I want to kiss you. Do you have any idea how much I've wanted to kiss you?"

Her hand darts out, curling around the fabric of my shirt at my belly. "How much?"

I inch closer. Our bodies line up. I press against her, so

she knows the answer to the question. "So much that it's all I think about. So much. I've wanted it for so long."

When I dip my head toward her, her eyes float closed with an expression of both utter contentment and rampant longing.

Here, under the umbrella, as the rain drums on the streets of Paris, I brush my lips to hers.

And it's everything I've imagined it would be.

She melts into my touch, and I take my time, my lips tracing hers, her breath ghosting over mine. Our bodies slide together. We are what we've wanted to be: lovers who can't wait to touch. She tugs me even closer, and I know this kiss is about to blast through the atmosphere. I'm sure I can't hold back any longer. The moment for slow and sweet has passed, and now that we've touched, a dam is going to break.

I'm going to devour her lips.

She's going to consume mine.

We're going to skip the rest of the day, stumble to her apartment, fall against the door, and at last come together. I can feel the pressure building inside both of us, like a gasket about to burst. As I clasp her face harder, my lips eager and urgent, her teeth clicking against mine, a loud trill sounds from my pocket.

"Ignore it," she murmurs.

But it's the ringtone from my boss.

I groan. "Fucking hell."

I separate from her, and it's like an affront to the fabric of the universe.

"Hello?"

"Glad I caught you. Can you come see me?"

19

Joy

I stopper frustration. I bottle longing. I mix sensuality.

My afternoon is bathed in replay of a kiss that ended too soon, so I do what I know how to do. I try to capture it. To reproduce a moment in time. What is the scent of a kiss you desperately need more of? What is the smell of something that tempts you too much?

You tell yourself you'll resist.

You believe so heartily that the past mistakes will ground you. They'll keep you from even tiptoeing into something risky. Relationships are fraught with danger, after all. They lead to closeness, and closeness leads to losing yourself. But when you've refrained and restrained, and you're twisting and turning and wanting so much . . . at last, you give in.

You surrender to it.

It's not that I can't fight it. It's that I no longer want to.

That kiss is still on my lips. I run a finger over my

bottom lip absently as I work. I'm both here and there. Both in the lab and under the umbrella, the rain pattering around us.

I'm daydreaming about his lips brushing against mine as I combine odorant molecules like a chef might do with spices, trying to craft the illusion of wandering down the street in the rain, the scent of possibility heavy in the drops. A little of this, a little of that, some molecules from an earthy mix, some more from a citrusy, airy one, another from the essence of jasmine.

I draw a deep inhale.

It's not yet there, but it's something.

There's a knock on the door. I look up to see Marisol in the window. I motion for her to come in. She enters, a thoroughly professional smile on her face. "How's everything going? I've been sending progress reports to the corporate headquarters raving about you."

"Thank you," I say, speaking in French. "I am grateful."

She nods appreciatively and gestures to the vials and tubes in front of me. Switching to English, I give her a quick update on what I'm working on.

"May I smell it?"

"It's not finished yet."

"I don't mind." She strides to me, and I offer her the little tester. She wafts it under her nose and murmurs, "*C'est fantastique.*"

The fact that she said that in French—a perfectly au naturel reaction—gives me a little thrill.

"You need to keep working on this," she adds.

"I will."

We chat more, and she thanks me again for my time and leaves. When she's gone, I daub the tiniest bit on my neck, then I head out for the night. I'm meeting Elise for a drink. Wine is a requirement at times like these. When a man kisses you breathless, then takes off before you can make any plans, you're legally required to drink buckets of vino.

At a brasserie, I order two glasses, and Elise nods her approval at my choice and my efforts to speak the language with the waiter.

"Your French is much better. Your *classes* must be working," she says, sketching air quotes. Her brown hair is twisted high on her head in a bun, and since she came from the office, she's sleek and elegant in a pencil skirt and a clingy white blouse. Her stilettos are a foot tall.

"They seem to be," I say.

"And I can tell you're actually taking classes. I'd have thought you were spending all night fucking."

My eyes widen. "Elise."

She tuts me. "Oh, please. You know that's what you want to be doing. I'm amazed you're learning anything beyond the best positions for multiple orgasms." She winks, looking librarian-sexy in her black glasses. "Seriously, tell me what's going on with the Brit."

I give her the quick version of the last several weeks then detail today's turn of events. She sighs delightedly. "And you swooned, and now you want to know what's next?"

"Yes."

She scoffs. "Men are so frustrating, but even so, please tell me you're not going to play the 'will he call me, won't he call me' game?"

I furrow my brow. "No. I know he'll call. I was more concerned—"

She grabs my cheeks, cupping them. "I love you. I absolutely love you."

"What was that for?" I ask when she drops her hands.

"For being bold. For knowing you're not going to play

a waiting game. Women spend too much time waiting for men. When you want something, you should go for it."

"I'd like to think I'm done with games. I suppose the only real question is—how risky is this? He's still my translator, and I want everything to go well while we work together for the next month until the assignment ends."

The waiter brings our wine, and I thank him, then Elise offers her glass to clink with mine. "To friendship, and to the possibility of a new lover for you."

"I'll happily drink to both," I say and take a sip.

Elise sets her glass down. "This is what I think about the level of risk. You're going to have great sex with him, right?"

A ribbon of heat unspools in me as I imagine the kind of sex we'll have. "Of course."

"Then, by my estimates, great sex should keep you going for a full month. You have nothing to worry about. By the time the shine is off, the job will be ending and you'll be able to look back without regret."

But I don't like the ending she's writing for our story. In a wobbly voice, I posit what may be the truest risk of all. "What if I want it to keep going?"

She draws a deep breath. "Then, you'll need to let him know you want a full-time lover—personally, I'm partial to the part-time ones. Until then, you simply enjoy every second of the time together, and you live for the moment. Moments are all we truly have."

Her voice downshifts to a tune I've never heard before. It's almost melancholy, and it's so unusual for my outgoing and daring friend. I raise my glass, trying to lighten the mood. "May some of the next moments in life contain fantastic orgasms."

Elise tips her glass to mine. "Those are my favorite moments."

But as she drinks, I swear I see something else in her eyes. Something sad. Something that makes me wonder why Elise believes so strongly in living for the moment.

I'm not sure I'll garner the answer today, so I reach into my bag for a tiny tube. "Pilfered it from the lab," I whisper, handing it to her.

"Naughty girl." Her eyes twinkle, the sadness wiped away.

"Something new I'm working on. Tell me what you think."

She uncaps it, and runs the top under her nose. "Mmm."

Her murmur makes my heart do a little jig. That's the sound of someone pleased. She closes her eyes. "It's a summer evening, when I waited for a man to meet me at the fountain. The sun dipped lower in the sky as I checked my watch. The water and the stones behind me were damp and earthy, and my heart filled with longing, then desire, when he arrived and kissed me like the world disappeared."

When she opens her eyes, she offers a wistful smile. "He's long gone, but this perfume is here to stay."

20

Griffin

Getting called into the boss's office is never a good thing.

It's not like I have a history of being some sort of hooligan at work. I just find the less the boss needs to see me, the better I'm likely doing.

Especially since Jean-Paul pushed off the meeting. Shortly after he called me away, he messaged to say he couldn't meet till five. Now it's five, and all I've been able to think about for the last few hours is that he's reassigning me. Or Joy's company is sacking me. Or Marisol found out I'm crazy for Joy, and she thinks our relationship is inappropriate.

Which doesn't sound likely at all, but my brain is a Tilt-A-Whirl, whipping through scenarios. All of them start with this tension in my chest and this pit in my stomach and this stupid fear that I've put Joy and myself at risk.

Even though nothing has happened.

Even though there are no explicit rules forbidding a relationship between us.

Still, the mind slapdashes where it fears to go the most.

I take a seat in Jean-Paul's office.

"Glad you could make it even in the rain. It's brass monkeys outside today, isn't it?" He winks, clearly proud of himself for dropping that Britishism into his conversation with me.

"It's absolutely brass monkeys."

"And I hope I didn't interrupt anything."

No, nothing. Just the best kiss in my entire life. Just my entire afternoon where I sat in a café and stared at my phone constantly as I worked on written translations and contemplated what the hell to say to the woman I'm mad about, all while I worried about my FUCKING job. "Not at all. Always happy to chat. What can I do for you?"

"That's the question, isn't it?" he says with a wink, as if he's going to tell me Today's Tawdry Tale. Leaning back in his chair, he clasps his hands behind his head and parks his feet on the desk. "Tell me about your work at L'Artisan."

I raise an eyebrow, wondering why he'd need to know those details, since I send him regular reports. Unless Marisol has complained. I sit up straighter and give an overview of my work, from the team meetings, to Joy's one-on-one conversations with her scientists, to the translations in the lab.

"And would you say your work has helped?"

I furrow my brow, almost wishing he'd toss out one of his inappropriate comments about a wife of his so I'd know this conversation was normal. But it doesn't feel normal. It feels like a precursor to bad news. "Absolutely. The company has embarked on a number of new projects. It's introduced new processes through the woman I work with. Her staff is doing well at implementing the protocols, she tells me." Maybe I'm selling it too hard. Maybe I'm like a credit card peddler in a shopping center now. But hell, I've witnessed the changes Joy has brought to her company in eight short weeks. She's fantastic. "Plus, Joy is doing well and conversing, and she's actually learning French now, too," I add, though I don't say that she's getting special lessons.

"Interesting." Jean-Paul hums, looking mildly impressed. "Most of them just want someone to be their mouthpiece. She must be a sharp lady."

"She is." I try to tamp down the personal pride I feel.

"My second wife was like that. A pretty little American. She was dying to learn French. Good thing I was willing to introduce her to all the *joys* of our language."

I nearly groan inside.

Be careful what you wish for. Now he's going on and on about how he taught his second wife more than the language. How he taught her the spice of life. When he's done, he slaps a palm on the table. "But you know how it goes with women. She wanted more and more, and it all just went to bollocks, right?"

Second idiom in five minutes. I'll have to tell Christian our boss is in rare idiomatic form today. "Totally bollocks."

He wags a finger at me. "Right you are. Too right," he says, affecting an English accent on the last one. I decide to award him a third point. "Anyway, I don't mean to be cheeky"—and a fourth now—"but I wanted to share some good news. I checked in with the client, and my contact there indicated they were so thrilled with your work that they're going to hire Capstone for more work as they bring on new American employees, so thank you for being a great ambassador."

I swallow down my surprise. "Is that so?"

He rises and offers me a hand to shake. "They think you're as fantastic as all get-out. Wait. That's an American saying. I'm going to have to hire you for my own idioms now."

"Well, that'd be the cat's whiskers, Jean-Paul," I say with a smile.

He laughs. "Well done. Blimey, well done."

"Not sure blimey fits, but hey. You must be knackered at the end of the day," I say, keeping up the volley.

His smile spreads across his wrinkled face. "You are a top translator. The best. Go take yourself out to dinner on me."

He hands me a gift card. I stare at it in disbelief for a moment, then I thank him. When I leave, I breathe a sigh of relief.

As I head down the stairs and into the Paris twilight, I can't help but feel I got away with something. Instead of a reprimand, I have fifty euros on a gift card to spend at a restaurant.

And as I walk down the street toward the river, I grin.

And I laugh.

Maybe I did get away with something. Maybe I'll keep getting away with it. I'll certainly try my hardest.

* * *

"One egg crepe with cheese."

Christian places the order at the crepe stand near

Deux Magots, then turns to me as he waits for his favorite crepe-maker in the city to make a savory dish. "Here's the thing. You know the risks. I'm not telling you something you don't know. The question becomes what happens when you leave for the other side of the world?"

"When I leave, I leave," I say coolly, because what else is there to say? There's a real expiration date to me, and I can't pretend it won't come. I've no clue when I'm returning, especially since I should be able to pick up written translation work remotely, feeding my bank account as I travel.

"Ah, so she's cool with it?"

I scratch my jaw, and glance down the street, trying to remember how Joy has reacted to the prospect of me leaving. "Pretty sure."

Christian arches a skeptical brow. "Pretty sure?"

"She knows I'm going to Indonesia."

"Right. But does she know you're *staying* there?"

I sigh. "I don't even know if I'm staying. I'll probably wind up someplace else."

He draws air quotes as he repeats, "Someplace else." He shakes his head. "For a man who makes a living translating words precisely, you're being awfully imprecise on this matter."

"You didn't even think I should get involved with her," I fire back.

"And you didn't follow that advice, did you?" he says, laughing.

"Not really."

"My point is this: now that you're involved, don't you think you ought to at least let her know this can only be a short-term thing? Be direct with her."

I stuff my hands into the pockets of my jeans. "I have to imagine she knows."

He rolls his eyes. "Don't imagine. Just be clear, like you should have been from the start."

"It's never been pertinent before."

"I'd say it's pertinent now." He claps me on the back. "I think you have your work cut out for you, mate. Good luck with that one. I wouldn't want to be you telling a woman you're hot for that you need to clock out in a month."

As I flash back to the day I ran into Joy when she was still Judy to me, I'm reminded that she wasn't looking for anything. That hasn't changed. She's still not looking for anything, and neither am I. We're Archie and Judy, and they were fine with a whole lot of "not looking for anything" together as they explored.

"It's all going to be fine. Neither one of us wants anything more."

Christian laughs as he takes the crepe and bites into it. "Right."

* * *

As I walk along the river, I run my thumb over the list of ten. I've completed three, I'm working on a fourth by teaching Joy French, I do the postscript on an ongoing basis by keeping in close touch with my parents, and I'm about to check off one more item.

Item number nine.

Take a chance on something that terrifies you.

The funny thing is, going for it with Joy doesn't scare me at all. It excites me. It enlivens me. Maybe this means it doesn't quite fit the bill, but I don't care.

I'm going to cross it off anyway.

9. *Take a chance on something that terrifies you.*

Griffin: The night is young. Do you want to pick up where we left off? Because it's literally all I want to do. And I know you like it when literally means literally.

21

Joy

I've swallowed a nest full of butterflies.

Wait. Butterflies don't live in nests.

They live in a swarm.

Actually, that's not right, either.

It's called an army. I remember from one of my science classes.

I set a hand on my belly, trying to quell the army inside it.

What is wrong with me? I'm thirty. I shouldn't be this nervous. But it's not nerves. It's excitement. It's the thrill. It's the wild, fantastical feeling when you fly upside down on a roller coaster.

But with an army?

I scratch my head as I wait.

Screw it. I need to know what it's called. As I pace across the iron footbridge in Canal St-Martin's, the emerald leaves of the trees glistening from the earlier showers, I unlock my phone. "Google, what is a group of butterflies called?"

She answers in her pleasing robotic voice. "A group of butterflies is called—"

Fingers brush across the back of my neck. "A kaleidoscope."

I don't just shiver. I shudder. My bones melt. Heat swirls through me. *That voice. That accent. This man.* I turn around. Soft moonlight frames his face. "How did you know that?"

He shrugs, a grin lighting up his handsome features. I want to run my fingers along his jawline. But I don't yet have the permission to touch him freely whenever I want. "Marine biology," he answers.

"Butterflies aren't marine life."

"True," he says, then takes a liberty I haven't. He runs the back of his fingers across my cheek. I gasp, and then it turns into the start of a moan. "I don't know, then. I suppose I picked it up somewhere along the way. Maybe because it sounds prettier than a swarm." He takes a beat then says it again, "Kaleidoscope."

It's both beautiful and sensuous, like everything he says to me.

"It is prettier," I say breathlessly, because his fingers are on my face. His body is inches away. The air crackles between us and my body hums as if I've tuned in to his frequency. There's something in the air tonight, and it's the anticipation of a night that's not ending.

It's only beginning.

"I'm glad you could meet me here. Do you know why I chose it?"

I shake my head, swallowing past the dryness in my throat. I want him to quench my thirst. A cool breeze flutters by, and I shiver. He tugs the collar of my pink jacket closer together. "Are you cold?"

"Not in the least." I lean my hip against the green railing.

"I've been working on a list of my own since I met you. A list of places."

"What sort of places?" I'm floating, as if I'm watching this moment from later tonight, or tomorrow, or a few years from now. I'm living in the present, but I'm also keenly aware that this is a time I will return to, over and over. This is one of those pivots in life. When you see everything through this prism.

"Places to kiss you."

I close my eyes for a second, my knees going weak. I can't touch the ground. I'm falling, sinking so far under I will lose myself. And I want to be lost in this night. He reaches for my arm, steadying me.

"Where?"

"I want to kiss you at Moulin Rouge. I want to kiss you at the top of Notre Dame. I want to kiss you in one of the covered passages, down a quiet hallway, where our footsteps echo as we escape the crowds. We'll find a deserted doorway, and I'll pull you into it and kiss you like crazy."

This is desire. This is what poets write about. This is what songwriters croon for. This feeling, and the sense that it can't last forever, but you want it to. You want to cocoon yourself inside it with your lover.

"God, yes," I say with a groan that's nearly ripped from my body. I want him so much. I want him to kiss me, to take me, to fuck me. I don't know how to contain this much longer. I don't have room for it. I'm going to burst with lust.

"I've wanted to kiss you on bridges," he says, running his hand down my arm. "Kiss you at cafés and in museums. I wanted to devour these perfect lips at the flower market." He brushes his fingertip over my top lip, and I go up in flames. *Portrait of a Melting Woman. Canvas: Paris. Medium: flesh and desire.*

"I've wanted you to kiss me everywhere," I say, grabbing his shirt. "I've wanted all those kisses. In front of the Eiffel Tower. Under a streetlamp. On my roof."

It's his turn to groan. A sexy, dirty, masculine sound that reminds me we aren't just playing kissing games. We are a man and a woman on the edge.

There's only one agenda tonight.

"I want to take you everywhere," he growls, threading his fingers through my hair. "Kiss you on every street corner."

"In front of every shop."

"But most of all, I want to kiss you here." He runs his finger along the side of my neck, and I stretch, giving him room, giving him all the room to rain kisses down my neck, and he does.

Oh God. He does. His lips sweep across my skin as night falls, as I fall, as this kiss reverberates in my body, as it echoes in my bones.

He touches the hollow of my throat. "And here." He presses his lips there, and I murmur.

This man is going to reduce me to nothing but lust and a wish for him to take me home and strip me bare.

"And here," he says, dusting his finger over my top lip. "This is my favorite place to kiss in Paris."

"Please," I whimper, and then we stay like that, hovering as if we're holding a pose, lips brushing against lips.

We slam into each other. He pushes me against the railing, and I grab at him, clawing at his shirt, yanking him close. He crushes his lips to mine. A brutal, searing kiss. It's hard and it's ruthless and it feels like being claimed.

We can't go back to who we were. There's no more time to act as if we're only friends. He kisses me deeply and passionately and madly, and I kiss him back, and we don't just kiss with our lips. Our whole bodies are in this. He's grinding against me, and I'm jerking and tugging and pulling him closer.

But I can't get close enough to him.

I clasp his face, my thumbs on his jaw, his hands in my hair, and we devour each other. I feast on his lips, and he seems to revel in my mouth, and I'm going to climb him. I'm going to jump him and climb him and do filthy things to him in public. I ache for him. My body is begging, crying for him to fill me. I've never ever felt like this. Never wanted someone in this kind of bone-deep, soul-crushing way. I can't take it anymore.

Judging by the way he breathes and groans and grinds against me, by the way his tongue fearlessly explores my lips and mouth, by the way his hands rope through my hair, he's as lost as I am.

Or maybe we're both just finding what we want.

"How close are you?" I ask.

"A few blocks away."

"Take me there."

22

Griffin

She's never been to my flat before. It's small, unassuming, and roughly the size of a car. But I'm not giving her a tour right now. I have one place I want to go. *Her.* The second the door closes, I yank her against me.

"Clothes. Off."

She nods, fiddling with the buttons on my shirt, sliding one open, then the next, then another. I tug at her top, yanking it off.

And . . . holy fuck.

Her bra is emerald green, and I'm already in love with it. It's lace, see-through, and it holds the two most wonderful sights in the world. "This, too. I've only had ten thousand fantasies already about your tits."

"Pervert," she says with a naughty grin as I unhook her bra while she undoes my shirt.

Her bra falls to the floor, and the most perfect breasts I've ever seen are inches away from my hands.

And then, yes, in my hands. I knead them, squeeze them, fondle them. "Spectacular."

"Why, thank you," she says, then, as I dip my face to the glorious land, sucking one rosy nipple between my teeth, she cries out.

No more teasing. No more sarcasm.

Her noises are pure lust, and they make me even harder.

I lick and suck as she moans. I lavish attention on each teardrop breast, making sure they're properly adored by my mouth. Then, she grabs my hair hard and yanks my face up. Her green eyes are fierce and blazing with desire. She slams her hands to my chest, running her fingers along her pecs, over my abs, and down toward the waistband of my jeans. I groan. It feels so fucking good to have her hands on me, to feel her fingers exploring my body.

Her eyebrows wiggle. "Have I mentioned how much I like six-packs?"

"No, you haven't. How much?"

"So very much." She slides closer, her hands working their way to unbutton my jeans, pushing my briefs down. My cock announces how incredibly happy it is to see her with a full-on salute. She takes my hard length in her hand, and I swear, time stops for a few mind-bending seconds as she touches me for the first time. My eyes close as I savor the intensity of this moment. There's no place else I'd rather be but rocking into her soft, talented hand. "So much it makes me want to have my hands all over you," she says playfully, then squeezes hard.

I hiss. Electricity sparks all over my skin. "If you wanting to get your hands on me comes from having a six-pack, then I'm absolutely grateful I followed that one to the letter."

She laughs as I smile, then we both go quiet as I thrust into her hand again.

Her voice is a dirty whisper. "Your dick is beautiful."

I grin as I open my eyes. "You know that sounds even hotter in your sexy American accent."

"Stop it. My accent isn't sexy."

"It so is. It turns me on. Especially the last thing you said. Maybe say that again, yeah?"

She grips me harder. "Your cock is beautiful."

"Mmm. Yep. Totally hot accent, and that's also my favorite thing you've ever said to me."

She squeezes on an upstroke. "Now get your beautiful cock inside me, Griffin."

"Scratch that," I say, groaning. "That's my new favorite thing."

I grab a condom from my wallet, push my jeans down, and kick them off. Then I regard her, leaning against the door, half-dressed, tits out, lips bruised and bee-stung. I wave the condom at her. "This is a problem we need to fix right now. Full nudity is required, Joy."

She's topless, but her jeans and heels are still on. "Allow me to rectify the situation." She unsnaps her jeans and pushes them down. Then, because I'm a gentleman, I kneel and pull them off the rest of the way, helping her step out of them, till she's in nothing but a scrap of green lace, because of course, Joy wears matching lingerie.

And it's beautifully, deliciously, slippery wet lace, as I discover when I slide my hand between her legs. Lust jolts my entire body as I feel how slick she is, even through her useless, pointless knickers. I draw a deep, satisfied breath as I tease my fingers across her. "I want to feel this all over me. I want my fingers inside you, my tongue on you, my cock in you."

A tremble moves through her body. "*Je suis excitée.*"

I blink up at her, surprised she used those words correctly. "I didn't teach you that," I say with a quirk of my lips.

She grins naughtily. "I learned it a while ago. I can finally use it properly."

"You used it fucking perfectly," I say as I slide the waistband slowly down her hips. "I believe these knickers have done their service. I think it's time we give them a proper good-bye and get them right the fuck off."

I tug them down her legs then leave them on the floor with her clothes. I kiss my way up, and she shudders as I travel along her soft skin. And there, at the apex of her thighs, is the paradise I've fantasized about. One trim red landing strip leads to the promised land. My fingers play with the soft curls as I trace a path to her center. "Enjoy every day, and eat it like a fruit," I say in a low, dirty whisper. Then I press a kiss to her clit, and she makes the sexiest, most sensual sound I've ever heard, an *ohh* that makes my cock twitch, makes me ache even more to be inside her. Her hands fly to my hair, and she yanks me closer, her breath coming in sharp, erratic pants. She rocks against me, and I feel like she's almost there already. The possibility of her coming on my mouth intoxicates me. I flick the tip of my tongue faster, groaning as I lick her, tasting her sweetness, savoring the evidence of her desire.

But seconds later, she pushes me away. I give her a look from my spot on the floor. "You don't like it?"

She drags her hand down her breasts. "I like it too much."

"I didn't know that was a thing."

"It's a thing when you go down on me like that."

I laugh. "Like how?"

"Like you're devouring me."

"Fuck." I can't resist her. I press another hot kiss to her clit and then rise. "I want to devour you."

"I want you inside me."

Well, I can't argue with that, so I grab her, hoist her up on my shoulder. She squeals. "What are you doing?"

"Wall-fucking is great, but I've got a mind to spread you out on the couch by the window. I've wanted to fuck you so the neighbors can see."

The shutters are open, and a spring breeze wafts in, the curtains fluttering. "Your neighbors are Peeping Toms?"

I set her down on the gray couch by the window. "Joy, it's Paris. We are all voyeurs here."

She shivers and runs her hand between her breasts. "Then let's give them something to see."

I groan as I watch her touch her belly now. "Including me," I rasp out. "I'd like to watch you fuck yourself sometime."

Her eyes darken with lust as her hand slides between her legs. I tear open the condom wrapper as her eyes drift away from me, like she's giving me a private audience into her personal fantasy. Her knees fall open as she touches herself. My chest burns, and my body heats to record temperatures. She's the most sensual woman I've ever seen, ever known. I want to just stare at her, to watch her as she pleasures herself.

But I know she wants more. *I* want more. I roll the condom on and kneel on the sofa, tugging her down the cushions, spreading her out, opening her legs.

Then I stop. I slap a palm to my forehead. "What was I thinking? No one can see us like this."

Quickly, I switch us around, so I'm seated on the couch, and she's on my lap. I tip my forehead to the open window. The view's not much, but at least it's a perfect sightline across the courtyard and into the other flats.

"Is this better for you?" she teases, glancing toward the window.

"It's better for everyone. But it'd be better for me if you could get on my dick right now."

She sucks in a breath as she adjusts her position, straddling me and staring at my erection with rapt attention and glossy eyes. Grabbing the base, I rub the head of my cock against her slickness. She leans her head back and moans, a dirty, gorgeous note, like sex and music all at once.

I moan, too, then I curse when she sinks down on me, taking me all the way. With her hands on my chest, she works to find her rhythm. Rising up, grinding down, swiveling her hips.

Watching her is pure eroticism. It's like she knows every inch of her body. Knows what she wants. Knows how to find it. And knows how to use me to get there. With a sway of her hips, a grind of her pelvis, she moves on me in a sensual dance. Up and down, and she stays there for a moment, sitting on my cock, sucking in her breath.

Raising my hips, I thrust up into her. So wet, so hot, so perfect.

She moans my name, wraps her arms around my neck. "Don't be gentle with me."

Her dirty mouth sends a charge down my spine. It ratchets up the lust rattling through my bones. "I won't."

I grab her hips, dig my fingers in, and move her on me. I adjust my left hand so my thumb glides across her clit, and she gasps. Every sound she makes sends a bolt of desire through my body. I'm burning everywhere, heat flaring over my skin as we fuck by the window. Her mouth falls open. Her eyes squeeze shut. Her hair slides down her back. And her tits bounce magnificently.

Majestically.

This is the snapshot of everything I want right now. To have her like this and to be used by her for pleasure.

This woman I've spent my days with. Spent my evenings with. Spent all my words on. This woman I want so much more of. White-hot pleasure blasts through me as our bodies grind and thrust. She clutches my shoulders, digging into my neck as I push up. She stares down at us, at the way she rides my cock, how she slides up and down on me. She trembles at the same time as she moans. Loud and dirty and hungry. "Harder."

She said not to be gentle, and if there's one thing I pride myself on, it's making sure a woman gets what she wants. One hand moving to her hair, I grab a fistful of those lush red strands and I tug.

"Oh God," she yelps. And then she moans—a long, lingering sound signaling the edge of bliss.

"Again," she begs, her voice raspy.

I let go of her hips, bring both hands to her hair and my teeth to her neck, nipping her, biting her.

She cries out her pleasure, and I rope my fingers in her hair once more, gathering it in my fists. I tug it back, tugging her down harder on me at the same time. Like that, I control her moves, and the exquisite torment on her face tells me she loves it.

I meet her eyes. "This is better than my fantasies."

"Do you fantasize about me a lot?"

"Every night. Every morning. All the time."

I yank her hair again. Hard. Rough. Demanding.

The way she likes it.

She's saying God's name as her eyes squeeze shut, and

her lips part in a gorgeous O, and then she's silent for one long, lovely, suspended moment until she cries out.

When I hear her orgasm, there's no doubt the neighbors will, too. The sound of her passion rattles my own climax free. Pleasure thunders down my spine, barrels into my thighs, and I come.

I say her name because it feels like that. Like erotic, filthy, fantastic, can't-believe-I'm-finally-having-her joy.

* * *

Eventually, she gets the tour. It lasts all of thirty seconds, since this is French real estate, after all.

"It's my mum's sister's flat, so I lease it from her. Aunt Sophie, who was known for giving me the most amazing treats during the holidays," I explain as I show her the minuscule bedroom.

"Sophie sounds like my kind of relative."

"She is."

"And does this mean the Thomas family gets to keep this flat for generations?"

"Yes, it's our prized possession."

Something flickers across her eyes when I say that, like a spark of hope. I'm not sure what's on her mind, but honestly, with her naked in my place, it's pretty hard for me to think straight. She spots a framed photo on my bureau of Ethan and me after the race we ran. Her eyes widen and she points. "Your brother was good-looking."

"You're not allowed to say that," I say in mock seriousness as I pull her onto the mattress.

"Oh, c'mon. You two must have been lady-killers."

"Wait. So you were stark raving mad at me on the street earlier today about item number two on his list, and now you want to know if we were tomcats together?"

She swats me. "I did not get mad at you, and I definitely did not turn stark raving mad. Plus, if memory serves, you kissed me right after you told me, so I guess your plan to make me jealous worked."

"Will it work again? I'm not above doing whatever it takes to get these lips on mine."

She shrugs impishly. "You'll have to try harder. First, tell me something I don't know about you."

I lean back into the pillows, tucking my hands behind my head. "I love lunch. Like, fucking adore it."

She laughs. "Everyone loves lunch."

"No, seriously. That's not true. People love breakfast or people love dinner. Lunch is the most underrated meal in the world, and I love it madly, and deeply, and truly."

She drags her hands through her hair, still tangled up from me. "My sister and I used to sneak out for lunch when we could."

"Sneak out?"

"That's what we called it at least. Mostly we just met for lunch at In-N-Out Burger."

I raise an eyebrow. "What's that?"

"Seriously? What's that? You don't know?"

I shake my head. "I presume it's a burger joint?"

"It's only the greatest burger joint in all the land. From coast to coast. Sea to shining sea. They also have great milkshakes. Someday, you'll go to the States and you'll understand the joys of In-N-Out Burger."

"Someday I will," I tell her, then we talk more, as moonlight filters across the sheets. She tells me about Allison, and I tell her more about Ethan. Even though only one of them is alive, somehow the conversation doesn't hurt quite as much as it would have a few months ago.

Maybe this is what it feels like to move through grief.

You never truly get over the loss of someone you love. But you get by, you get through, you get around.

That's why I don't say anything tonight about what comes next for me. Sometimes, you just want things to go perfectly. And they do for the rest of the evening. Because we can't keep our hands off each other, and soon enough we're not talking about family. We're talking about each other.

I prop my head in my hand. "You know we're seeing each other tomorrow, right?"

"At work?"

"And after."

"For language lessons?"

"And for this," I say, running a hand down her hip.

"Presumptuous much?"

"Woman, I have orgasms to give you. Don't deny me."

She tugs me close. "Say it in French."

And I do, whispering dirty, filthy things in her ear, as I move her under me, and slide into her again. "*Je te veux tellement.*"

I want you so much.

She moans.

"Say it to me," I command.

She repeats my words. "*Je te veux tellement.*"

"Now tell me to fuck you hard. I know you know this one."

Her back bows as she murmurs, "*Baise-moi fort.*"

I bring her to the edge again, telling her, "*Jouis avec moi.*"

Come with me.

Soon, she does, as the moon shines and Paris sleeps, as we're entwined together at last.

23

Joy

One of the things I love most about being a modern woman is we know we can have it all. The job, the family, the kids, the love affair, the great sex.

I don't have kids, obviously. But I'd like to think I'm winning on a few of those other points right now. After finishing up in the lab, I grab my phone and tap out a message to my sister.

Joy: True/False. It's possible to have your cake and eat it, too.

Allison: I've never understood that saying. Isn't having it and eating it the same dang thing?

Joy: You know what I'm saying. Do you believe we can truly have it all?

Allison: Absolutely. But having it all isn't free, sister. :)

Joy: What's the cost?

Allison: Usually money. Usually you can only have it all if you're rich. But sometimes you can if you're really lucky.

I wonder if I could be one of those lucky women. When I leave the office on Friday evening, it feels that way. The job is going well. L'Artisan is thrilled with the work I've been doing, and I feel as if I'm entering a whole new level of success on the job front. Finally, I'm able to move up and use all my skills. I'm at a place where I can thrive and uncover new opportunities.

Then there's this city.

I walk down the boulevard, threading my way past buildings that have witnessed centuries of lives and battles and loves, past shops that peddle mouthwatering treats, past people who experience the world in a different way than I did mere months ago. The most romantic city on earth is starting to feel like my home.

Plus, I'm learning a new language. My tongue forms words and sentences that I'd never have crafted before.

Then, there's the man I'm meeting tonight.

The man I'm head over Jimmy Choos for.

I didn't come to Paris to fall in love, but Paris had other plans for me.

* * *

After I shower, dry my hair, and slip into a sapphire-blue dress that hugs my curves, I toss a wide scarf over my shoulders. I consider the options on my mirrored tray, then go for the caramel and white musk notes in Candy by Prada, spritzing on a tiny amount.

I head to Montmartre.

Griffin waits for me outside Moulin Rouge, the windmill behind him, the bright red lights somehow making those blue eyes of his even bluer. He says nothing as I walk to him, only stares at me predatorily. How odd that I saw him hours ago when I wore a pencil skirt and white blouse at the office. Now I'm in a clingy dress that he'll strip off later tonight. That's how he looks at me. As if he's already undressed me. I feel naked before his gaze, and it thrills me.

When I reach him, he wraps an arm around my waist, dips me, and kisses me.

I swoon.

There's no other way to describe it. He has me in his arms, and he's taking my breath away on the street outside the world's most famous cabaret, and my head is a fantastically static haze. He kisses me like we're in the movies, like this is one of those kisses a photographer will capture, and it'll become a classic black-and-white photo. Women will post it online with captions like *I'll have what she's having.*

And I'm having it. The kind of kiss that makes my head spin. That makes my heart thump. That turns me on from ankles to eyebrows.

When at last our lips separate and he pulls me up, I blink at him, sighing contentedly. "You're too much."

He laughs. "I'll assume 'too much' is a good thing."

"You're cake. I'm having you and eating you," I say dopily, because I think I might be high on him.

"So much talk of eating things," he says, running a hand through my hair as his soft lips travel to my neck. "And yet I still need to eat *you* again and again."

That spark flares through me, and I'm already dangerously wet.

We head inside, taking a seat for the show, where we spend the next hour entertained by dozens upon dozens of women in sequins and feathers dancing and kicking to bright, bold, and sometimes seductive music. Their sumptuous costumes shimmer on the stage, the cherry reds, glittery golds, and shiny silvers adding to the decadence of the evening. This place is, and has always been, a portal to the hedonistic, an invitation to dance till dawn, to sleep in past noon, to drink and live and be so very merry.

Griffin's hand is on me the whole time, moving from my leg, to my hand, over my shoulders. As I watch, I exist in a state of heightened awareness. I'm a hummingbird, wings buzzing, waiting to dip my beak into the honey water.

When we leave, we wander through the hilly streets of Montmartre, past cafés where the clink of wineglasses and bits of conversation float past my ears. I pick up phrases here and there, crystal clear in my brain for once, and I grab Griffin's arm, my eyes widening.

"I'm starting to understand what they're saying," I tell him in French.

He smiles and kisses me. "Your dream is coming true."

My heart flutters. I want to tell him I have new dreams. I want to tell him he's part of them.

Something holds me back, though. Maybe it's my own

ancient fears. My worries over what happens when you let someone in. How you start to give up the parts of you that matter most. If I'm going to keep giving the most precious real estate in my heart to him, I want to know him more, and understand what drives him.

We stop in a small park and grab a bench in a quiet corner, away from the Friday night revelry. But before I can ask him what I most want to know, he squeezes my fingers and says, "I want you to see what's on the list."

I straighten my shoulders, surprised at this sudden declaration, even though it's as if he's read my mind. "You do?"

He nods. "You're important to me. I want you to understand my life, and my choices."

His words are heavy, anchored by a weight I don't fully understand. He sighs, rubs a hand over his jaw, and I tense more. Something is on his list that I won't like, and I don't think it's about other women. It's about him. It's about us.

I brace myself for hurt. "I want to say you don't have to tell me, but I think I might need to know," I say softly.

He swallows and brushes a strand of hair away from my cheek. "I'm leaving."

My ears ring. My head hurts. A cold, hard echo reverberates in my body, like a crash of cymbals. I must have heard him wrong. "What?"

"I'm leaving Paris. When the assignment at your company is over."

I blink, and if I were standing, I'd stumble. Instead, my hands curl around the wooden slat of the bench, holding on tight. "You're leaving?"

He nods. "When I go to Indonesia. . ."

"You're not coming back?"

"I don't think so," he says, heavily.

I nod a few times, my brain slowly processing this new input. It's like someone dropped a molecule of bleach into a vanilla-scented perfume. "Wow."

He rubs his palms along his slacks. "I'm sorry."

Those words hit me hard. They make me feel like Richard did. Responsible for his fate. I paste on a smile. "Don't be sorry. I was just surprised. That's all."

"I should have said something sooner." Running a hand up my arm, his fingers tiptoe over my shoulder. My body has the audacity to form goose bumps. "But I had no idea where we were going, or if we were ever going to happen, or really what to say other than that I was going there for the race."

I take a calming breath. "You don't need to clear things with me. This is your life. You need to live it the way that makes sense to you."

"Joy . . ." His voice is tinged with sadness.

"Are you planning to live in Indonesia?" I ask, drawing all my strength.

He nods. "For a little while. I've been saving the money to do this. But I'll also travel all around. I've always wanted to."

Like that, understanding lights up my brain, like neon signs flicking on at night.

At the museum, he said, *I want to go everywhere.*

At dinner when he told me about the marathon, his words were, *I've always wanted to go there, spend some time wandering around when I'm done.*

I should have seen this coming. He's been clear enough. I thought he meant he'd take trips, but perhaps I only wanted to believe he would take trips, because they have a beginning and an end.

He's never lied to me.

I've lied to myself.

I've chosen to believe the fairy-tale version of falling in love in Paris. Not the real one, where I meet a man who has too much wanderlust, a man who's living a life he and his brother plotted. A life only one of them can live now.

"Do you want to see the list?"

"Yes," I say with a gulp because I need to know what I'm up against. Once upon a time, I believed my own reticence over relationships would be our biggest barrier. Now I know the highest hurdle is one that I can't, and won't, tear down.

It's time, it's space, it's distance. It's family, it's love, it's honor.

It is intractable.

He takes a piece of paper from his wallet and unfolds it. I hold my breath, waiting. Once he spreads the paper open, it's like seeing a ghost. The handwriting is his brother's. It's a scratchy and uneven scrawl, the penmanship of someone who could barely hold a pen anymore. It breaks my heart.

1. ~~Live in Paris for a year.~~ *Check.*

    2. ~~Sleep with all the French women.~~ *Check.*

    3. Visit Indonesia. Run a marathon there. Travel across the country, then everywhere.

    4. Pack your bags, wander the globe, and eat macarons, or whatever you want because you can, since you'll . . .

    5. ~~Have six-pack abs. You can do it. I was almost there. Hell, show me up and go for an eight-pack.~~ *Check.*

    6. Help someone you care about achieve their dream.

    7. Have your caricature drawn in Place du Tertre. Preferably a highly amusing image that would have made me laugh.

    8. Sleep under the stars.

9. ~~Take a chance that terrifies you.~~ *Check.*
10. *Drink champagne along the Seine when you bid adieu.*
P.S. *Be nice to Mum and Dad. It's hard for them.*

I laugh at the same time that a sob works its way up my throat then escapes. I drop my head in my hands, and let a few tears slip down my cheeks.

Griffin rubs a hand on my back. "Are you okay?"

I nod. "It's just sad." I don't mean him leaving, though that is intensely sad. I raise my face, a new tear streaking down. "I'm sorry your brother's not here. I'm sorry this happened to him."

Griffin dusts his lips over my cheek, kissing away the evidence of my tears. "It's okay. I mean, it's not, but what can you do? Don't cry, sweetheart. I hate to see you sad."

That only makes me want to cry harder. The *sweetheart*. The endearment. The way my emotions matter to him.

But this isn't about me.

This is so much bigger than him, than us.

This is about a promise to the person you love most. The person you love unconditionally. It's a dying wish to do what someone else can't.

Gathering myself, I draw a deep breath, swallowing past the harsh lump in my throat. It's not my loss. It's his, and I'm acting like I own it. I lift my chin, keeping my voice even. "Why are some underlined?"

"Those are the ongoing ones. I should always be nice to Mum and Dad, right?" he says with a smile.

"Of course, but it's sweet Ethan pointed it out."

"He worried about them. And it's not hard to be nice to them, but it's important, and that's why I try to talk to them often. To stay in touch."

"And the other one underlined is the one about helping someone achieve their dreams. I guess I'm still a work-in-progress," I say, a quirk to my lips.

He wraps his arm tighter around my shoulder, leans his face to me, brushing his lips against mine. "Yes, I like that you're ongoing. I like that you're not there yet. It means you still need me."

More than you know. "I have so much to learn."

"I'll get you there."

And then you'll leave. Then you'll take off.

But I don't say that. I'm a grown-up, and that's the role I need to play. I fasten on a smile. "And then you'll be on your way to Indonesia. You'll do the marathon and travel, then you'll wander and eat macarons. So that's three and four."

He nods. "Which leaves me with three left to do here, I suppose."

"Sleep under the stars. Why haven't you done that? That seems like something you could do any night."

"True, but I don't think that's what it means."

"What do you think it means?"

"We used to make lists of all the places we wanted to go. We had this huge map of the world with pins stuck in future destinations, and we'd say that we'd sleep under the stars if we had to." His eyes look faraway, and he's slipped back to the past, to memories that are bittersweet. "Or if we wanted to," Griffin adds, a cheerier note to his voice. "We always gave ourselves an out. If we had to, or if we wanted to."

"So, it applies to traveling," I say heavily, and it seems many of these items do. But that's who Griffin and his brother were, I'm learning. They were boys bitten with the bug of adventure. Then, they became men, unable to pack their bags and take off. And so, now, one of them must.

I move down the list, running my finger over the caricature one, and the champagne item. "I know someone who can help you with these final two."

He raises an eyebrow playfully. "Oh, do you?"

I dance my fingers over my chest. "I happen to adore champagne, and I also know a great caricaturist."

He laughs heartily. "How on earth do you know a great caricaturist? That's so random."

I wave broadly at the streets in front of us. "Hello? Montmartre? Place du Tertre. Elise lives near here, and when I was on my way to her home, I had a drawing done a couple months ago. I'll take you to see the guy. It'll be fun."

"There you go. Done." He mimes making a check mark.

I squint. "But I don't understand why you didn't do that one yet. It seems easier."

He shrugs. "Maybe because it's easy. I figured I'd tackle the others first. Besides, this was one I knew I could do anytime, I suppose."

Part of me desperately wants to believe he hasn't had his caricature done so that he'll have a tether to Paris. I want to believe he loves Paris as wildly as I do, and when the time comes to say good-bye, he won't be able to. The tie to this place will be too strong.

But that's a fool's hope.

I've been a fool before.

I can't do it again.

I'll be a rock. That's what I know how to be. This man is teaching me a whole new language. The least I can do is be by his side as he finishes his brother's bucket list. He needs to see this through. It's not my place to hold him back with a heart too full for him. It's my place to help guide him there, a gentle hand on his back, an encouraging word, and a fantastic time before he waves good-bye. Send him off in style, even if it makes my heart ache more than I would like.

So much more than I would like.

I lace my fingers through his and walk to the nearby square, where charcoal artists draw elongated faces. But it's late, and most have gone for the night.

"We'll come back another time," Griffin says, and a faint kernel of hope dares to take shape inside me. The hope that there will be another time, another chance for us.

A ragtag group of musicians plucking away on violins and cellos play a French tune, the words melancholy but the melody upbeat enough. Griffin takes my hand and spins me, and we dance under the moonlight, the stars winking above us, the old-time music becoming our soundtrack.

"Now all this dancing makes me want to do one thing only," he says as the song ends.

"What's that?"

"Make love to you."

Uber has never made it to my place so quickly.

In my bed, we speak less than last night. We tease less, too. But here in the dark, as he climbs over me, runs his hands down my naked body and enters me, I don't need words to know what he's feeling. I see it in his eyes. In the intensity of his gaze. I hear it in his sounds, his noises. He hikes up my leg, opening me more, moving in me. He doesn't look away, and it's almost too much.

But too much of him is what I want.

Even if it hurts.

Even if I know it's ending.

When we're like this, tangled together, our bodies slick

and hot, our breath wild and erratic, our lips parted, it doesn't feel as if we're counting down.

But once we come down from our high, I'm keenly aware that I'm crossing off days on the calendar until the man I'm in love with leaves.

24

Griffin

The first time I traveled to Paris, I was three.

My mum took Ethan and me to see where she grew up, before she left to live in England. Shockingly, I don't remember a lick of that trip. But the photos are enough to make me shudder. Mum dressed us in prissy little shirts that no child should ever wear.

We visited again when I was six and Ethan was five. Apparently, we were little shits then. The story goes that we nicked a little Eiffel Tower keychain from a young boy selling them by the carousel near the famous landmark. I've always suspected the story was apocryphal, told at dinner parties by my parents to entertain the guests. But there is a photo of us in front of the tower, and my dad wrote a caption on it: *Little troublemakers.*

We visited many times over the years, seeing Mum's sister, who now lives in Brittany. We'd check out the sights and the famous landmarks, and go to the open-air markets. Though I did all that with my family, I also looked elsewhere on those trips. Down alleys, around corners, in the passages. Always seeking unknown treasures and odd little curiosities.

As a teenager, when I went about the city on my own, I started keeping track of all the unusual things I saw— level markers, corner guards, antique signs. I was like a surveyor conducting an inventory of Paris, recording all the things that caught my eye.

Funny that I never noticed the angels Joy keeps telling me about.

I'm still not an angel person. I don't believe they're watching over me, and I definitely don't think my brother is an angel. That's just not how I'm wired. But since Joy mentioned the very first one on the door knocker, I've been intrigued with their presence. Because I'd missed them. Because I failed to notice them on my journeys around Paris. That's why over the next week I research them online, marking where to find them.

When I hop on my bike one afternoon, I ride around the city, visiting a pair in the window of a luxurious mansion, another blowing a horn on the frame of a hotel, and one more in a Japanese garden, that came from the remains of a church bombed in Japan during the Second World War. The damaged angel sculpture was sent here as a symbol of peace.

I stop at the last one, staring for a long time, as if I can find a special meaning in it. But I don't know what to make of the angels scattered around the city, unless it's as simple as this—each one whispers a story of how Paris came to be. Some offer clues about art and music. Others tell of how the city moved through war and revolution. Still others speak of survival, lasting among the wreckage.

Maybe that's what links these winged statues—they're

a new form of connect-the-dots in this city. I smile as I hop back on my bike, pleased that I've figured out this little riddle.

I'll miss discovering oddities like this, puzzling them together to learn what they mean. I'll miss many things about this city, I realize as I ride along the river. The bread, for starters. I don't know that there has ever been better bread in the entire world. I'll miss the streetlamps, the cafés, the sidewalks themselves. I'll miss that everywhere around me there is beauty, even if it's simply in a shop window.

I'll miss the people. Marie at the bakery, Julien by the river, even Jean-Paul and his absurd stories. I'll definitely miss Christian and his devil-may-care spirit.

Most of all, I will miss the woman I've spent so many hours with over the last few months. As I ride aimlessly along the Seine, I think back to the day many weeks ago when I was ready to take off and explore Indonesia before the marathon, finishing my training on the island. Instead, what frustrated me at the time gave me three months with Joy.

Three unexpected months I wouldn't ever want to give up.

I only wish it were longer. I wish we'd started sooner. I wish it were fair to ask for something from her that I know in my heart is wholly unfair. Even so, there's a part of me that longs to ask Joy what she'll be doing six months, maybe twelve months from now. If she might want to somehow make a go of this. But I honestly don't know when I'm coming back, or if my journeys will take me elsewhere. Is that even fair? To ask someone to wait for you when you don't know how long you'll be gone?

I slow my pace as I near Julien's green stall by Notre Dame. Hopping off the bike, I lean the metal frame against the stone wall by the river. He raises his chin and barks at me. "Where is your lovely woman? I'd rather look at her pretty face than your ugly mug."

Yeah, I'll miss his gruffness, oddly enough.

"Nice to see you, too." I clap him on the shoulder. "And to answer your question, I'm taking her out tonight. I'm meeting her friend, and she's meeting one of my mates."

He huffs, parking a weathered hand on the faded green wood on one side of his stall. "She likes you more than you could know."

I tilt my head. "Why do you say that?"

"You must have charmed her. That's all I can figure. She was here the other day."

"She was?" I smile, picturing Joy here, perusing the wares.

"She bought some postcards. She asked me questions. How long have I worked here, how I was doing?"

The grin spreads as I imagine Joy practicing her language skills. "Were you nice to her, old man?"

He scoffs. "She was about ready to have a nightcap with me."

I laugh, amused. "Don't steal my girl."

"Does she know how much you'll miss her when you do your stupid run in some stupid country that isn't France?"

"Why don't you tell me what you really think?"

"You're a fool."

"You're extra salty today."

"You have a woman you love, and you want to leave. You're a fool."

"Love?" I ask, narrowing my eyes, surprised at his quick verdict. "The woman I love?"

He waves a hand dismissively. "Young people. You don't realize what you have."

He's wrong. I do realize it. I see it plain and clear.

But there are choices that aren't mine to make. There are promises I made more than a year ago.

That day will never fade.

"What can I do? Anything. Just name it. I'll do it for you," I told Ethan when he took his last turn for the worse. The infection had done irreparable damage to major organs and the doctor had just told us there was nothing more they could do. The fighting was over. The infection had won.

"You don't have to do anything for me."

"Let me," I pleaded, desperate to be his voice, his legs, his last chance.

"You want a bucket list?" There was the faintest laugh in his voice.

"Yes. Yes, I do."

"You've gone mad."

"I mean it. We were going to do everything. We had plans. What would you do if you could? I'll do it for you."

"You mean it?"

I nodded savagely. "Yes, I'll do anything. Except skydiving. Anything but skydiving."

Silently, he watched me for a long moment, studying my eyes as if searching for something in them. He found whatever he was looking for, perhaps the permission to ask me to do what he couldn't. Because then he smiled amidst the tubes and beeping machinery of his hospital room. "Okay. Let's do it. One last list."

I scrambled for a pen and paper, and he started to write. The pen wobbled in his weak fingers. My heart splintered, and I choked back a tear. "I'll do it."

Ethan shook his head, his grip tightening, harder than I'd seen him hold a pen.

The lump thickened in my throat. "I need to get some water."

I excused myself for a moment, ostensibly to head to the water fountain. Jamming the heel of my hand against my eye, I wiped away the evidence, then returned to his room, and watched as he managed to write it all down. Ten items, and a final postscript.

I blink away the harsh memory, and gesture to the shelves of books and small notecards. "Anything here she wanted?"

Julien surveys his goods, then taps a notecard with a photo of Monet's garden. "She liked this picture. She bought it for herself. Maybe she doesn't need you to buy her things."

My shoulders tense. His words clang around in my head.

He's right. He's ridiculously right, but not about buying things. About Joy needing me. She doesn't need me, not truly. She's independent and capable and bold, and she's learning a whole new language. She won't want to wait for me. I need to excise the idea of even asking her to.

Instead, I'll make the most of the last few weeks with her.

I buy a few of the small notecards of flowers, grab a pen from Julien, lean against the stone wall by the river, and write a note.

But when I look back at my words, I can't say that. I can't ask that. I tuck it into my wallet, and write another.

An invitation.

* * *

Ivy climbs the white walls at the back of the six-room boutique hotel, while songbirds chirp in the night air. Music pulses low and sensual, and absinthe flows freely in glasses at this outdoor enclave, a secret nighttime garden that Joy uncovered deep in the heart of the hip Oberkampf district in Paris. It's at the Hotel Particulier Tenth, nestled among verdant trees and lush bushes, off a quiet side street with an address nearly impossible to find.

Her friend Elise knows the owner. I have the impression Elise knows everyone worth knowing in Paris.

"So, this is the woman who says days should be eaten," I say as we're introduced.

"So, this is the man who's so enchanted my friend," she says, her chocolate-brown eyes skeptical behind her glasses, almost as if she doesn't quite trust me. Elise has a sisterly protectiveness to her, even though I doubt Joy needs it. She's the kind of woman who can fight her own battles.

I tip my forehead to Joy, next to me. "The enchantment is entirely mutual."

Elise raises an eyebrow appreciatively and nods at me. "Good. Then you've passed my test for the night."

I wipe my hand across my brow. "Whew. I was worried."

"A woman needs a friend to keep her man on his toes."

Joy laughs and sets a hand on my arm. "By the way, have I told you Elise has been appointed in charge of all the inquisitions in my life?"

"No. I'm in charge of the fun," Elise corrects playfully from atop her towering heels. I suspect they add four, maybe five inches to her height. I also suspect she's the type of woman who could run in heels and never wobble. She has that air about her.

"Fun? Did someone say fun? I believe that's my

middle name." Christian is here. He strides across the patio, stopping next to Joy and Elise. I make the requisite intros, and Joy throws her arms around him, hugging him like an old friend, then to Elise I explain that he's a translator, too.

"French to English?" Elise asks my friend.

Christian shakes his head. "Yes, but no. I specialize in the Scandinavian languages."

Elise roams her eyes over his tall, blond frame. "You do look something like a Viking."

Christian laughs. It isn't the first time a woman has said that to him. "Denmark is my first love. Copenhagen-born."

"A Dane with a British accent. You look like Alexander Skarsgård, and you sound like Tom Hardy. This might very well be fantasy made flesh," Elise says, waving her hand to fan herself.

He smiles. "Why, yes, I'd love to take you home right now."

Joy laughs loudly. "And clearly it's time for us to go."

Elise shakes her head and pats Joy's shoulder. "Don't be silly. I can admire your man's friend and make sure you get drunk on absinthe at the same damn time."

"You're a multitalented woman," Christian says, and Joy and I step back, grabbing a spot on the outdoor couch and ordering absinthe.

"Copenhagen is a lovely city," Elise says to Christian. "I traveled there a year ago. I took one of those canal tours."

"What was your favorite part of the tour? Seeing the palaces? Hearing the stories of all our crown jewels?"

Elise chuckles, shaking her head. "Neither. I most enjoyed when the boat glided past a private dock, where a very fit, very muscular Danish man was doing handstands naked on the dock."

Christian taps his chin, his expression serious. "Was it right by Nyhavn? A little past the outdoor food market?"

"I believe so," Elise says with a curious smile. "Do you know this gentleman? Is he the Mad Naked Handstander of Copenhagen?"

"Mad? No. More like fit, handsome, and well-hung."

She scrunches her brow. "You've been admiring his package, too?"

"So, you *were* indeed admiring it?"

"There was a lot to admire," she says with a happy shrug, and Joy nudges me as we watch them like spectators.

Christian taps his chest. "That was me."

A laugh bursts from Elise. "What?"

Joy turns to me with wide eyes, whispering, "Was that Christian?"

I shrug, laughing quietly and listening to Christian's answer.

"Well, I suppose it's entirely possible there could be other tall, fit, muscular men who have homes on the water in Copenhagen, and do handstands, yoga, and other acrobatics naked in an attempt to entertain the canal tourists with other *crown jewels*," he says, and Elise laughs. "In fact, I have a few good mates who also engage in this pastime. But there's a good chance it was actually me."

Elise whistles. "Then I'm even more pleased to meet the man whose photos are already on my cell phone."

The waiter arrives with our drinks, and I thank him, then wrap an arm around Joy and nuzzle her. "Looks like they're getting along without us."

She stretches her neck, inviting me to kiss her more. "That means you can entertain me."

I brush my lips along her throat, kissing up to her

chin, along her jawline, then to her ear. "How do you most like to be entertained?"

"With your tongue," she whispers.

I groan. "Now, you're going to make it so very hard to stay here."

She reaches for our glasses and hands me one. "Just think how worked up you'll be when we finally leave."

Raising her glass, she takes a drink and murmurs her appreciation. The sound of her pleasure over the drink is sensual and dirty, and turns me on even more. "I'm already worked up."

Her eyes wander down my body, and she raises an eyebrow. "Good. Now, think about what it'll be like when we head to my flat, I go upstairs ahead of you, and you find me naked on the rooftop terrace."

We last thirty minutes, and then I make an executive decision. There's not much reason to stay here any longer when there are tongues that need to be used for entertainment.

25

Joy

Eighty-four steps are worth it.

For the view.

For the June breeze, after the last few weeks of rain and chilly nights.

And for this possibility.

A glass of white, burgundy lace panties, and a cushioned chaise lounge. Soft music floats from my phone, and the lights of the city give me the best art in the world to gaze at while I wait.

I don't wait long.

I only asked for a few minutes.

The door is unlocked, and soon I hear the creak of wood, the groan of the door closing, then footsteps on the stairs leading to the roof. The little hairs on my arms stand on end before he even reaches me. My body hums, and thrills race over my skin.

He turns the corner at the top of the steps, and his

eyes blaze with a desire I can read even in the dark, even from ten feet away.

I'm the stage, and he's just turned on all the lights. They spotlight me, and tingling awareness and longing prickle across my skin. I'm the peach left on the table, and he's going to take it, bring it to his lips, and bite into it.

A harsh, wild breath dares to escape my lips as he walks over to me. To complete the seduction, I bring the glass of wine to my lips as coolly as I can, steadying it and taking one more drink.

He reaches me, so much heat in his blue eyes. "How does it taste?"

He's asking about the wine. But there are so many other meanings. "Try it."

I offer him the glass and he takes it, drinking some down as he sits on the end of the chaise. He hands the glass back to me, and I set it on the table.

He curls a hand around my ankle.

My shoes are still on. Sling-back black heels.

He eyes them, running his fingers over the top of my foot. A pulse beats between my legs as heat pools in my center. Already, I'm wet and aching for him. I don't know how I'll go without this kind of sex, this kind of intimacy, this kind of expectation.

I'll miss it savagely when he's gone in a few weeks, and I fiercely want more of it already.

"Nice red soles," he says, admiring the shoes.

"Nice everything," I say to him, since he's fully dressed.

Firmly, he presses down on my right ankle, forcing me to drop my leg, to open myself for him.

A growl sounds as if it's ripped from his throat as he stares at me. His eyes zero in on my panties. "Look at you. So wet already."

He grasps my other ankle and moves it, positioning

the heels of my shoes at the edge of the chaise. My legs are parted for him.

"Take your clothes off," I tell him, but it doesn't sound like a command. More like a desperate plea.

He shakes his head at the same time he strips off his shirt in one fast move. I sigh greedily as I admire his skin in the moonlight. The hard planes of his pecs, the grooves of his abs. The six-pack. Thank the Lord for the six-pack. I bow down before its gloriously hard design and shape.

"Can't wait anymore." He bends to the chaise, crawls up it, and tugs off my panties in one swift move. He untangles them from my shoes and tosses them on the terrace. I groan his name like a woman possessed when his tongue flicks across my wetness.

I melt under his knowing touch. It's not the first time he's done this to me. I've enjoyed the sight of his face between my legs many nights. I've savored it, and come for him.

He knows what to do. He knows how to touch me. He licks a lingering line up my center then presses his hands to my thighs, spreading me open. He makes me vulnerable to him, to the moment, to the pleasure.

But that's exactly how I want to be.

I want to let go. I want to give in. I've never known sex could be like this. I've never felt intimacy this intensely before.

In the past, I've been guarded, cautious, protected the pieces of myself as best as I can.

But with Griffin, he can't seem to get enough. He wants so much, craves so deeply, and gives so freely of pleasure. It unlocks something inside me. The way he touches me, the way he talks to me, makes me want to let go. I reach for the lever on the side of the chaise, and I lower it, going flat.

He murmurs as he presses his whole mouth to me.

I cry out. I love when he consumes me. I love when it feels like he's going to lose control from tasting me. I arch into him, rocking my hips as he kisses me so intensely, so passionately that I know he's going to draw an orgasm out of me in mere seconds.

My hands find their way to his head, and my fingers thread through his dark hair. They curl around his skull, and he seems to mirror my moves. His hands scoop beneath me, cupping my ass, pulling me closer. It's like he's drinking me in. My eyes float closed, but somewhere in the back of my mind, I tell myself to open them.

To watch.

I want to remember not only what this feels like, but what it looks like.

Streaks of moonlight dance across my belly. The lights of the Eiffel Tower twinkle against the night, reflecting across his arms wrapped around me. Shadows shroud his face, buried between my legs as he licks and consumes.

His tongue is everywhere. Lapping me up, kissing me, flicking against the most sensitive spot.

I can't hold back, and I don't even try to. I rock up into his face, fucking him as he fucks me with his tongue, his lips, his mouth, with his desire.

Pleasure curls low in my belly, tight and pulsing. It pulls and tenses, and starts to radiate in my bones. Sounds fall from my lips with abandon. Incoherent noises and groans. Obscene cries of lust as I part my legs farther, grab him harder. The white-hot sensations build higher, coil tighter.

I'm on the edge for minutes, it seems, crying out, telling him *I'm coming, I'm coming, I'm coming*. Because it's endless. Stars blaze before my eyelids. My mind is a hot blur. And the pleasure literally won't stop. It crashes down on me, and finally pulls me under into its gorgeous, blissful embrace.

I surrender to it, and to him.

I'm breathing hard, panting, flushed from everything when I blink open my eyes to find him naked and standing next to me, his cock eager to join the festivities.

"Give that to me," I say. "I want you in my mouth."

I sit up, my head spinning as I kneel on the cushion, drawing him in. He groans when my tongue swirls across the head, then I suck him, and within seconds, he's thrusting. I tell myself to relax, to take him deep. He grunts my name as I bring him in farther, wrapping a hand around the base and cupping his balls as I suck.

"Christ," he groans. "I could come in your throat right now."

I look up at him, a twinkle in my eyes, I'm sure. For a brief second, I let him go. "That's the idea."

He sighs and pushes me back down on the chaise. I move to kneel between his legs, but his hand hits my shoulder. "Wait. Let me eat you again."

"You have an enormous appetite."

"It's not the only thing that's enormous," he says with a wink.

And then we move and shift so that he's mostly on his back, and I'm mostly on my side, and I'm entirely in a filthy new plane of heaven as I take him deep in my mouth, while he spreads my legs open and licks me again.

He's gentler this time, since I've already come. But it's just as good at this slower pace. It's good in its own decadent way. And it's better because I can feel him pulsing in my mouth. Then, again, he shifts us. He's flat on his back now, and I'm on top of him, my legs draped over his shoulders. He groans as he licks me more intensely, spreading my cheeks, his fingers kneading my ass as he works me over once more.

I'm on fire. I'm sizzling from head to toe. But I want his pleasure, too. I desperately want his release in my mouth, on my tongue, over my lips. Somehow, it turns into a wild, delirious race. We're loud and greedy, sloppy and hungry. I suck him deep, not stopping, never stopping, even when I feel my body race to the edge. But he's there first. His thighs tense under me. His cock thrusts deep in my mouth. His balls draw up in my hand.

And then I taste him, hot and salty. I swallow it down as he digs his fingers into my flesh and spears me with his tongue.

I cry out, and I'm lost once more in the sea of bliss, six stories above the ground as I come again, high above the city I love.

* * *

We don't stop there.

A little later, we're at the railing of the terrace, the neighbors across the river surely getting their peep show as I curl my hands tight around the iron posts. His hands wrap around my hips. I'm bent over for him, and he's fucking me hard. Relentlessly. The way I like it. I love feeling all of him, deep in me, pounding in me. *Bare.*

We had the safety talk, and I love that there's nothing between us now.

He grabs my hair, twisting it around his fist, and excitement bursts in me knowing he's going to tug hard. It's the thrill of what's to come. He pulls, yanking my neck back, and I yelp in pleasure. He goes deeper in me, and I moan like an animal, feeling him, feeling everything.

A smack on my ass. A swat on my cheek. Another tug

on my hair. His fingers on my clit. His cock hitting me in places I swear have never been touched, not like this, not so deeply.

It's raw and powerful, and he fucks me ruthlessly, fucking my whole body, and soon I can barely take all these sensations. They soar and fly all over my body, until they curl inward and burst.

One more powerful climax, and he follows me there.

* * *

"I'm not sure I can move ever again," I say, running my fingers down the fine hairs on his chest.

"I have nowhere to be, and I'm pretty sure I can call in for food. We don't need to leave."

I laugh lightly. "Good, because my legs are jelly."

"I'll order a few blankets, too. We'll camp out here. We'll wake up to croissants for breakfast, and we'll do it all again tomorrow." He dusts a kiss on my cheek. "And the next night, and the next."

He makes it sound so possible, as if time is a river, flowing endlessly. We'll dip our ladles in and drink it up, anytime, anywhere. We'll swallow it all, and we'll stay in this state of glittery bliss we both seem to want.

But we don't have next nights and next nights. Our time is closing in on itself.

I shift gears because right now I can't bear more talk that seduces me, that tricks me into thinking we're a river when we're a moat. I raise my face and meet his eyes as I tap-dance my fingers across his belly. "What's the story with the macarons from your list?"

He laughs and parks a hand under his head. "Ah, the macarons. By the way, kudos for not pronouncing it as if it rhymes with raccoons."

"Since it doesn't." I laugh. "And now, do tell."

"Mum's sister, Sophie, always bought me macarons for Christmas."

"That's rather sweet, and a little feminine, to be frank. Did she get you perfume, too?" I tease.

He pinches my nipple, and I pretend to yelp. "Speaking of perfume, you do know the way you smell is completely intoxicating, yeah?"

My heart dances a little flip-flop. Finally, a man who loves my perfume. "I'm not interested in living an unscented life," I say. "And I'm so glad I can wear perfume again."

He knits his brow. "You couldn't before?"

I shake my head. "My ex hated it. He said anything scented gave him a headache. I didn't want him to feel worse, so I stopped wearing it with him. I'm glad I don't have to hold back who I am with you."

"Did you have to hold back in other ways?"

I nod. "At times, yes. I was so consumed in his issues for the last year that I didn't devote as much time and energy to work as I wanted to. I wanted to rise in my career, and even though there weren't a ton of openings at my company at the time, I also didn't pursue any. I was so concerned about him."

"I don't believe you should ever hold someone back, someone you care about." There's a faint note of worry in his voice. "I wouldn't ever want to do that to you."

"You don't hold me back," I say, since he seems to need the reassurance right now. "You've only helped me."

"Good. It's the same for me. Also, I think I'm addicted to your *scented life*. Every day, it's like a discovery with you." He drops his nose to my neck. "Some days you smell like candy. Sometimes like caramel. There are days when you're a flower, or a garden. And sometimes you smell like sex."

I crack up. "That's probably just after you've fucked me."

He grins wickedly. "Yes, but sometimes you smell like sex because I'm thinking about fucking you." He taps his finger on his chin. "Maybe that's all the time, then."

"Oh, good. I want to walk around life smelling like a man's dirty dream."

He wraps his arms around my waist. "*My* dirty dream. And tonight, the way you smell has been driving me wild since I saw you in the garden."

A thrill races through me. "Really?"

Burying his nose in my hair, he inhales deeply. "You smell like . . . jasmine."

I freeze. "Shut up," I whisper.

He pulls back. "No. I mean it."

"That's in my perfume."

"So I was right." His smile is electric.

"You are." I tap his nose. "And you once said your sense of smell was wretched."

"Maybe it's come back because of you. Maybe you brought it back."

My heart thumps a little harder. I try to tell myself it's only the sense of smell. It's the one deemed least important. It's not as if he were blind or deaf and I magically returned those senses to him. But just as he's taught me how to experience the world through new words, perhaps I've shown him how to savor what makes the world delicious.

"Maybe I did. By the way, the perfume I'm wearing tonight?" My pitch rises in excitement.

He meets my gaze, waits for me to say more.

"It's a little something I cooked up myself."

His smile widens. "You made it? You crafted your own perfume?"

"It's something I'm playing around with," I say, and I can't mask a note of pride, not after the way he responded to it. "It's not done yet, but I'm testing out some formulations."

He growls sexily and kisses my neck. "My God, this has been my favorite. This can bring a man to his knees."

"Well, you were pretty randy tonight," I tease.

"I'll be even randier in the middle of the night."

I laugh and place a hand on his chest. "And you're avoiding the macarons. I want the full story of Aunt Sophie and the macarons."

He groans. "Sophie liked to give us things she thought we'd taken a liking to. Well, there was one time when she was babysitting us and she had her favorite lavender macarons with her, and since I have a sweet tooth, I gobbled them up. Ethan wouldn't touch them. Too purple, he said. She had to rustle up some cheese and crackers for him. For Christmas that year, she gave me lavender macarons and he got a cheese board."

"And he teased you about the macarons instead of you giving him a hard time about cheese?"

"Of course. He teased me relentlessly. Because they were girly. He thought lavender macarons was the height of having something on me."

"Did you even like them?"

Dragging a hand through his hair, he laughs. "Actually, they were pretty tasty, and the cheese was quite bland. But in his mind, I was the poor sod who had to suffer through the pretty little lavender macarons. And so, he managed to take the piss out of me even on his deathbed," Griffin says, and I tense for a second, thinking we're heading into darker waters with that last word. But he's smiling, and so I relax. He's not sinking under. He's laughing at the memory, and the sight of him like this feels like the sun warming my shoulders. He's coming out on the other side of grief.

He takes my hand in his. "He always made me laugh. And you're pretty funny, too, my gorgeous American beauty, who smells like sex and flowers and candy and everything I want in the world."

Something inside my heart rattles loose, like a bird escaping its cage. Flying free.

He's everything I want in the world, too.

I squeeze his fingers. "Hey, Archie."

"Hi, Judy."

With my free hand, I brush his hair away from his forehead. "I'm falling in love with you."

It's not hard to say. It doesn't take a lot of courage. It's just the truth, and I want him to know, no matter what comes next.

A smile crosses his lips, lighting him up like the night sky. "I'm madly in love with you."

"Yeah?" I smile dopily, and this is the bliss I want to live in. *This.* This feeling in my heart. The way I can't get close enough to him.

He nods and threads a hand in my hair. "I didn't mean for it to happen, but I was pretty much gone for you the day I met you."

My heart is glowing now, I'm sure, shining so brightly the airplanes above can spot me. "It was the accent, wasn't it?"

He laughs and shakes his head. "Nope. It was your attitude. You were so bold, and I loved it. I still do. I love it more every day. You made it so insanely impossible not to fall in love with you."

My smile can't be contained. "You really should have

made yourself more irresistible because it's pretty much the same for me."

But then my smile falters when I remember once more our inevitable ending. This can't last. This crazy, giddy feeling is a splash of fireworks in the summer sky. Awesome and sparkly and then gone in a heartbeat.

"I'm going to miss you like crazy. You know that, right?" he says, rubbing a thumb over my cheek.

"I know," I whisper.

"Like crazy," he repeats, his voice lower this time, tinged with sadness. "We only have two weeks left."

As if I'm not painfully aware of the days on the calendar scrolling by. "Fourteen days," I say solemnly.

"Let's make them amazing. It's all we can do, yeah?"

A lump rises high in my throat and threatens to yank down all the waterworks from my eyes, like the rainstorm I once longed for but am now trying to avoid. I swallow them whole. "Let's do it."

And because I can't take this anymore, I can't take the aching in my chest, I cover it up with a fierce kiss. I hold his face and claim his lips, and I pour every ounce of my sadness into his mouth.

It's needy and hungry, like a confirmation of what we both know. We're in love, and we're ending, and we'll make the most of these last two weeks, and we're going to be okay with all the oddities and curiosities in our love story. We're the out-of-place elephant on the roof of the church. We're a sundial that doesn't work. We're the clock that's only right twice a day. We're ice cream that tastes amazing, but we can't have it for every meal. We can't have it much longer at all.

When we break apart, he stretches out an arm, reaches for his jeans, and grabs something from his wallet. It's a notecard. An illustration of a bouquet of lilacs adorns the front.

"Open it," he tells me.

I do as I'm told and read his words out loud. "*Spend next weekend in Giverny with me. I want to go someplace with you where I've never been. I want to experience a place with you for the very first time. I want to take you there and see it through your eyes, too. Will you go with me?*"

My throat tightens, but I will myself to relax, speaking softly. "Obviously, the answer is yes."

I slip away to the bathroom, and when I return he does the same, but he rejoins me on the roof with a blanket, and he brings me close on the chaise.

When we wake, he taps my shoulder, squinting as dawn tugs at the cool morning sky.

"Number eight."

I furrow my brow.

"I get to cross it off. *Sleep under the stars.*"

"I thought 'sleep under the stars' was for traveling."

He shrugs and smiles. "I've decided this counts. Because it's for when we had to and when we wanted to. And this is a 'wanted to' situation."

This should make me happy. That he's bending. That he's flexible. That he found a loophole of sorts and made this night under the stars *count*. That I *count* enough to be something deep and meaningful to his dreams.

But I also know it means he's one step closer to packing his bags.

26

Griffin

The nights are intoxicating. We make love past midnight. We fall asleep together on the terrace. In the mornings, we stop at the bakery and grab croissants. We go to work together, and even at the office the moments feel deliciously stolen.

We slip out for lunches, and sometimes those lunches take place at nearby hotels. Yes, we have nooners, and they're fantastic. One evening, we return to Place du Tertre, and Joy finds the caricaturist.

"I'll commission your portrait," she says playfully, then asks the man to draw me.

Her French is great. She's not fluent. But she's learned so much so quickly that number six on my list is now crossed off. She's not a work-in-progress anymore. She's made it to where she wants to go.

She whispers something to the artist, and he laughs, then keeps sketching.

When the charcoal cartoon is finished, the man shows it to me. "My forehead is huge, and my hair is ten feet tall," I say with a laugh, then my eyes drift down. The man has drawn something in my hand. A lavender macaron.

I laugh louder. "This is brilliant. Now you're taking the piss out of me, too."

She wiggles her eyebrows. "Looks like I can get your goat, too."

The look of glee in her eyes cracks me up. Funny, how that's what Ethan predicted for this item.

7. Have your caricature drawn in Place du Tertre. Preferably a highly amusing image that would have made me laugh.

He was right, and as I check it off and we leave, I can't help but feel time speed even faster. Ruthlessly faster.

It's as if a bartender set a gigantic piña colada in front of me, and I'm not stopping until I finish the last sip. But that's the problem. We're nearing the end of the glass, and I desperately want to get drunk on another one.

*   *   *

When I run past the Salvador Dali sundial on Rue Saint-Jacques a few days later, I curse it. Because it doesn't work. It's a cruel trick, in a way, to make you think time doesn't matter.

That's a lie.

As my feet fly along the pavement, I find myself filled with regret. Regret that I didn't pursue something with Joy that first day I helped her with her flat. Regret that I didn't kiss her that Sunday afternoon at Île de la Cité. Regret over all the times I wanted to tell her how I felt, but I held back.

I'll never retrieve those lost hours now, and I want them more than anything. Because they'd mean more time with her. I want so much more. But the days don't stop coming just because we want to slow their pace.

Maybe that's why there are so many damn sundials in this city. It's like a *DaVinci Code* secret, and the revelation is that time is the only thing that matters. It's the ultimate non-renewable resource, and I've squandered it.

Soon, I run past Shakespeare and Company bookshop, where I meet up with Christian. He's been out of the country on an assignment for the last several days. He joins me for the final two miles. At last we finish, grab some waters, and down them at the river's edge, the sun dropping low in the afternoon sky, burning off the day. Spring is ending, and summer is weaving its way to the city, bringing blue skies and sunshine.

It doesn't suit my mood, so it pisses me off. I look away from the sun. "The other night. Joy's friend?" I ask, since I need to switch gears to something besides my situation. "Anything there?"

Christian wiggles his eyebrows. "Elise is great."

"And?"

"And nothing happened, to answer your real question."

"That's so unlike you."

"I've been known to hold out from time to time."

"She seemed keen on you. She must have wretched taste."

"The worst," he says, with a laugh. "And the keenness is mutual."

"Then why not make a go of it?"

He pushes his palms to the ground, the sign to slow down. "Settle down, mate. All in due time."

But that's rubbish. There's no time to waste. "Good thing you can see her whenever you want," I mutter.

He shrugs and scratches his jaw. "You could see Joy whenever you wanted."

"Yes, I have a private jet at my disposal to whisk me around the world."

"That's not what I mean, and you know it."

I glance at my watch, ignoring the comment. "I need to go pack some more."

"You're really doing this?"

"My lease is up."

He scoffs. "It's your mum's sister's flat."

"I told Sophie I was going. She's known for a couple of months—since I bought the plane ticket. I might be her nephew, but it's still real estate she can rent. And she's in the process of doing so."

Christian arches a brow. "Ten euros says you could get it back from her."

I look away from him, staring at the water, wishing for an answer. Hell, I wish Ethan had left an answer. A proviso, an addendum. *Hey, if you fall in love, ignore my wishes. Love, your little brother.*

"Doubtful. Besides, it is what it is."

He sighs and says nothing. He gazes at the water, too. A minute later, he speaks. "Listen, I'd get you a parting gift for when you go, but the best gift I can give you is this: I'll look out for your girl and make sure she isn't too sad."

I narrow my eyes.

"Calm your tits. I don't mean it like that. I'm not putting the moves on her. I mean I'll be there if she needs anyone to lift heavy objects or read a fucking contract."

I laugh and clap him on the back. "I appreciate that. Especially the heavy lifting. That's what friends are for."

When I head to my flat, I pack a few more boxes. I

don't have a lot of stuff. Most of my possessions I'm sending home to store at my parents'. The furniture is Sophie's.

As I stare at the walls, it's looking emptier, less lived in.

I guess item number one is truly coming to a close. *Live in Paris for a year.* It's nearly done. I sink down on the couch, log onto my laptop, and check on my flight reservation. My finger hovers over the *request a refund* button. Today's the last day to cancel without a fee.

"Damn it," I mutter. Why isn't my brother's postscript: *if you complete six or seven items, we'll call it good*?

I drop my head to my hand, wishing I was willing to ignore his requests. Wishing I knew how.

Honestly, for the first time ever, I want to be a selfish prick and say I've done enough. I want to say I've done all I can. I want the permission to choose Plan B, whatever the hell that is. I don't know what it would be, but maybe someone else does. Maybe someone who loves him as deeply as I do, and likely more. I call that person.

"Hi. Is everything okay?"

I smile. "Yes, Mum. Just packing and whatnot."

"How is it going?"

Awful. "Fine. How are you?"

"I'm great. Your dad and I are on our way to the movies. We're seeing a comedy. Can you believe it?"

I rub my ear as if there's water in it. "Come again?"

She laughs. "I've gone mad, right? We're going to a Dwayne Johnson film on a Friday night."

"Yes. When did you become a fan of Dwayne Johnson? For that matter, when did you start liking mainstream movies? I thought you were Miss Art Cinema."

"People change," she says, and I can hear a smile in her voice. Even from this distance I can tell it's authentic. "I found I needed comedy more than sad films with unhappy endings. I like popcorn flicks that make me laugh now."

"Including those with beefy actors, evidently."

"Seems that way," she says, laughing, then she clears her throat. "Griffin, love. I'm sorry to do this, but can we chat later?"

I sit up straighter, startled a bit. I can't remember a time when she's ended a call first. "Sure. Call me when you're through."

She takes a breath. "We're meeting some friends after. I'm not sure when I'll be home."

"Right. Of course. Have fun."

When I hang up, I'm left with the oddest feeling. I've been blown off by my parents, who are living their lives. My parents are heading to the cinema, going out with friends, and I'm sitting here in a nearly empty apartment, getting ready to leave the woman I love.

I click back to the web browser with my ticket on it. The clock on the browser ticks. A few more hours. I stare at the countdown for one minute, then another. My mind wanders to earlier today. To that broken sundial that gives no clue as to when you're supposed to be somewhere. I'd be aimless if I relied on that damn Dali.

But this computer clock?

This one says something, loud and clear.

It's not too late.

I straighten my shoulders, awareness hitting me hard and beautifully, all at once.

These are *found* hours. I stand and pace across the hardwood floor, weighing my options. Because I have options.

I have time.

Time to change my mind. Time to change my plans.

Time to ask Joy to go with me. Time to ask her to wait for me. Time to postpone this trip.

My heart thumps a little harder with that realization.

I look at my watch.

Joy has a dinner with Marisol tonight, and I'm meeting her at her place later. I won't squander these hours until I see her. I'll use them to devise a Plan B.

27

Joy

Marisol slices her chicken and brings a piece to her mouth. After she chews, she waves broadly behind her, indicating the small restaurant in the heart of St. Germain des Pres where we're dining. "I'm so glad you could have dinner tonight."

"This place is fantastic. The salad is one of the best I've had so far in Paris," I say in French, since I want to impress her.

She raises her eyebrows in appreciation. "Well said."

We chat more about the company, the products I'm overseeing, and life in Paris. I tell her I'm learning more French every day, and growing more comfortable with the language and the city.

She smiles. "I'm so glad you've enjoyed it."

I flinch for a moment, noticing she used the past tense. "I am enjoying it," I say, since I want to make sure she knows this is a present tense thing for me. Paris is where I live. Paris is what I love.

"And I've enjoyed having you here."

My chest pinches. I set my fork down when I hear that word. I part my lips, unsure where to start, but quickly decide that this company didn't hire me so I could beat around the bush. I choose directness. "Is there something I need to know?"

Marisol laughs nervously. "As a matter of fact," she says, setting down her utensil, "I wanted to have dinner with you to talk about what's next."

"Okay, let's talk," I say, since I signed a one-year contract, and I haven't even hit the three-month mark yet.

"First, we love your work."

My heart is a stone. It sinks heavily in my chest. That's the professional equivalent of *it's not you, it's me.* "Thank you." I tense, waiting for the shoe to drop.

She neatly tucks her blonde strands behind her ears. "And you've been absolutely amazing at L'Artisan. So much I don't want to see you go."

"I don't want to go," I say cautiously, as worry threads deeper into me.

She sighs heavily. "It pains me to do this, but I wanted to let you know the company will be making an offer to take you back to the United States."

My brain goes haywire. Lights and buttons and noises whir in a cacophony. This isn't in the script. This isn't what comes next. It's completely out of left field. "I don't understand."

"The parent company loves your work here, and they've been reading the progress reports I've sent." She flashes a rueful smile. "Perhaps that was my mistake. To let them know how very talented you are. Now, it seems there's been an opening in the Austin office, and they're going to offer it to you."

That's everything I wanted several months ago. I blink,

trying to process this unexpected news. "They are? To run the fragrance lab?"

She shakes her head. "No. To run the perfume lab."

My eyes widen. Everything around me slows to a crawl. The waiters walk sluggishly. Noise ceases, and the moment closes in on itself. That was my dream job forever. I swallow past the shock and try to restart the motor. "Are you serious?"

"Yes. That's the plan. There have been some changes at the corporate office, and they're putting together an offer for you. You'll likely have it on your desk on Monday morning. You have to know I'd love to keep you here if there were some way, but I don't know that we can compete with their offer. We're the same company, yes, but we operate somewhat autonomously as a French division, as you know. We don't yet have a perfume lab."

"And they do," I say, with something like wonder in my voice. I know that lab. I've stood outside the door. Gazed inside. Hoped and prayed and longed to lead it. I wouldn't just be a fragrance chemist. I'd be a perfume composer. That would be passion meeting work in the most wonderful coupling. My heart dares to speed up at the prospect of crafting what I love for my job.

I adore creating scents.

But I'm in love with perfume.

She raises her glass of water and takes a drink. "They have a great lab, and it seems when I wrote the report about your new formulation in progress, they were so impressed they wanted to take you from me."

Her lips curve into a frown. Then quickly, they quirk up in the most wistful congratulatory smile I've ever seen. She's letting me go, if I want to. She's giving me permission to go home.

But where is my home now?

* * *

On the walk home, I text my sister.

Joy: What would you do?

Allison: Don't make me choose!!!

Joy: But you helped me decide to go to France!

Allison: No, you already knew you wanted to go. I just confirmed what you wanted and gave you my support.

Joy: Stop being reasonable and logical. What should I do? Tell me!!!

Allison: You know I want to see you. You know I want you home. I'm not unbiased here. You can't ask me to decide.

Joy: I miss you.

Allison: I miss you.

Joy: But I love Paris.

Allison: There's that.

Joy: But honestly, will it be too sad for me to stay?

Allison: I don't know. I'd like to say it'll only be sad if you let it be that way.

Joy: But on the other hand, will I regret it if I don't take this chance?

Allison: Or will you regret it if you do?

Joy: OH MY GOD, THANK YOU FOR MAKING THIS HARDER.

Allison: Look at it this way—you are free to make this choice for YOU. Only for you. Not out of guilt, not out of obligation, not for a man, not for love, even. But for yourself. Do what your gut tells you.

Joy: My gut is quiet.

Allison: It'll speak soon enough.

Joy: But what if it just says it wants a croissant?

Allison: Then that's your answer. :)

But truthfully, the answer is I don't know.

* * *

Griffin's jaw drops. "Wow. That's tremendous, and totally unexpected."

"I know, right?" I say, as I flop down on the chaise on my terrace, the stars winking faintly above us.

"Are you going to take it?"

I shrug. "I don't know. I love it here so much. But the chance to run a perfume lab? That's a dream come true."

He nods thoughtfully, as if he's trying to convince himself. "Yeah, it would be amazing," he says, but the words come out funny, as if he's not sure how to say them.

"It would be amazing," I repeat, because that's simply a fact.

"When will you decide?" He takes my hand in his and rubs his thumb over my palm.

"Supposedly, I'll have the offer in a few more days."

Another nod. He swallows this time. Exhales. Scrubs a hand over his jaw. "That's . . ."

But he doesn't finish.

I squeeze his hand. "What would you do if you were me?"

I can ask him freely now since there's no pressure, no expectation. It's not as if we're going to be together when I make this choice. I can make this decision for me, and only me, as my sister said. I can choose my career without losing myself. I can rewrite the mistakes of my past.

"When would they want you back?" he asks, and the question comes out rough, as if there's gravel in his throat.

"Probably in a month, Marisol said." I furrow my brow. "Are you okay?"

"Yeah. Absolutely. Just, wow. This is wow," he says, tapping his fingers against his skull then spreading them wide open, as if this is blowing his mind. Maybe it is. "You'd move back home."

Home.

That word echoes between us. For a while it felt like home was here with him. But we're a vacation. We're an escape. He's not my home because he's leaving, and I may as well take off now, too. How fitting that we came together in Paris like a chemical reaction. We combusted, and now we're repelling. We're shooting away from our epicenter, both of us, drifting farther apart. Maybe it was meant to be this way.

Home isn't him and me.

It's elsewhere.

I squeeze his hand, asking again, "What would you do?"

"If it's your dream come true, you should go for it," he says, his voice thick, almost as if it's clogged with emotion. "I don't want to hold you back."

I tilt my head to the side, curiosity gripping me. "How would you hold me back? You won't even be here."

He winces and looks away.

"You won't be here, right?" I ask, pressing. For a split second, my heart leaps. Has he changed his mind? Is he staying? I wait patiently for an answer.

His eyes shine with sadness, and I try to read their meaning. But they're a language that won't translate for me.

So, I go first. Taking a tentative step. "If you were here, it would be different."

He closes his eyes and gathers me close.

Griffin

"I know," I say as I wrap her in my arms and press a kiss to her lips.

I can't risk speaking more. I can't say what I want to say. Because I can't let her make this choice for me. That goes against everything she needs in life. Everything I said I'd do. I told her I wouldn't hold her back. She doesn't want me to hold her back.

She wants to be free to make her own choices.

There's no asking her to stay.

There's no asking her to go with me for a few weeks.

There's no putting off the trip so we can steal a few more months.

There's only a "down the road."

When we pull apart, I offer that. "Maybe we can see each other in Texas someday."

"Yeah, maybe we can." She smiles faintly.

Sometimes, I suppose life insists we stick to Plan A.

Perhaps we were always inevitable—inevitably drawn together and inevitably thrust apart.

I can't ask her to stay in case I come back sooner. I can't ask her to have a go of things when I'm done. That's like asking her to live an unscented life.

Later, after another bittersweet coming together, I finish what I started.

With a few minutes to spare, I confirm the ticket once and for all. There is no Plan B.

* * *

We play a game on the train to Giverny on Saturday morning. I pretend I don't speak French at all. Joy has to do all the talking for us. She buys the tickets at the Saint-Lazare station. She gives them to the conductor and asks where the seats are. She inquires when we will arrive.

On the train, she buys two bottles of water, and she asks the woman across the aisle if she knows the time.

It's simple stuff, but she does it all.

"You might not even need this language anymore," I say with a smile, even though I find it immeasurably sad that she's learning French only to go home to a place where she won't need it.

"I'll find an enclave of French speakers in Austin," she says, and if that doesn't make it clear she's leaning toward returning to America, I don't know what does.

"So you're going back to the United States?" I ask as the train rattles into the station, nearly an hour from Paris.

"I don't know. It's hard to imagine a chance like this coming along again."

"That's the thing about chances. When they come your way, you need to take them."

She raises her bottle of water in a toast. My plastic bottle smacks against hers, making a dull echo.

Yes, it seems she's going back to the States.

We were always a moment in time.

And if I've learned anything from carrying this list with me for the last year—if I've learned anything about *why* I carry it—it's to make the most of every single moment. "Hey, Joy. What do you say we focus only on good things this weekend?"

"Only happy talk."

"Deal?"

"I'd say you've got a deal."

29

Joy

June is flamboyant.

This month is such a show-off, sashaying around with its warm breezes and lush flowers that blaze with red, cherry, and ruby petals. I snap photo upon photo of the kaleidoscope of flowers in Monet's garden. It's a pinwheel of colors. It's a painting. It's lushness come to life.

No wonder the artist drew such inspiration here.

"Once you see these gardens it's no surprise that he painted so many variations of them," I say as we wander past flowerbeds that do their best impression of emeralds, garnets, and sapphires.

"It makes you wonder how he painted anything else at all," Griffin says.

He points to the forest-green bridge, curling over a shimmering pond. Water lilies float on the surface, bobbing aimlessly as they luxuriate in the afternoon rays. "Where would you take it?"

"I'm not picky. I'd take it wherever it went. I'd like to see London at some point. Amsterdam, too. Tokyo sounds like fun. Everywhere. But I might also take it right back to the Jean-Paul Hévin chocolate shop in Paris. Or, wait." I snap my fingers. "I'd go to the market to buy walnuts and bread. I might even take it to Montmartre sometime and wander through the hilly streets." I stop in front of an archway lined with pink roses. "Where would you take the bridge?"

He rolls his eyes. "Don't ask a ridiculous question."

I furrow my brow. "Why is that ridiculous?"

He dots a kiss on my forehead. "I'd take it to see you, obviously." My skin warms, but I can't linger in the sentiment because he tugs on my hand. "Come on, we don't want to miss anything."

As we wander through extravagant foliage, making sure we don't miss a single petal, I ask him to tell me more about his parents. He talks about the new movie kick his mother is on, the efforts his dad makes to cook, and how they've mentioned recently they want to visit Iceland. Was the travel bug passed on to him from his parents, I ask? It's entirely possible, he says, and as he describes the trips he and his brother planned, something snags in my brain, like a moment of déjà vu. I'm not sure what it is, or how to place it, but my mind is desperately trying to latch on to *something*.

He seems to sense it, tilting his head. "You went quiet. What's on your mind?"

"Something feels eerily familiar about what you said. I can't figure it out, though."

"It'll come to you at three in the morning. That's when all the unsolved riddles are answered."

As we stroll under a weeping willow, the conversation

shifts again to another level of happy talk. "What makes you happiest?"

His answers come swiftly. "Running. Eating ice cream. Kissing you." He drops his voice to a whisper and moves his mouth near my ear. "Fucking you." I blush, and he raises his voice, continuing. "Hanging out with friends. Laughing. Finding something unexpected. What about you?"

"My sister. Shoes. Bright colors. Rain on cobbled streets. Kissing you in the rain on cobbled streets," I say, and his quick smile in response thrills me. "Endless gorgeous views. Lazy conversations that seem to meander nowhere, but let you truly know someone. And pretty, luxurious, decadent scents, but you know that."

"I do, and I know, too, that someday you'll be accepting an award for your creations."

I give him a look as if he's crazy.

"You will," he says, with cool confidence. "And you'll even accept it in French. I can see it so clearly."

I roll my eyes, even though, inside, my heart is springing, loving the idea.

"You're going to be at the top of your field. I believe that. You're going to be the best at what you do. You'll make some amazing new concoction. It'll be splashed all over magazines and necks and wrists, and it'll be this new infatuation that everyone wants."

"You're crazy." But I can't stop grinning.

"Someday, it'll happen."

I whip my head in the direction of a delicious smell. I'd know it anywhere. A flower, slinking its way unexpectedly around the weeping willow. "This is my favorite. Honeysuckle."

He leans in close and murmurs his appreciation. "This smells like desire."

"It does?"

He nods and brings his mouth to my neck, kissing my throat. "Completely."

And that's when I know what my concoction is missing. It's right under my nose.

My favorite.

When he pulls away, I tell him, "I came to Monet's garden to explore, and now I'm reminded of what I love."

"Me, too."

* * *

The room is dark. Moonlight filters through the open window, the curtains fluttering.

There are a million things that could be said, and yet there's nothing more to say. Nothing more to talk about. He runs his thumb over my bottom lip, then presses his mouth to mine. Every move tells me he's memorizing me, lingering in one of our last kisses.

It takes my breath away. It makes my knees weak.

This kiss is the reason kissing was invented. This kiss is the sky breaking open. It's why we run through the airport to stop a plane.

Why we *run, run, run* to stop a lover from leaving.

For this.

This kind of intimacy. This kind of need.

It's the reason we tell stories of how memories make us feel.

We separate, and he rakes his gaze over me from head to toe, as if he's photographing every curve, every dip and valley. Running his hands from my shoulders down my bare arms to my waist, he's imprinting the feel of me.

I'm his, and I'm not his at the same damn time. For tonight, for a few more nights only, I belong to him.

He strips me naked, and I take off all his clothes.

But we don't make love like two sad sacks. We make love the way we always have. Standing up, on all fours, bent over the bed.

We do it rough. We do it hard. We don't cry in sorrow. I only cry out when he makes me come again and again.

Then, when there's barely anything left in me? That's when he spreads me out on the bed and enters me slowly and luxuriously, hiking up my knees, going deeper, so much deeper than before.

"Please," I moan. I don't even know what I'm asking for. But I keep asking. "Please, please, please."

"Anything," he says. "I'll give you anything."

"You." It's a feather of a word.

He moves faster, harder, and my world blurs, spiraling away from me. "Come with me," he growls, and he says it over and over, in English this time, and I can't miss the extra layer of meaning I want to hear.

Come with me. Come with me. Come with me.

I want to tell him I would. I want to tell him I'm already there.

But then the pleasure takes over, curling and wrapping around me, and I clutch his shoulders, pulling him close, and I let go, sliding into blissful oblivion.

* * *

I blink open my eyes, and sit up straight. It's three in the morning. Griffin is sound asleep, peacefully snoozing. There is no more déjà vu. I know what was weighing on my mind in the garden.

The question now is how to tell him.

I search for the right moment on the train ride back to Paris. I'm still formulating the words in my head. The things I want to say. But it hardly feels like something that can wait. I test it out as the train rolls closer to the city.

"I was thinking about your bucket list in the middle of the night."

"You were?"

"I have a theory about it."

He arches a curious brow.

I tell him my theory.

When I'm done, he scoffs. "No. There's no way that's it." He squeezes my hand and does a one-eighty. "Now, have you decided what you're going to do when you get the job offer?"

The conversation is over just like that.

I put it out of my mind.

* * *

He's right. The job offer is amazing.

He's right about something else, too. Honeysuckle is the missing ingredient. I add it the next day, and work on the formulation until I can imagine it seducing me in a store when I spritz it on. I would buy this in buckets. I would buy it in droves. I would give it to everyone I know.

I bring a tester to Elise that night, and her brown eyes light up when she tries it. "And what are we going to do with this delicious sensual cocktail now?"

"I don't know."

She pats my shoulder. "That seems to be your answer lately. But I beg to differ."

"You do?"

She nods. "The job offer. The perfume. You say you don't know, but you do."

"Oh good. Please tell me."

She shakes her head, and smiles knowingly. "I'm not

going to tell you. You know." She taps my breastbone. "Right here, you know."

Maybe she's right. Perhaps I do know what I want. The trouble is, it's too hard for me to think about what I want when Griffin's still here. I don't want to make the same mistakes that I did before. Looking back, it was easy to think I was stuck with Richard. In reality, I let myself be pulled under. I let his madness cocoon me. I chose to be saddled with guilt and regret. Griffin was right that night when we wandered past the Eiffel Tower. *We always have a choice*, he said.

I'd thought I was doing the right thing at the time. I might very well have been doing the right thing.

But now, I can choose my path in my own way. I can make the choice that suits me. That's what I've needed—not to lose myself in a man.

When my man leaves, I'll decide.

30

Griffin

A soft gleam from the streetlamps casts its filter over the city. The light is one more thing that makes this city unique. The gaslight makes everything glow.

I'll miss it.

At the edge of the river, I raise a glass of champagne in honor of number ten.

10. Drink champagne along the Seine when you bid adieu. Check.

I clink the crystal flute to Joy's.

The next morning, I arrive at the airport as the blue light of dawn spreads over the sky. I check my bag, print my boarding pass, and sling my backpack on my shoulder.

As travelers race by, wheeling suitcases and pushing carts, Joy asks me once more if I have my sneakers for the race.

"Trainers," I tell her.

"Sneakers," she insists. "Say it once with me. *Sneakers.*"

I do as she asks because it makes her laugh, and that's a sound I want to bottle and keep with me.

Then her laughter ceases, and she cups my cheeks. "Be safe. Be good. Have so much fun. And drink lots of water during your marathon."

"I will."

"I'll check online to see how you did. So, no dropping out," she says, wagging her finger.

"I can email you and let you know, too," I say, a note of hope rising up as I offer once more to stay in touch. Somehow. Some way.

She shakes her head. "Not yet. Soon maybe."

"I know," I say softly and pull her close. We agreed to go silent for a few weeks. She said it would help her make her decision, and I have to respect that. She has to do this her way.

"I love you," I murmur into her hair.

"I love you," she says, kissing my neck, my jaw, my ear.

I cover her mouth with mine, kissing her hard one last time. I'm so glad I took a chance that terrified me when I kissed her the first time. I will never regret that. It gave me this fierce love.

When at last we separate, she brushes her hands over the neck of my shirt as if she's straightening it out. "Now, go." Her voice hitches. "Or I won't be able to say good-bye."

Don't. Don't say good-bye, then.

"I'm going. I'm going."

She runs her hand down my shirt. "I'll miss you, but you know that."

Ask me to stay. Ask me to stay and I will. I have no more willpower with you. If you ask me to stay, I won't go. "I'll miss you more than you can know."

She shakes her head, swallowing hard. "Go. You'll tempt me to steal you."

Steal me. I'll steal you, too.

"But I know you need to go. You need to do this. Do it. Then, come find me." She offers a faint smile on those last words, and I want to hold on to them for as long as I can.

"I will." I kiss her one more time, and then before either one of us can stop this, I walk away.

I don't know if I will find her. I don't know if she'll want me to, or if she'll have moved on to her new life in Texas with some cowboy or oil tycoon.

But I can't linger on that. I have a promise to keep. A promise that I won't hold her back.

An hour later, I board my flight, and as the jetliner rises in the sky, I close the shade, shut my eyes, and try in vain to blot out the regret.

31

Joy

It would be a bald-faced, big-ass lie if I looked in the mirror and said my eyes looked great. Today, they most decidedly do not. But that's what makeup is for. To cover the tears I shed on my rooftop last night. Of course I cried. Fat, salty tears. Of course I'm sad. Like someone punched a hole in my heart.

Of course I need Jackie O sunglasses today.

And yet, I'm not miserable.

I'm not devastated. I've had enough time to cry.

I've been processing the end of us since we began. We fell in love while we were breaking apart. We were simultaneously coming and going. Maybe, when you live through a bittersweet love, it makes the ending easier.

As Elise would say, some relationships only last for the blink of an eye, but that doesn't make them any less worthwhile.

It was worth it. Every moment was worth it.

And now it's Sunday evening, and I'm hungry.

I leave, and once I reach the street I ask my friend a question. "Google, where is the nearest brasserie with excellent salads?"

"The nearest brasserie with excellent salads is on Rue Jacob."

"Thank you," I say to my phone after we finish conversing in this country's native tongue.

I changed the settings recently. I no longer speak to Google in English. I talk to her in French, and she answers me in that language. It's our little bond, like a shrink-patient privilege.

I turn down the block, following her directions, and find she's taking me to one of the passages, a covered arcade. Mosaic tiles line the floor. The archways high above span two or three stories, and as I turn down the hall, I pass a shop peddling old-fashioned wooden toys, a bookstore with arty titles, and a shop selling maps.

I'm a digital woman. I don't want a map to pin to my wall, or a globe to spin. But as I gaze at a blue orb in the window, staring at the distance between Paris and Bali, I'm keenly aware of how big our world is.

And how very small, too.

The world is a massive place that can swallow you whole.

Or you can embrace its vastness, right along with little provincial joys. Like dinner at a fine café.

As I take a seat at the table, glancing at the empty chair across from me, I wait for the tears to lock up my throat. I steel myself for the vise in my chest, squeezing my heart.

But when the waiter arrives and asks me what I want

to drink, I've no time to mourn. I have to order, and I no longer have a safety net.

I ask what the specials are. He tells me. I ask how the chicken is prepared. I'm informed. And then I order a wine and a salad with sliced chicken. When the wine arrives, I thank him, and take a drink. I watch as couples stroll along the tiled floor, as mothers hold hands with daughters, as groups of friends scurry in search of a drink.

Once my food arrives, I take a photo and post it to my feed. #Dinnerinthecityoflights #oohlala #bonappetit. I want to remember this night. I want to look at this photo and recall how I feel right now, the sadness that lingers along with the happiness I was lucky enough to experience before I said good-bye to him.

And even though I'm alone, I don't feel lonely. Not as I eat, not as I walk down the street to my flat later that night, and not as I head into work the next day, saying hello to my colleagues and, for the most part, managing to talk to them in their language.

It's not perfect.

I'm not fluent.

But I'm good enough to get by now.

After work, I stop by the market to pick up some fruit, and as I head down the stalls, a gray-haired woman asks if I dropped a scarf. She points to a sky-blue silky scrap on the ground.

"That's mine. Thank you so much." I pick it up, and toss it around my neck, even though it's not cold. But it is fashionable, and for that reason alone, I adore this accessory.

I head to the Metro, navigating seamlessly. Later, after I climb the steps to my terrace, I drink in the city at my feet.

I know. I've always known.

I miss him fiercely. I miss him wildly. And I know what my heart wants—to have it all.

I call Elise and ask for her help.

32

Griffin

Sweat slicks down my chest.

The sun fires bullets of heat.

No relief is in sight.

I long to tear away from the group of runners and dive into the endless blue sea temptingly nearby. In the first ten days on the Indonesian island of Bali, I've already gone scuba diving, seen the waterfalls, and hiked up a mountain at dawn to view the sunrise. Each was enjoyable in its own way, and each was a little bit empty, too.

Because I did them alone.

But every day I've run, and now, when it counts, I hit the twenty-mile mark. My feet are screaming at me, shouting that they'll never permit this crap again. But even so, my heart is pounding strong, and I never let up. I run through the sand, I run through the town, and I run while the sun bakes my shoulders. Another mile, another one more, and I'm nearly there.

As the finish line looms into view, I expect to be clobbered with memories.

With images of my brother.

But those don't come.

Maybe this makes me selfish, but I'm grinning and muttering, "Holy crap. I'm doing it." I'm fulfilling the dream I had when I was younger. But life got in the way, and I never got around to running a race.

Now, I'm finishing a marathon.

One foot in front of the other.

Every footfall aches, and every footfall sings.

And when at last, more than a decade after I decided to do this, I cross the finish line, I punch the air. I let out a whoop. I feel like the most selfish prick in the world, but not for long, because it's too awesome a feeling to accomplish something I've always wanted to do.

As I slow my pace, grab some water that a volunteer hands to me, and walk instead of run, my whole life comes into focus.

Everything is bright and clear.

The past, and the future.

Bali is but a whisper.

Joy was right. Everything she told me on the train ride home from Giverny is true. Goose bumps rise on my skin with the staggering realization that the list was never about my brother.

33

Joy

Christian slaps his hands together like a coach, rubbing one palm against the other. "C'mon. You can do this, kid," he says, adopting an American accent and smacking me on the arm.

Elise rolls her eyes from her perch on her living room couch. It's seven thirty in the morning on a Monday, but they're prepping me one last time. "Oh, come on now. You're not her football coach."

He narrows his eyes. "You mean proper football, I trust? The world's greatest sport, right?"

Elise laughs. "Joy is from Texas. I mean the one you despise." She turns to me. "From the top."

I take a deep, calming breath. I square my shoulders. I practice once more what I want to say to Marisol when I meet with her in two more hours.

My words aren't what I'd say if I had Griffin translating

for me. I don't have him to rely on. I have to go it alone. I keep it simple so I can say it myself.

When I'm done, they both slow clap.

"You're ready," Elise declares. "Now go convince her to let you have it all."

* * *

I show Marisol the tester bottle. "This is the perfume I made over the past three months. I want to introduce it here in France. I want to keep finding ways to bring innovation to L'Artisan. I want to introduce new products here, and to help oversee them. If you'll have me, I want to stay. If you like this mix, I'll do everything I can to make it a success for you."

Marisol blinks. "You want to stay?" She points to her desk. "Here, in Paris?"

Nerves fly up my throat. I want to stay so desperately. I came to Paris for a new experience, and that experience has changed me. I didn't just fall in love with Griffin. I fell in love with the city. I fell in love with a whole new language. Paris feels like home.

"I'm not done with Paris. And I hope Paris isn't done with me."

Marisol squeals. It's the strangest sound from such a proper woman. But she actually squeaks, then rises from her chair in a flurry. She strides over to me and wraps me in an unexpected hug. "I accept the continuation of your employment."

When it comes to chances that don't come around often, this is the one I'd most regret if I let it pass by —the chance to stay here.

I don't doubt that it would be wonderful to run a perfume lab in Austin. But here in front of me, I can keep learning a whole new language. A whole new way of living. I might not be overseeing a fleet of scents, but if I can guide one to market, it'll be more than a dream come true.

She dangles the glass bottle between two fingers. "By the way, do you have a name for your composition?"

I have a name, and I have a story. It is all my bitter-sweet days when I wander across the cobblestone streets, damp with rain. It is the sweet floral mists from the flower market that enchant my senses. It is the chocolate notes that waft through the air at a shop that's close to heaven. It's the smell of the first kiss and a last kiss. It is the promise that somehow, someday we will meet again. "For now, I'm calling it Come What May."

She nods and smiles. "I like that. It's both sad and happy at the same time, but it ends on a dash of hope."

Yes, that sounds like exactly what it is.

When I leave the office that night, return to my street, open the pink door, and climb the uneven eighty-four steps, I know what the woman in the pink-checkered suit on the plane told me has come true.

Paris is where you go to reinvent yourself.

34

Griffin

Sometimes something is so obvious, you're not sure how you missed it.

But that's because it was hidden in plain sight.

Like all those damn angels that followed me around the city while I never noticed them.

That evening, I dig my toes into the coolest sand, the ocean lapping at my feet. As I watch the stars winking in the sky, I read between the lines on the list I memorized long ago.

Ten items and a postscript.

A bucket list.

A dying wish.

But it's not that at all, it turns out.

Joy unlocked the code before I did. She discovered the real meaning, but I wasn't ready to hear it. I dismissed her theory, stuffing it away. It took running twenty-six miles halfway around the world to see that it was never a bucket list I carried with me.

It was instructions for living.

For how to live without him.

Ethan didn't ask me to complete those ten items. He only gave me this list when I told him I'd do anything for him, when I begged him for it. He'd looked at me, studied my eyes, and knew what I needed. Something to live for. Reasons to be happy without him.

"Okay. Let's do it. One last list."

It was a list for me, a list of all my hopes and dreams. It was guidelines on how to live a rich and beautiful life. He wrote me a treasure map for how to make it through his death. He was so clever, even up until the end. He knew I'd need a nudge, so my dreams were veiled in the guise of his dying wishes.

I'm the one who wanted to run a marathon. He'd already completed one.

I'm the one who longed to live in Paris, and he made sure I did it.

He told me to travel the world because I'd led the charge in planning our adventures when we were kids.

He knew I'd want to laugh with friends, so he put the caricature item on the list. He knew I'd want to help others, so he put that on the rules to live by, too.

I have lived most of these ten wishes.

But I don't want to live all of them anymore. I'm not consumed with the same clawing need to visit all the corners of the world anymore. I no longer suffer from an incurable case of wanderlust.

I've been cured. I uncovered a new dream right before my eyes.

I have a new wish—to be with the woman I love, wherever she is.

I wanted her to ask me to stay, but that's not enough. I need to put my heart on the line for her. She never held me back from going, and I won't hold myself back any longer. If she's going to be in Texas, that's where I'll go.

But there's one more thing on the list I need to fulfill.

I need to take a chance that terrifies me.

I thought I'd done that. I thought that pursuing Joy counted. But even when I crossed it off, it never fit because wanting to be with Joy never terrified me.

The true risk is letting go of this list and flying without an instruction manual. Navigating without a map. But the time has come to find my own way. I raise an imaginary glass like I did when I said good-bye to Paris, but now I'm saying good-bye to the man I was—a man motivated by a promise, driven by the past.

It's time to choose something entirely new. Something no one wrote down. But it's what I want most in the world.

Now, I need to figure out how quickly I can get to Texas.

35

Joy

Lest anyone think I'm just a lush who loves the vino, let the record reflect that I do consume my morning fuel roof-side, too.

I bring the ceramic mug to my lips, and down some of the life-sustaining beverage as I watch the city wake up. Boats glide along the water, and the morning mist burns away from the tower. I glance at my phone. I'm due at the office in an hour, and I need to make it on time. I head to the stairs, stopping briefly at the chaise. Images flash and pop of all the dirty deeds this chair has witnessed.

"Oh, the stories you could tell," I say in a flirty whisper, bending down to kiss the top of the pillow as I pretend the chair can talk.

A piece of paper catches my eye.

Tilting my head, I study the corner of a flowered card poking out from beneath the lounge. I reach underneath and find the card Griffin gave me when he invited me to Giverny for the weekend. Did I leave it here on the roof that night when he asked me to go? I suppose it's possible.

I pick it up and head down the steps, flicking it open when I reach the living room.

I stumble and grab hold of the railing, gasping as I read.

Words that shock me.

Words that aren't an invitation to Giverny at all.

This is another card entirely. Maybe it fell out of his pocket? Maybe he always intended for me to discover it? Or was it never meant to be seen?

I run my finger over the blue ink of his handwriting.

A part of me wants to stay with you. A part of me wants you to ask me to. If you did, I'd do it. Cancel the trip, curl up with you, and be happier than I've ever been before. That's how I am with you. And another piece of me wants to steal you away with me so we can be together. It feels impossible, but it also doesn't. Say I'm not crazy.

My heart hammers against my rib cage. It rattles the bars. It jumps and bangs, begging me to listen. He wanted to stay with me before he knew about my job offer. He wanted to stay even after he learned of it. As I flash back to the night after my dinner with Marisol, I recall his face perfectly, the sadness in his eyes, the thickness in his voice.

"I don't want to hold you back," he'd told me.

"How would you hold me back? You won't even be here," I'd said.

When he didn't answer, I'd pushed back. *"You won't be here, right?"* I remember hoping, wishing his mind had changed.

Had it already? Had he planned to cancel his trip but

then stopped when he learned of my job offer? My heart is a cyclone of emotions. It spins and whips, and there's only one thing to do.

Run to the computer.

Tell him.

Take a chance.

Bring him home.

Scrambling to my laptop I flip it open, find his email, and tap out a message.

Re: You're not crazy

On the terrace, I found a card you never gave me. It made me fall a little bit more for you, if that's even possible. But it is, and that reminds me that I don't think we're impossible at all. I'm still here. I'll be here. I'll be waiting for you.

Joy

* * *

He doesn't reply. For a minute. Then another five minutes. Ten godforsaken minutes later, my inbox is still stupidly empty. It doesn't replenish itself in the next twenty minutes with anything but offers for coupons and news of shoe sales while I finish getting ready and head to work.

At the office, it's radio silent.

By noon, I've nearly worn out the fingerprint on my index finger from hitting refresh constantly. Still no reply. Not a word, not a peep.

By the end of the day, my nerves are frayed thin, my emotions strung tight, and my sister is surely spent from replying to messages from me all day long, even though it's seven hours earlier where she is.

I grant her a reprieve from man-talk.

Joy: Enough about boys. When will you come visit me? The French fries here are even better.

Allison: *French* fries. Snort. I should hope so.

Joy: Answer the question.

Allison: When you invite me. :)

Joy: You're invited. Catch the next plane!

Allison: How about next month instead?

Joy: Deal.

Allison: Also, please arrange numerous dates with hot French men for us.

But I won't be riding shotgun on that request. There's only one hot Frenchman I want, and he's British, too.

I set my phone down and return to my work. Charles helps me with the final formulations for Come What May. We speak in a mix of French and English, and we've finally figured out how to communicate without burning down the lab.

When I leave that evening, I nearly rip my phone from my purse to check it again. Outside the building, I smack into Elise.

"You're stalking me?" I tease.

"I am. Now, I want you to go home, put on a pretty dress, and wear your finest shoes, because I'm taking you out tonight to celebrate."

"You could have called and told me that."

She links her arm with mine while I steal a glance at my email. No replies. "I know. But that's not my way. I wanted to see your face."

"I like your face, too."

"Besides, it's my job to appear randomly to remind you why you stayed in Paris. Because you have friends here, and a rich and lovely life."

"You're acting odd today."

"I'm never odd."

She strolls home with me and we chat, catching up on her work and mine, then admiring displays in windows, pointing out where we want to eat the next weekend. I ask her about Christian and whether she's ever going to tell me if there's something going on between them.

She winks. "Maybe. Maybe there is."

But we've reached my home. "Do you want to come upstairs and wait?"

She shakes her head and gives me a kiss on each cheek. "I'll wait for you at the café at the corner."

I walk upstairs, my head bent over the phone the whole time. It's been more than eleven hours. What on earth is Griffin doing? Zip-lining with monkeys? Swimming with dolphins? Lolling on the beach with beautiful women in bikinis?

I howl in jealousy at the thought.

Twenty minutes later, I text Elise that I'm on my way down. It's late June, and this peach sundress I put on is perfect for a night out with friends. Strappy sandals are on my feet, and summer is in the air when I push open the pink door.

I stop in my tracks.

All the breath in my body escapes me. My eyes are playing tricks on me because this only happens in the movies.

36

Griffin

I cross the street, wild excitement stirring inside me. It's the thrill of hope. It's the rush of a brand-new start. It's everything I feel when I see her face—exuberance, desire, and this great and wild love.

She stands, dazed, in front of her pink doorway, eyes wide open. My Joy, framed by the boldest of bold colors, just the way she likes it. A vision in peach and pink and all that red spilling over her shoulders.

When I reach her, I say two simple words. "*Bon soir.*"

"*Bon soir.*" It comes out breathy, full of wonder.

Her lips part as if she's trying to say more, but no words come. Instead, she raises her hand, tugs at my shirt, then flings her arms around me. I reciprocate, pulling her close.

She melts against me, and it feels spectacular. This is a welcome home the likes of which men climb mountains for. I'm not sure what I did to deserve it, but as she draws her nose down my neck, inhaling me in the way that only she can, I know I'll take it.

Every day.

She lets her arms fall from me, places her hands on my chest, and looks in my eyes. Her gaze is curious, quizzical. "Did you get my email?"

I nod. "About an hour and a half ago, when I landed. There was no Wi-Fi on the seventeen-hour flight."

Her brow furrows. "Wait. What? You only got my email an hour ago and you're here?" She points to the ground, as if she needs to make sure I know where we are.

But I know. Hell, do I ever know where I am and where I want to be.

"I was already on my way," I say, running a hand up her bare arm. I'm a starving man. I've gone too long without touching her. I need contact. Need to feel her skin. She shivers as my fingers reach her shoulder. "I thought you were in Texas. I was sure you'd taken the job there, and I was about to buy a ticket all the way from Bali to Austin."

"You were?" she whispers.

"I was. I was going to find you wherever you were."

"In Texas?"

"You say that like it's the height of insanity."

She shakes her head as if she's shaking off water. "I'm just surprised."

"Joy, if you'd gone to Mount Everest I'd have purchased a ticket there. If you were in the Arctic Circle, that's where I'd have traveled to."

A grin crosses her lips and seems intent on staying there. "How'd you wind up here, then?"

I brush my fingers back down to her wrist. "I figured it would be wiser to call a friend before I bought a ticket, so

I rang Christian and he told me you'd decided to stay, so I came back."

"Because of me?" Her voice wobbles.

I thread my fingers through hers, clasping tight. She squeezes back. "Yes. Because of you. It's all because of you. You were right on the train, and I wasn't ready to hear it then. I had to fly five thousand miles and run another twenty-six before I was whacked with the it's-so-damn-obvious stick."

"Did it hurt?" she asks playfully, and that pitch-perfect dry sense of humor is part and parcel of why I'd fly five thousand miles again and again to see her.

"It felt good. Sometimes a man needs to be whacked with the sheer obviousness of his life. It was so crystal clear, and now I have a new list. Do you want to hear it?"

"I do."

I let go of her hand, take out a sheet of paper from my pocket, unfold it, and clear my throat.

Five things I want to do . . .

1. Be with you.
2. Love you every day.
3. Give you heaps and heaps of screaming orgasms whenever you want.
4. Wander the world with you, or just explore Paris together. Whatever the world is to you, I want to be by your side.
5. Drink champagne on your rooftop as we say good-bye to the crazy idea that we weren't meant to last, because we are.

P.S. This list also includes the ongoing, always and forevermore invitation to visit chocolate shops, bakeries, and any market you wish whenever you wish, as well as more orgasms.

P.P.S. Have I mentioned orgasms?

She throws her arms around my neck once more. "I do believe you can have it all."

I arch an eyebrow. "Are you saying you want to have your cake and eat it, too?"

"Cake is always a good idea."

"So is falling in love. So is staying in love. So is staying together. What do you say we do that?"

She quirks up her lips, and her bright green eyes twinkle with mischief. When she answers me, she's not speaking the language she knows best. "I'd say you have yourself a deal."

I cup her cheeks, hold her face, and kiss her. Like that, we make the world disappear. It's us, kissing on the street, coming back together.

Coming home.

She's who I always want to return to. Every night.

When at last we pull apart, she's breathless and flushed. It's a look I like seeing on her. It's a look I want to make sure she always wears.

She nibbles on one corner of her lips and glances at her watch. "Elise is waiting for me. I should go tell her you're having me for dinner."

I laugh. "She already knows."

"What?"

"I might have been impulsive in surprising you. But I'm not stupid. I called my mate, he called your friend, and they made sure you'd be home when I was arriving."

"You clever man," she says appreciatively as she

unlocks the pink door. "I guess she's not waiting for me at the café on the corner."

"No, I don't think she is."

"So, seventeen hours on a plane," she muses as she tugs me to the staircase. "You must be exhausted."

"Yes. I want to go to sleep straight away," I say drily, since nothing could be further from the truth. I slept soundly on the plane. "Any chance I could crash here?"

She laughs. "Yes, feel free to crash on my couch. I'll be quiet."

"You've never been quiet," I say, and I smack her ass as she heads up the steps.

"You're the one to blame for all my noise."

"I'd like to always be the one to blame for that."

Soon, we're up all those damn stairs. The door bangs shut, and our hands grab at each other. I can't stop kissing her, can't stop touching her.

"I don't know how I thought I could do without you," I say.

"Don't then."

I push up her skirt, tug down her knickers, and press her hard to the wall. In seconds, my jeans are undone, and I push in as her body welcomes me. I still when I'm inside her, letting the fantastic reality of my life set in. I'm back where I belong.

A shudder racks my body as I start to move in her. She ropes her hands around my neck and pulls my face closer, kissing me the whole time. Her red lips never stop claiming mine—rough, fierce, demanding.

I hike up her leg and wrap it around my hip, going deeper. She moans, loud and long, noisy, like she promised she'd be. She sounds like she's getting lost in us again. Like she did every time. Like I want her to do all the time. I want her to get lost with me so I can be the one to find her.

Soon, she's trembling, and I watch as her pleasure moves through her, as she dissolves into my arms, and before I know it, I follow her there, and we come back together.

"Thanks for the postscript," she murmurs.

I laugh as I tug her close. "You always get the postscript."

* * *

After another time, and yet another, we flop onto her couch, spent. She plays with my hair, and my stomach growls. "You must be hungry," she says.

I lift up her skirt. "Why, yes, let's do it again."

She swats at me. "Hungry for dinner."

"Sure."

Fifteen minutes later, we're at the café around the corner, where she orders for us then sets down her menu. "So, you're back in Paris. Did Sophie keep her place for you?"

I shake my head. "She rented it."

Joy taps her chin. "Hmm. Interesting."

"Is that interesting?"

"You've come back to Paris without a place to live. You must really like me."

"Hmm. I guess I do."

"It's going to be hard living on the streets, isn't it?"

"So rough. But I'll make do."

"I can toss you a blanket if you need."

"Oh, please, don't put yourself out. I have a bench I plan to sleep under."

"That sounds fabulous." She spreads her napkin on her lap. "But just in case that doesn't work out . . ."

"You have something else in mind?"

She shrugs as she smirks. "I suppose you could live with me."

I reach for her hand. "I would love to climb eighty-four steps every day and every night with you."

She narrows her eyes, stares at me. "You're not going to run off to Iceland or Russia or the Amazon, are you?"

"I have everything I want right here in front of me."

"Good. Because I'm not going anywhere. Turns out this city suits me."

"It suits you perfectly."

She slides her hand across the table. "Stay with me."

"I will."

As we dine, and talk, and laugh, and then stroll back to our home, I'm aware every moment that this is exactly where I want to be.

Here, now, and for always.

EPILOGUE

Joy

I wrap a ruby-red scarf tighter around my neck and pull a white knit cap over my red hair. December has arrived, bringing snowfalls, nights in front of the fireplace, and the endless need to warm up under the covers.

Now, though, I'm venturing outdoors.

Sometimes, on Saturday afternoons, I surprise Griffin.

I like to show up on the tail end of his tours.

He's still translating, but he's also doing something he loves even more. He's introducing tourists and natives alike to the curiosities of Paris that are hidden in plain sight. He's not operating boat rides along the Seine, or leading trips through the Louvre. Others can do that better and enjoy it more, he has said.

But there's no one—not a soul in the whole wide world—who knows the corners of Paris better than him, the spots with unexpected delights that can be found all over this metropolis. A few times a day, he'll guide travelers to the oddities of our city, showing them the street that runs under a residence in the 17th arrondissement, bizarre sculptures that jut out of buildings, sundials that do work, and sundials that don't do their jobs at all. At other times, he mixes up his repertoire and takes his customers on tours of the best chocolate shops, always ending at what I call heaven with a cup of hot chocolate.

That was my idea. After all, who doesn't like chocolate?

Sometimes he leads tours in Spanish, sometimes in French, often in English, and occasionally in Portuguese, since he now knows that language.

That was his dream, and he stayed the course.

Perhaps he was always meant to be an explorer. His journeys have simply become more local, in the city we both now call home. But we've managed to break out our passports a few times in the last several months. We're not world travelers, but we saw the Northern Lights in Iceland, and they were as majestic as a queen's glittery crown. We flew to Copenhagen last month and wandered through the charming streets, and we're taking off for Tokyo in a few months to finally see what Griffin calls the neon city.

"It's more fun going places with you," he'd said when we watched the stars in the cool night sky near the Arctic Circle.

"Everything's better together," I'd replied.

Life has been good here, too. Come What May is rolling out in time for the Christmas season, and I'm hopeful it'll be a hit. My sister and parents will be visiting for the holidays, and I plan to take them shopping at all my favorite outdoor markets and the most fantastic department stores, too. After that, Griffin and I will take the train to London to see his parents for New Year's.

Really, what more could an American girl in Paris ask for? I'm speaking the language capably every day, mixing up concoctions in the lab during my working hours, and coming home to a man who makes me laugh, who makes me smile, and who loves to whisk me away. Sometimes, we take a trip around the world and we don't even have to go anywhere. That's what making love with him feels like.

I guess I've always been a goner for a man with an English accent.

And now I get to listen to one pretty much whenever I want.

Yes, that's what I call having it all.

Today, I join in when he shows a group of Americans from San Francisco the angel I spotted in Île de la Cité one fine Sunday afternoon many months ago.

"I'm not sure this angel means anything," he says, pointing to the cherub carved into stone above an awning. "But it means something to me. The woman I love noticed it one day when we ate ice cream and wandered these streets. I'd never seen it before, not in all my travels. I learned then that some things are right in front of us, and we just have to look up."

He gives them all a few moments to look up, snap photos, then say good-bye.

When they disperse, he takes my arm and links it through his. I ask how his day has been.

"You tell me, you little spy."

"I like to keep you on your toes with my random appearances."

"And you do. You always do."

I raise my face and meet his gaze. "What do you want to do tonight?"

He narrows his brow as if considering my question. "Sip champagne on the rooftop?"

"That's always a good idea," I say as we stroll by the oldest clock in Paris.

The golden hands tick tock their way around the face. "That clock is when I knew I wanted to be with you," he says, a happily wistful tone to his voice.

"It is?"

He nods. "I remember thinking about time, and how we can't ever retrieve lost hours. But we can make the most of the hours in front of us, and I wanted to spend those with you. It took me a while to sort out how that would happen. But now I have, and I want to keep savoring every minute." He takes a beat, snapping his fingers as if he's remembering something recently forgotten. "That reminds me. I had another idea for what to do tonight."

"What's that?"

He drops to one knee and flips open a maroon velvet box. My heart beats so loudly I can hear it, I swear, and a rush of breath escapes my lungs. Warmth spreads all over me as I gaze at a gorgeous diamond solitaire.

"Let's get engaged tonight," he says, holding my gaze. "I love you madly, Joy. I love you so much I'd follow you around the world. I'd make you the center of my world. That's what you are to me, and as we've made new dreams together, I have one more. Item number six. For you to be my wife."

My smile is as wide as the river. I drop to my knees, throw my arms around his neck, and cry the happiest tears of my life. I murmur one word as my answer. "*Oui.*"

Fitting that it's the same sound as an English word I rather love.

We.

That's what we are.

ANOTHER EPILOGUE

Griffin
Six months later

The bubbly liquid slides down the crystal flute, and I hand it to Joy, setting the bottle on the table.

She raises her glass as the sunset flares behind her, the last remnants of the day tugging streaks of deep pink into the horizon.

"And what are we toasting to tonight, Mr. Thomas?"

I clink my glass to hers. "Hmm. Could it be that you now have three last names?"

She leans her head back and laughs, a rich, bright laugh that I love. "Assuming I use them all."

"Oh, please. What could be better than introducing yourself as Joy Danvers-Lively-Thomas, the best perfumer in the world?"

"That does have a nice ring to it," she says, taking a drink of the champagne.

"Speaking of rings . . ." I hold up my hand, the platinum band on it sparkling under the fading light, then thread my fingers with hers. I take another drink, set the glass down, and pull her next to me on the chaise. "That takes care of number five on my list."

Drink champagne on your rooftop when we say good-bye to the crazy idea that we weren't meant to last, because we are. Check.

She brushes her lips to mine. "Can I have my postscript now, please?"

"You can always have that."

And I make sure she always does.

THE END

Curious about Christian and Elise? They have a story to tell in PART-TIME LOVER, releasing in June! Read on for more on that standalone romance! Also, be sure to check out COME AS YOU ARE, a sexy, swoony standalone romance with a masquerade ball, a Cinderella twist, and a billionaire hero who will sweep you off your feet. You can sign up directly for my newsletter to receive an alert when these sexy new books are available!

Upcoming Releases

ABOUT PART-TIME LOVER...

I'll say this about Christian — he made one hell of a first impression. When I first saw the strapping man, he was doing handstands naked on a dock along the canal. His crown jewels were far more entertaining than anything else I'd seen on the boat tour, so I did what any curious woman would do — I took his photo. I might have looked at the shot a few dozen times. Little did I know I'd meet him again, a year later, at a secret garden bar in the heart of the city, where I'd learn that his mind and his mouth were even more captivating. But given the way my heart had been trampled, I wanted only a simple deal — No strings. No expectations.

Our arrangement worked well enough until the day I needed a lot more from him...

* * *

Let me just say, this whole part-time lover thing was her idea. I'd have gone all-in from the start, but hey, when a gorgeous, brilliant woman invites you into her bed, and only her bed...well, I said yes.

But then, one hysterical phone call from my brother later, begging me to find myself a wife so grandfather's business stays in the family, and I need a promotion with Elise. **Turns out a full-time husband suits her needs too,** and a temporary marriage of convenience ought to do the trick, until we can simply untie the knot...

As long as no one finds out...
  As long as no one gets hurt...

As long as no one falls in love...

But our ending was one I never saw coming.

PART-TIME LOVER will be available everywhere!

Chapter One
   Elise

A year ago

Something about the last night in a foreign city makes you want to do crazy things. You want to drink it all in, and taste every single dish on the menu. After all, tomorrow you'll be gone.

Left with only memories.

The last night is the last stop on the merry-go-round of memory-making.

The last afternoon is, too, and as the sun careens mercilessly towards the horizon, it's a reminder that I need to jam everything in.

"Do you feel like going a little bit wild?" I ask Veronica.

She wiggles her eyebrows. "If you mean day drinking, we've already done that."

I wag my finger as we stroll down the middle of a cobbled street. "One glass of wine at lunch does not constitute day drinking."

"No? That seems the very definition."

I link an arm through hers. "One glass is simply a beverage at lunch. The meter doesn't start on day drinking until you hit two glasses, silly goose."

"How good to know the scale for lushness," she says drily as she stops to stare a handbag in the Prada store window.

I give her a few seconds to worship at the altar of designer goods. "In any case, I was thinking we ought to do something we've never done before."

She snaps her gaze from the far-too-expensive leather item she'll never buy, and presses a hand demurely to her chest, batting her hazel eyes innocently. "I'm not that kind of girl."

I laugh. "As if."

"I know. You like your sausage too much."

"As do you. You're practically a butcher," I say as we sidestep a pair of strapping, chiseled blond men, who look like twin models for "Scandinavian Design's Catalogue of Men—Denmark" edition. Their blue eyes linger on both of us, and one smiles and offers a confident, "Hello."

"Hello to you, too," I say with a grin.

They continue in their direction, and we head in ours. "Should we just wander down the streets and say hello to random hot men?" Veronica offers.

"I don't think that's an entirely bad idea, but no, that's not my notion of wild."

This urge to have one wild night is in complete contrast to the purpose of the three-days-in-Copenhagen getaway Veronica insisted I needed.

It's been a year since . . .

I shake away the dark thought.

Anniversaries of horrible days require trips. And day drinking. And refocusing on things that you control.

"If I want to explore the travel sector more at work, I need to know even more about this city, so I can advertise it better. What if we take one of those buffet boat tours?"

She laughs. "What's a buffet boat tour?"

"A buffet of landmarks. All-your-eyes-can-eat." As we near the wide square at the end of the block, I point to the red booth advertising canal tours. I play my ace. "It's like a crash course in Copenhagen, and we'll make sure we haven't missed a single thing. It'll help me win new business. You know I need to focus on work."

She flashes a smile of understanding. "Anything for you when you prey on my sympathies." She marches up to the fire-engine red booth and purchases two tickets for the next tour, and we head down the concrete steps to the boat.

The blond guide with aviator shades and shoulder-length hair flashes a bright smile as we step onboard, his nametag glinting in the afternoon sun. "Good afternoon, ladies."

"Lars, she's no lady." Veronica points to me and winks.

"Ladies or not, you're both welcome on my ship as long as you promise to enjoy the sights."

"We will. Also, you're handsome, Lars." Veronica is shamelessly a flirt.

"Thank you very much, and I'll enjoy the sights as well." It seems Lars is a flirt, too. His blue-eyed gaze lingers on my friend with the hourglass figure and pretty eyes as we take our seats.

We wait for the boat to fill, but only a handful of others join us. An older couple, sports hats, cameras on their necks, and matching *I Heart Copenhagen* sweatshirts. There are also a gaggle of twenty-something women with long legs and college sweatshirts, and some Japanese tourists.

I lean back in the cushioned seat, dropping my sunglasses to shield my eyes as the boat peels away from the dock. As we slide over the placid water, Lars regales us with tales of royal families and scandals, pointing out the city's sights. I lean closer to Veronica and whisper, "Will you pick up where you left off with the handsome boat captain?"

Lars suffers from an affliction common to many men in Denmark. He's a cut above average in the looks department. Let the record reflect, the Danes make the best-looking men.

"Of course. I'm going to talk to him when the tour ends."

"Excellent. I love your planning skills."

The boat slides under another bridge then motors through a more residential area, passing homes on the water, and private docks every few feet. My eyes hungrily eat up the view. My current hometown of Paris is my love, but I could get used to weekends in Copenhagen. It's a delightful mix of old and new, like a Swiss alpine town mated with a futuristic sky-rise city.

As I gaze at the sun-soaked homes, I imagine lazy afternoons drinking strong coffee on the deck, reading delicious tales under the rays. That seems like a recipe for happiness for the rest of my days.

I want to feel that way. *Happy.* It's been so damn elusive for the last few years, and for a fleeting moment, it feels as if I grasp it again, so I'm no longer teetering on the edge of grief and shame.

But that's why I'm here, to move past that terrible duet.

I try valiantly to simply enjoy everything in front of me: the buildings, the water, the view.

As we round the bend in the canal, I blink *at* the view.

Holy hell, the unexpected view.

Nearby is a private dock.

On that dock is a man.

He's performing a downward-facing dog, and his rear is facing us.

What a spectacular ass.

It's not covered in sweatpants or basketball shorts.

It's au naturel, as finely sculpted as the statue of David.

He's a dog all right.

I sit up.

I practically stand. I lean on the edge of the boat, agog. I won't even pretend I'm not looking. I'm ogling.

The Japanese friends whisper and point. The couple shifts closer to get a better look. The college girls titter and laugh.

We slide along on the calm water, and now we're fifty feet away from a sight way better than the Little Mermaid statue, more magnificent than the royal palace.

He bends forward, pressing his palms into the wood, lifting his legs, and flipping them upside down.

Full. Frontal. Birthday suit.

He's a tall drink of man, and I'm so very thirsty.

"Look," I whisper to Veronica, though of course she's already engaged in the fine art of gawking. "Did you know the Mad Naked Handstander of Copenhagen was on the tour?"

She sighs contentedly. "I am so glad you forced me to go to the buffet." She parks her chin in her hands, watching the tall upside-down creature.

"My favorite part of the buffet is dessert," I say, as my eyes gobble him up.

It's an angle you don't see men in that often.

I suspect most people don't look good like this when naked and in such an unusual position.

But this man wears nudity well.

"I enjoyed the rubies and emeralds in Rosenborg Castle, but I like these crown jewels even better," I say.

And hey, perhaps I'm perving, but I'm an equal-opportunity spectator at this private dock show. I don't merely peer at the centerpiece of his physique, resting majestically against the grooves of his abs. My eyes take a most happy stroll up and down his carved body, from the planes of his stomach, to his strong thighs, to his arms ripped with muscles. His face is hard to read at 180 degrees, but I see the shape of his cheekbones, carved by angels.

Then, he moves. He walks on his hands. Back and forth.

Like he's performing.

Showing off his most unique skill set.

I chuckle louder.

Then louder still when he holds himself up on one hand only, waving to us.

"What a show-off," Veronica says.

Lars clears his throat. "And sometimes, we see the unexpected sights of Copenhagen."

I do what any curious onlooker might do. I grab my phone, and snap.

Snap.

Snap.

The man stands, takes a bow, and waves.

My chest heats up. The temperature in me flirts with mercury levels. He's a stunner. My God, he's like Skarsgård, from this distance.

And, because I believe in speaking my mind, I cup my hand over my mouth, and shout, "Bravo. All of it."

He doffs an imaginary top hat and takes a bow. "My pleasure." His voice booms across the water, his accent a British one.

Sparks unexpectedly race down my chest. That accent is delicious. "Oh no. The pleasure is truly all mine."

His lips curve up in a smile. A wickedly handsome one. "Then meet me tonight at Jane!"

Veronica nudges me. "That's a club. Say yes. Say it now." Her voice is marked with urgency,

"You're insane," I whisper.

"This is the wild thing to do. Not a boat ride."

Is she crazy?

As the boat motors on, the idea seems both intoxicating and dangerous. Stupid, maybe, too. For a second, I imagine asking Lars to stop the boat. Skarsgård would jump in the water and dolphin his way over to me, parking his hands on the edge of the boat, and flashing a gleaming smile, his hair wet, his face covered in droplets of water.

Oh hell, I want to say yes to the naked man.

He barks at me once again, shouting a street name that starts with a K, since every word here has a K in it, and ends with something like haven. "I'll be there at seven."

I swallow. Is he mad? Am I? Or am I doing what I've told myself I should do for some time now? *Seize the day.*

I cup my hand over the side of my mouth, and call out, "Perhaps I'll see you at seven."

Once one of the most beautiful views ever fades from sight, Veronica arches a well-groomed eyebrow. "You're going, right?"

A prickle of nerves skates down my spine. "I am?"

"Did I detect a question mark?"

"Don't you think it's dangerous to have drinks with a man you don't know?"

Shaking her head, she rises, flicks her chestnut brown hair off her shoulders, and strides purposefully to the front of the boat. Once Lars finishes a tale about the Danish navy and their warships, he lowers his shades, drops his mic, and cocks his head to the side.

Veronica says something to him I can't hear.

But his eyes tell me everything. He's said more than "perhaps."

As she saunters back to me, a determined look in her

eyes, she's daring me to go. She's chosen her own adventure for tonight.

Flopping down in the seat, she declares, "You better get your ass to Jane on whatever street that was." She pokes my shoulder. "You have a date, and so do I."

Why is it that last nights in foreign countries make you do crazy things?

I mean, *think* crazy things.

Clearly, I'm not actually going out with him.

I might have a bath in the marble tub at the hotel, sip a glass of champagne, and lose myself in a new book, the story of a young couple who travel to Rome and get lost and found.

"It's insane."

Veronica grabs my arm, her eyes imploring. "You're not going to his house. That would be insane. You're going to a bar. That's safe."

But is it? Is it safe for my heart?

Once I ask the question, though, I know the answer.

It's only one night. There's nothing safer.

And that's why there's nothing fate can do to stop me. I'm making this choice.

PART-TIME LOVER releases on June 4 on all retailers!
Next up is COME AS YOU ARE, releasing April 16! Here's a brief excerpt....

She's flirting with me, and she has no idea who I am, and I have no idea who she is. Yes, this mask was a brilliant idea in my list of brilliant ideas. The music picks up speed, and I twirl her around once more.

"So tell me, where did you learn to dance?" she asks.

"Don't laugh."

"I'll probably laugh."

"YouTube."

She laughs sweetly. "Seriously?"

I nod. "I figured I needed a life skill beyond math, numbers, and computers. I learned how to dance online."

She curls her hands over my shoulders. "You're a nerd." The words come out as if she just said I was a rock star or a pro quarterback. She says it with affection and, honestly, a whole lot of desire.

"Shocking, isn't it, that I'm a nerd?"

"A hot nerd, to be precise," she adds.

I bring her closer. "So are you."

"You're a very hot, witty nerd."

I'm damn close to kissing her on this dance floor. But I'd rather get her away from everyone else. I lean in to whisper, "Same to you, you incredibly sexy hot nerd I want to kiss."

She lets out a murmur, and when I pull back to meet her eyes again, I ask, "Have you seen the library here?"

"There's a library?" Her pitch rises.

"Yes. Why don't we check out the books and you can tell me more about your Monopoly strategy and the taxi apps you didn't fund?"

"Why, yes, your grace. I'd love to."

I laugh. "I'm not a duke."

"Can we pretend you are?"

"Of course, Angel. I can be whoever you want."

As long as it's not me.

ABOUT COME AS YOU ARE

I couldn't have scripted a more perfect night.

For one fantastic evening, at a masquerade party in the heart of Manhattan, I'm not the millionaire everyone wants a piece of. Fine—multimillionaire. But who's counting all those commas? Not me, and not the most intriguing woman I've ever met, who happens to like dancing, witty banter, and hot, passionate up-against-the-wall sex as much as I do. There's no need for names or business cards. And that's why I'm eager to get to know her more, since my mystery woman seems to like me for me, rather than for my huge...bank account.

Everything's coming up aces. Until the next day when things get a little complicated. (Newsflash — a lot complicated.)

* * *

He's charming, brilliant, an incredible lover, and right now I want to stab fate in the eyeballs.

I've had one goal I've been working toward, and lo and behold, my mystery man is the very person who stands between me and my dream job. A job I desperately need since my hard-knock life has nothing in common with his star-kissed one.

But it's time to put that fairytale night behind me, and focus on learning what makes him tick. Too bad it turns out his quirks are my quirks, and his love affair with New York matches mine.

And as we spend our days together, I discover something else that feels like a cruel twist of fate — I'm falling for this naughty prince charming, and that's not an ending I can write to our story.

***

COME AS YOU ARE releases on April 16 and can be preordered on most retailers now!

ACKNOWLEDGMENTS

I am grateful to so many people put made the story possible. Thank you to Rose Hilliard for being the match that started the Wanderlust fire, to Michelle Wolfson for making all things possible, and to KP Simmon for guiding me to yes. A special thank you to Helen Williams, who was my British eyes and ears and who devoured each chapter. Thank you to Jen for reading along and weeping when I hoped you would, and to Lauren Clarke for loving this story and helping to shape it. Abiding thanks to the people who checked my French – Monique Daoust and Katie DSP. Thank you to the ladies who make the books shine – Karen, Tiffany, Lynn, Virginia and Dena. A special shoutout to several books that were immensely helpful in research – Planting Schemes from Monet's Garden by Vivian Russell, Curiosities of Paris by Dominique Lesbros, Coming to My Senses by Alyssa Harad, Perfume: The Alchemy of Scent by Jean-Claude Ellena, and Angels of Paris by Rosemary Flannery.

Most of all I am thankful to my readers, and to the city of Paris for giving endless inspiration.

ALSO BY LAUREN BLAKELY

FULL PACKAGE, the #1 New York Times Bestselling romantic comedy!

BIG ROCK, the hit New York Times Bestselling standalone romantic comedy!

MISTER O, also a New York Times Bestselling standalone romantic comedy!

WELL HUNG, a New York Times Bestselling standalone romantic comedy!

JOY RIDE, a USA Today Bestselling standalone romantic comedy!

HARD WOOD, a USA Today Bestselling standalone romantic comedy!

THE SEXY ONE, a New York Times Bestselling bestselling standalone romance!

THE HOT ONE, a USA Today Bestselling bestselling standalone romance!

THE KNOCKED UP PLAN, a multi-week USA Today and Amazon Charts Bestselling bestselling standalone romance!

MOST VALUABLE PLAYBOY, a sexy multi-week USA Today Bestselling sports romance, and MOST LIKELY TO SCORE!

THE V CARD, a USA Today Bestselling sinfully sexy romantic comedy!

The New York Times and USA Today Bestselling Seductive Nights series including *Night After Night*, *After This Night*, and *One More Night*

And the two standalone romance novels in the Joy Delivered Duet, *Nights With Him* and Forbidden Nights, both New York Times and USA Today Bestsellers!

Sweet Sinful Nights, Sinful Desire, Sinful Longing and Sinful Love, the complete New York Times Bestselling high-heat romantic suspense series that spins off from Seductive Nights!

Playing With Her Heart, a USA Today bestseller, and a sexy Seductive Nights spin-off standalone! (Davis and Jill's romance)

21 Stolen Kisses, the USA Today Bestselling forbidden new adult romance!

Caught Up In Us, a New York Times and USA Today Bestseller! (Kat and Bryan's romance!)

Pretending He's Mine, a Barnes & Noble and iBooks Bestseller! (Reeve & Sutton's romance)

Trophy Husband, a New York Times and USA Today Bestseller! (Chris & McKenna's romance)

Far Too Tempting, the USA Today Bestselling standalone romance! (Matthew and Jane's romance)

Stars in Their Eyes, an iBooks bestseller! (William and Jess' romance)

My USA Today bestselling No Regrets series that includes

The Thrill of It (Meet Harley and Trey)

and its sequel

Every Second With You

My New York Times and USA Today Bestselling Fighting Fire series that includes

Burn For Me (Smith and Jamie's romance!)

Melt for Him (Megan and Becker's romance!)

and *Consumed by You* (Travis and Cara's romance!)

The Sapphire Affair series...

The Sapphire Affair

The Sapphire Heist

Out of Bounds

A New York Times Bestselling sexy sports romance

The Only One

A second chance love story!

Stud Finder

A sexy, flirty romance!

CONTACT

I love hearing from readers! You can find me on Twitter at LaurenBlakely3, Instagram at LaurenBlakelyBooks, Facebook at LaurenBlakelyBooks, or online at LaurenBlakely.com. You can also email me at laurenblakelybooks@gmail.com

.

29050004R00186

Printed in Great Britain
by Amazon